See Something

Also by Carol J. Perry

SEE SOMETHING

A Witch City Mystery

CAROL J. PERRY

KENSINGTON
PUBLISHING CORP.

www.kensingtonbooks.com

KENSINGTON BOOKS are published by

Kensington Publishing Corp.
119 West 40th Street
New York, NY 10018

All Kensington titles, imprints, and distributed lines are available at special quantity discounts for bulk purchases for sales promotion, premiums, fund-raising, educational, or institutional use.

Special book excerpts or customized printings can also be created to fit specific needs. For details, write or phone the office of the Kensington Sales Manager: Attn.: Sales Department. Kensington Publishing Corp., 119 West 40th Street, New York, NY 10018. Phone: 1-800-221-2647.

The K logo is a trademark of Kensington Publishing Corp.

First Printing: June 2021
ISBN-13: 978-1-4967-3141-8
ISBN-10: 1-4967-3141-7

ISBN-13: 978-1-4967-3142-5 (ebook)
ISBN-10: 1-4967-3142-5 (ebook)

10 9 8 7 6 5 4 3 2 1

Printed in the United States of America

For Dan, my husband and best friend

New beginnings are often disguised as painful endings.
—Lao Tzo, fifth century BCE

CHAPTER 1

Mixed emotions. Is there a song about that? There ought to be. Anyway, I guess it would explain the way I felt one pretty June morning in my hometown of Salem, Massachusetts. My emotions, as I attempted to brush too-curly red hair into some sort of order, and tried to decide what to wear on this sort-of-special day, were decidedly mixed—a nagging sense of disappointment was somehow smooshed together with wide-eyed anticipation.

I'm Lee Barrett, née Maralee Kowalski: red-haired, thirty-three, Salem born, orphaned early, married once, and widowed young. All this introspection was brought on because my interesting, comfortable, and almost-glamourous job as field reporter at WICH-TV had recently (and quite abruptly) ended with an unexpected (and not entirely welcome) promotion.

My boss, WICH-TV station manager Bruce Doan had—at his wife Buffy's urging, I'm sure—hired her nephew Howard Templeton as my replacement. At the same time, Mr. Doan decided that our fair city needed a lot more emphasis on local programming, and that I—with a *very* moderate increase in pay—was exactly the right person to make that happen. So *poof*! Like magic, I was suddenly producer and program director for three already established once-a-week shows—*Shopping Salem*, *The Saturday Morning Business Hour*, and *Cooking with Wanda the Weather Girl*. The three would present no major problems. With established formats already in place, they could all be improved with spruced-up sets, along with some innovative promotion. Our weekday late-night call-in show—*Tarot Time with River North*—was darned near perfect just the way it was. Downright intimidating, though, was a new weekday production—still in the planning stages—an hour-long morning show for children.

I knew Howie Templeton. I'd helped with his training a few months back, before he'd landed a job with a small Maine station. Apparently—at least according to his aunt Buffy—he was ready to move to a larger market, like Salem. My question was, *Am I ready to handle* my *new assignment?* I've worked in front of and behind the TV cameras ever since my graduation from Boston's Emerson College. I've been a Miami home-shopping-channel show host, an investigative reporter, a field reporter, and a television production instructor. I'd even served briefly—and certainly without distinction—as a late-night call-in psychic on an ill-fated show called *Nightshades*. But producing a daily kids' program opened up a whole new—and completely unfamiliar—world to me. As usual, Doan likes his employees to wear more than one hat, so I got to keep my field reporter business cards. All that meant was that if by chance something worth some journalistic investigating came my way, I might get a shot at some on-screen face time.

I decided on a cool and comfortable blue A-line dress, headed into the kitchen, and turned on Mr. Coffee. After my NASCAR-driver husband Johnny Barrett's death in Florida, my aunt, Isobel Russell—I call her Aunt Ibby—had created this cozy apartment for me on the third floor of the old family home on Winter Street. We shared the big house with our gentleman cat, O'Ryan, who, at the moment, sat on the kitchen windowsill looking out. I carried my coffee and a manila folder marked "Kid Show" to the 1970s Lucite table, pulled up a chair beside the window, joining O'Ryan in his study of the immediate outdoors. There didn't seem to be anything particularly interesting going on out there to demand such rapt attention from the big yellow cat, so I opened the folder. There wasn't a lot going on in there either. Not nearly enough to get my new project underway.

"I think I'm off to a pretty good start," I said to the cat, who may or may not have been listening. "I have appointments today with both Ranger Rob and Katie the Clown." The pair were not strangers to television programming geared toward a juvenile audience. They had, in fact, been childhood favorites of my own. Ranger Rob Oberlin was an old-time guitar-strumming singing cowboy with tales of adventure on the range. Cute and funny Katie the Clown charmed kids with her deadpan clown antics and storytelling ability. Aunt Ibby had even bought me a Ranger Rob cowboy doll and a Katie clown doll, which had occupied the window seat in my childhood bedroom for years after the show had ended. I planned for cartoon videos to help fill up the time, and I hoped to get retired Gloucester fisherman Captain Billy Barker to act as occasional show host and—since he owned the city's largest toy store—as the main sponsor as well.

O'Ryan made a graceful turn on the narrow sill—the kind only a cat can make—and favored me with a quick chin lick, indicating that he'd been listening after all. "Mrrup," he declared. Sounded like a positive comment to me. My aunt and I both often talk to the big yellow striped cat—sometimes about some serious stuff. He's not exactly an ordinary feline. He once belonged to a witch named Ariel Constellation. Some say he was her familiar—and in Salem a witch's familiar is respected, sometimes even feared.

I slipped the slim manila folder into a briefcase, along with a couple of granola bars—in case this day didn't allow for a lunch break—and exited my kitchen into the third-floor front hall. O'Ryan beat me to it via his cat door and together we headed down the broad staircase stairs to Aunt Ibby's, where invitations to breakfast were pretty much a sure thing. It was early, but I knew she'd be up—either busy in her high-tech home office or in the kitchen working the *Globe* crossword puzzle. (In ink.) The first-floor foyer opens onto her living room, and the cat scooted ahead of me toward the kitchen to announce our arrival. I followed.

My slim, trim, and attractive sixty-something aunt is semiretired from her position as research librarian at Salem's main library. She looked up from her *Boston Globe*.

"Good morning, Maralee. Fresh blueberry muffins in the warmer. Coffee's still hot."

"Thanks," I said, helping myself to both. O'Ryan had

already busied himself with the contents of his special red bowl. "I have a busy day ahead of me. I may be home a little later than usual."

"I'm sure you'll handle everything beautifully," she said. "You always do. Shall I hold dinner for you, or do you have plans?"

"Pete may be coming over later. Not sure what time. He said he'd bring takeout. Chinese, I think." Police detective Pete Mondello and I had been dating for a couple of years, and the relationship seemed to get better all the time.

"You know I always plan for leftovers," she said. "If you get hungry, just come on down."

"I will." I put my mug and empty plate into the dishwasher, patted the cat, kissed my aunt goodbye, and left via her kitchen door to the back hall and out the back door. Outside, next to the garden fence, the air had a pleasant faint herbal smell. The humidity was low—my hair probably wouldn't frizz. Wanda the Weather Girl had promised fair skies and temperature in the low seventies. A perfect day for walking the few blocks to work. I glanced at my watch. Still early. A brisk walk might "clear away the cobwebs," as my aunt is fond of saying. The details of my new position could definitely use some clearing.

The Salem Common is at the end of our street. It's a big, beautiful oasis in the middle of a busy city at every time of year, but summertime is special. I admired the newly planted flower beds, bright spots of color among grassy paths. The old-fashioned popcorn wagon was in place, and happy kids crowded around the swing sets and monkey bars. Stacia, the pigeon lady, wearing a hot-pink muumuu, was seated on her usual bench, tossing treats to her expectant audience of cooing gray birds. Stacia had human company today—a neatly dressed brunette, hands folded in her lap. I smiled, realizing that the woman would choose another bench before long. Pigeons are good-natured but notably messy creatures.

The "cobweb clearing" aspect of my walk began to take effect almost immediately. I'd only gone as far as the statue of Nathaniel Hawthorne when I'd visualized a stage set that would work for both Katie the Clown and Ranger Rob. *What about a rodeo background?* I was pretty sure there'd be plenty of room within the station's vast ground-floor studio area for what I was imagining: some split-rail fencing, a make-believe bull chute, and a few rows of bleacher seats for visiting kids. Ranger Rob could do his cowboy routines, and what's a rodeo without a clown? By the time I'd passed the Catholic church, I'd figured out a couple of program crossover promotions. Maybe Wanda the Weather Girl could do a chuck-wagon cooking demo, or the *Shopping Salem* folks might give a little background information and a sales pitch on cow-boy boots or iron frying pans. I knew that Captain Billy would find toys and games to fit whatever daily themes we might come up with. I rounded the corner onto New Derby Street, hummed a few bars of "Home on the Range," and hurried toward the station, looking forward to the rest of the day.

I climbed the marble steps to the WICH-TV building, pushed open the door, and crossed the black-and-white tile floor to the vintage brass-doored elevator affection-ately known as "Old Clunky." The ride up to the second floor was no bumpier than usual, and Rhonda, the station receptionist, greeted me with a big smile. She extended her hand and dangled a key on a silver chain from one finger.

"Guess what? You finally have your own office."

I reached for the key. "No kidding! Where is it?"

"Come on. I'll show you." She hurried around the purple Formica counter surrounding her desk and grabbed my elbow. "You're going to love it. You're in there with all the big-time prime-time guys." She opened the green metal door leading to the WICH-TV newsroom. That's the newest, most up-to-date part of the old building. The lighting is good, the computers are reasonably new, and there's a neat row of glass-walled cubicles back there where the news anchors and the senior sales managers do their business.

Rhonda led me to one of the sparkling glass rooms—the one with "Lee Barrett, Program Director" in neat black letters on the door. I resisted the strong temptation to pull out my phone and take a selfie beside it.

"Why don't you just toss your briefcase inside," she said. "Your singing cowboy is already here waiting to see you. I sent him over to the soundstage where your new show is going to happen."

I did as Rhonda suggested, regretfully leaving my new office digs with a longing backward glance, and followed her to the ground-level stage where my favorite videographer, Marty McCarthy, was already at work with Ranger Rob.

"Hey, Moon," Marty called. "Your cowboy here sounds as good as ever." Marty still calls me "Moon" because back when I played a psychic I called myself "Crystal Moon" and some of the WICH-TV staff haven't forgotten it.

"I'm sure he does," I said. "Hi, Rob. Good to see you."

The old cowboy looked good too. Stetson hat at a jaunty angle and guitar slung casually over his shoulder, he'd lost considerable weight since I'd last seen him.

"Thanks for the opportunity, Lee. I'm anxious to get back to work. So's Agnes." Katie the Clown's real name is Agnes Hooper, though she still answers to "Katie" most of the time.

"She should be along any minute," I said. "She's really excited about the new show. I have a few thoughts about the set I'd like to run by you both. You too, Marty."

"Let's keep it simple, Moon." She shook her head, gray curls bobbing. "No moving parts."

"Just the bull chute," I announced with a smile.

"A bull chute!" Rob laughed and strummed a chord on his guitar. "When we have guests they can run out from the chute. Excellent! What do you think, Ms. Marty?"

"I think I'll look up 'bull chute' in the dictionary," she said, straight-faced, "to be sure you're not just shooting the bull."

Rhonda reappeared with Agnes/Katie in tow. "Hi, everybody," the petite woman called, hurrying to Rob's side "Hi, darlin'. Good to be back here, isn't it? Feels like home."

The cowboy's welcoming smile was broad as he broke into an upbeat version of "Send In the Clowns," then leaned down and kissed her on the cheek. "Hi there, honey bunch. Yep. It's good to be working together again."

"Good to be working at all," the little clown said. "Especially great to be doing a kids' show. Have we got any sponsors yet?"

"We're pretty sure about Captain Billy's Toy Trawler," I said, "and the sales department is working on signing up some of your old sponsors. Quite a few of them are still in business in Salem. I'm thinking about a rodeo background for the new set, and we might hang some colorful advertising banners along the split-rail fence."

"Good one, Moon," Marty said. "The sponsors will love it. But has Doan signed on for the expense of building the set?"

Heck, no. I just thought it up an hour ago.

I sidestepped the question. "He needs to see some sketches and cost estimates," I said. "We're working on it." I used the editorial "we." Nobody was actually working on it yet. Including me. I needed to get my ideas down on paper—like immediately. The current sets in the WICH-TV studio were pretty simple. Wanda's kitchen had been in place since I'd first come to work there, and *Shopping Salem* and *Saturday Morning Business Hour* were simple cubicles furnished with desks, chairs, and appropriate signage. Cosmetic improvements to all three would be simple and, hopefully, fairly inexpensive.

Building a new permanent set from scratch and within what would undoubtedly be a meager budget and a tight time frame—was going to be the first big challenge I'd face from my shiny new office.

But it wasn't the last. It wasn't the biggest. And it wasn't anywhere near the most dangerous.

CHAPTER 2

I could hardly wait to get into my new office—the first space of my very own since I'd come to work at WICH-TV. I took that selfie and sent it to Aunt Ibby. I sat in the swivel chair, and after looking through all sides of the glass room and determining that no one was watching me, I gave the chair a good spin. Couldn't resist. It felt good. I opened the drawers, one by one. Most were empty except for a full package of copy paper, some manila file folders, a box of yellow number-two pencils, a half-empty box of Crayola colored pencils, and a purple ball-point pen with the station's logo on it. A quick trip to Staples was definitely in order.

There was a wastebasket under my desk, a four-drawer file cabinet and a paper shredder against one wall. In one corner there were two club chairs upholstered in purple plastic with a white wicker table. (Buffy Doan is partial to purple and much of the station's décor reflects her taste.)

I pulled a sheet of copy paper from the stack, clicked the ballpoint pen, and began my to-do list. First on the list was *set design for kids' show.* Next was *name for kids' show.* After that came *suggested sponsor list for kids' show.* I wasn't sure I had things in the right order. Should the show have a name first? After all, I couldn't present Mr. Doan with a folder marked "Design for unnamed children's show." That wasn't the only problem. I had a good idea of what my rodeo stage set should look like, but have no artistic skill whatsoever. Who could I get on short notice to do a proper artist's rendering? The suggested sponsors list would be comparatively easy to put together. No matter what, by day's end I intended to have all my ducks—and clowns and cowboys and sponsors—in a row.

I decided to stick to my list—right or wrong. Set design first. The only artist I know personally is Dakota Berman—locally well-known for portraits, landscapes, and gravestone rubbings. I was maid of honor at his wedding to Shannon Dumas. (Shannon had been one of my students when I'd taught TV production at Salem's Tabitha Trumbull Academy for the Arts—known to Salem folks as "the Tabby.") Would Dakota do a TV set design for me? Worth a try.

I tried. He said yes. In fact, it was an enthusiastic YES! Seems that Dakota had been looking to stretch his artistic wings, and set design might open a few new doors for him. We made an appointment for him to come over to the station to check out the available space and to see how my rodeo idea might be implemented. His schedule was tight and he wouldn't be able to meet with me until after five, but I happily agreed that five would be fine with me. Anyway, I'd already told Aunt Ibby I might be arriving home later than usual.

On to the next item on my short list. *Name for kids' show.* Hmmm. That might be a tough one. I know titles are important, and I was going to have to come up with a good one—and do it before five o'clock if Dakota was going to be able to incorporate it in his sketches for the stage set. I opened the slim manila folder and pulled out a blank sheet of lined paper. "RODEO," I printed in block letters. "COWBOY," "CLOWN," I added, then looked around in my new glass-walled world, searching for inspiration.

Nothing.

There was a knock at my door. Ranger Rob and Katie peered in at me, each one smiling broadly, each clearly delighted with this new opportunity. I returned the smiles and motioned for them to come in.

"RANGER ROB" I printed on the lined sheet and waved a hand toward the purple chairs. "Come on in and sit down, you two. I'm working on a name for the show. Any suggestions?"

Rob sat down, but Katie stood across the desk from me and pointed to the paper. "Of course I'm reading upside down, but what's wrong with that title?"

"What title?" I frowned, turning the paper around.

"Ranger Rob's Rodeo," she said. "Three Rs. It's euphonious, don't you think?"

"It is," I agreed, surprised. "It does have a certain ring to it, doesn't it? What do you think, Rob?"

His grin gave his answer before he spoke. "I like it a lot. Especially the three Rs. You say you watched us back when you were a kid. You were one of my little buckaroos. Don't you remember my set on the old show was the Triple R Ranch?"

"That's right. I do remember. I'll bet a lot of today's young moms will remember it too."

A sudden burst of activity in the newsroom behind us caused the three of us to look in that direction. Once again, I appreciated the location of my new office. I'd be one of the first to know about any breaking news happening in Salem—and it certainly looked as if something was breaking.

Howard Templeton came barreling past my door, followed in quick succession by my favorite mobile unit driver/videographer, Francine. I felt a tiny twinge of jealousy. Chasing a breaking news story is exciting. I was already missing that part of my job.

"Excuse me a minute," I said, hurrying to the door and pulling it open. "Hey, Francine!

What's up?"

"Floater in the harbor," she called over her shoulder. "Looks like it wasn't an accident."

I closed the office door and walked slowly to my desk, struggling to stifle my natural reporter's curiosity. *Looks like it wasn't an accident? How?* "Some excitement going on out there," I said, keeping my voice level. "Where were we?"

"Picking a name," Katie said. "Ranger Rob's Rodeo. Do you think Mr. Doan will like it?"

"We'll find out," I promised. "But for now, that's it. Next I need to put together a list of possible sponsors. We'll start with some of your old sponsors. I think Captain Billy's Toy Trawler is a pretty sure thing. Any ideas?"

They each came up with some names, and before long

we had good selection of likely sponsors to hand over to the sales team, who'd undoubtedly come up with more.

"Good job, you two," I said. "Thanks for your help."

Rob and Katie left the office, his arm casually draped over her shoulders. Back when the two starred in the top-rated kids' show of my childhood, it was rumored that they were an "item." It looked to me as though they still were—and that made me smile.

I gathered up my notes on the proposed show name and possible sponsors—with a silent vow to pull them into an orderly presentation really, really soon—stuck them into the folder, jammed it into the top drawer of my desk, and hurried out the door and into the newsroom.

"Scott," I said, speaking to Scott Palmer—not one of my favorite people at the station, but the first reporter I happened to run into. "What's up with the drowning victim? Francine says it's not an accident."

Scott didn't look happy. "Seems that way. Their live shots should be coming any minute. The new kid seems to be getting all the plum assignments, or hadn't you noticed?"

I had noticed, but didn't see any advantage in belaboring the point. "Did you check the police scanner?" I asked. That's the first thing I would have done if I'd been the field reporter who got left behind. I was pretty sure Scott would have too.

"Yeah, sure," he admitted. "The guy probably drowned, but let's say he didn't jump into the water voluntarily."

"How do they know that?"

"Looks like his hands had been bound."

"Murder?"

"Seems so. Hard to swim if you can't use your hands." He pointed to a TV monitor on the wall. "Hey. There's the fair-haired nephew doing the stand-up. Looks like they're over near Collins Cove." We both moved closer to the screen. Howie Templeton stood on a stone wall, his back to the narrow stretch of beach where a Salem police department cruiser was parked on the sand. A crime scene investigation vehicle was visible on the street to the reporter's left and the familiar yellow tape was staked out along the perimeter of the stone wall.

"Must be low tide," Scott mumbled.

Templeton used a clip mic on his collar. I'd always preferred the stick mic myself. He looked good though. Confident. He'd learned a lot at that Maine station.

"This morning at around eight a.m., the Salem police received a 911 call about a man's body on the beach in the vicinity of Collins Cove," he said, his voice properly solemn. "Preliminary investigation indicates that the unidentified man was possibly a drowning victim. According to a police report, however, foul play is indicated. The medical examiner describes the victim as male, aged around forty, six feet tall, weight one hundred and sixty-five pounds, brown hair, blue eyes. He wore blue jeans and a white shirt. There was no form of identification on the body. No visible scars or tattoos. If you have any information as to the identity of this person, or if you have observed any unusual or suspicious activity in the Collins Cove area within the last forty-eight hours, please call the number on your screen. I'm Howard Templeton reporting for WICH-TV. Stay tuned for the latest updates on this breaking news."

"Possible homicide?" I said.

"No doubt about it," Scott said. "One of my contacts says there are rope marks on both wrists." He added a grudging, "The kid didn't do bad."

"He's learning," I said. "Looks good on camera too."

"You going to ask your cop boyfriend what's going on?"

"Of course I am," I said. "But he doesn't tell me much about police business." That was true. Pete rarely talks about his job unless I ask, and even then he doesn't tell me much about any ongoing cases he might be working. Of course I was going to ask him about the dead man— rope marks on his wrists—how could I not? However, with a sigh I hoped nobody heard, I returned to my new office, putting one-time field reporter thoughts about a brand-new murder investigation aside and concentrating on the job of program director.

That's what I did. Ignoring as much as possible the frantic activity going on in the newsroom behind me, I skipped lunch, ate my granola bar, and pulled together the material I had so far on the stage set and show name. I'd have to type it into a presentable form for Mr. Doan's approval. All I had to do then was wait for Dakota Berman. I used a few sheets of copy paper and one of the yellow number-two pencils and made a few rough—very rough—sketches of the way I thought the Ranger Rob's Rodeo set might look. I printed "Ranger Rob's Rodeo" in block letters on each one.

I took time out to watch the afternoon news, where Howie did another report on the murder, this one from the police station where Chief Tom Whaley gave one of his brief interviews. The chief doesn't enjoy doing these things and keeps them as short as he can get away with. Confirming for me what Scott had said about rope marks, the chief said that the medical examiner's report indicated that the drowning victim's wrists had been bound and the death was now classified as a homicide. The man was still unidentified, but now there was a two-thousand-dollar reward offered for information leading to the capture of the killer or killers. The chief also displayed an artist's pastel sketch of the victim. With light-brown hair and blue eyes, he was an average looking middle-aged man—nothing outstanding about him that I could see. I wondered if Dakota Berman had thought about doing sketches for the police department and made a plan to ask him.

I stopped watching TV and dragged my attention back to current duties. I thought about what Marty had said about looking up "bull chute." It wasn't a bad idea. I've seen one or two at rodeos and some on TV, but never had to give much thought to their actual construction or functioning. I turned on the computer, typed in "bull chute," and found plenty of images. It didn't look too complicated—a narrow blue gate with horizontal metal bars. There were a few for sale too, in the four-thousand-dollar range. We could safely forget about those. I'd most likely have to fake the gate with plywood and wooden closet poles, but the general effect would be okay—as long as we didn't use real bulls. I sketched the imaginary wooden blue gate with a blue Crayola, and watched the clock.

Dakota Berman showed up a few minutes before five. I was happy to see my old friend, and after greeting one another enthusiastically and catching up on what was new in our lives—me with the new job, Dakota and Shannon expecting their first baby—we got down to business. We walked to the empty set where the show would be staged, and he paced off approximate measurements. With pencil and ruler I marked feet and inches on graph paper as he called the numbers out. At the same time, I explained the basic idea behind the show. It would be aimed at kids on weekday mornings. I wanted it to be fun and educational at the same time. Back at my office I showed him the newest publicity shots of Rob and Katie, then hesitantly shoved my stack of copy-paper pencil sketches across my desk.

He pointed to the photos. "I remember them. I used to watch them when I was a kid. Is the little clown as cute as she used to be?"

"Those are fairly new pictures. They both look good. I know my drawings are rough, but they'll give you an idea of what I have in mind."

He shuffled through them. "Can you make me copies of your—um—artwork." He smiled. "I'll get right to work on this."

I stood and fed the papers into the copier. "Oh, Dakota? The police released an artist's sketch of the murder victim they found this morning. Do you ever work with the police on that kind of thing?"

"I haven't, but maybe I'll look into it. Don't tell me you're working on that murder besides producing this new show for kids!"

I held up both hands. "Nope. That's Howard Templeton's baby now. I'm trying hard to block out what's going on out there." I jerked a thumb over my shoulder toward the newsroom. "Not easy to ignore when it's practically in my lap."

"I'll bet. Well, I guess you're in a rush for this." He held up the sheets of copy paper. "I'll get back to you tomorrow afternoon with a preliminary. Okay?"

I breathed a sigh of relief. "That will be great. Thanks so much. Just attach your bill."

"How about we trade for a little commercial time for my gallery?" he said. "Think Doan will go for that?"

"I can practically guarantee it," I said. "Thank you. See you tomorrow."

By the time I'd straightened up my office and lined up my meager supplies neatly in their proper drawers, the early news broadcast was nearly over and Phil Archer replayed part of the earlier interview Howie had done with the chief. Still nothing new on the matter. The victim was still unidentified and no suspects had been named. I tucked my artwork and the notes on program names and possible sponsors into my briefcase.

I phoned Aunt Ibby to tell her I'd be along shortly. She'd been watching the news too, and peppered me with questions about the body they'd found at Collins Cove. I told her that there was nothing more to tell other than what Phil had just reported. "Good heavens, Maralee," she insisted. "You *must* know something more. You work with the *news* media. and this is a *murder* case."

"Aunt Ibby, if I knew anything else I'd tell you. Remember, I'm not a reporter anymore. I have other duties to think about now."

"Of course, but you know how interested I am in this sort of thing. Keep your ears open, won't you, dear?"

My aunt's intense interest in suspicious deaths was fairly new. She and a couple of her "girlfriends," Betsy Leavitt and Louisa Abney-Babcock, had recently become involved in investigating the murder of a man all three of them had known in high school. I promised to keep my ears open, said good night to Rhonda, and started for home.

It was nearly dusk when I reached the Salem Common. I took the shortcut—a diagonal path across the middle of the park instead of my usual sidewalk around the perimeter route. The popcorn wagon was gone and the hot-dog guy was setting up for his evening business. Stacia had left and the pigeons had probably gone to roost, but oddly enough, the woman I'd seen in the morning still sat there, alone on Stacia's bench.

Strange. Has she been there all day? I shrugged and walked a little faster. "None of my business," I told myself. "It's a public park. If she wants to sit there it's okay with me."

But it wasn't okay and I knew it. I turned and hurried back toward the bench and the lone woman.

"Hello," I said. "Are you all right?"

She looked up, facing me, pale blue eyes open wide, but didn't speak. I moved closer. "Are you all right?" I asked again.

She shook her head. "No."

I sat beside her, trying to avoid white splashes of pigeon poop. "What's your name?"

She began to cry. "I don't know."

CHAPTER 3

Hesitantly, I reached over and patted her shoulder. *She doesn't know her name?* I looked into her eyes. They looked clear, bright, not at all as though she was drugged or drunk or somehow impaired. "Have you been injured?" I asked.

She shook her head. "I don't think so. I don't know. Nothing hurts."

"Do you have a purse?" I looked past her, onto the seat beside her. "Maybe you have some identification in it."

"I already thought of that," she said. "No purse. No wallet. No money. Nothing much in my pockets either—except some tissues." She pulled out a wrinkled white square, dabbed at her eyes, blew her nose, and stuck it back into the pocket of her pink sweater.

"Do you know where you are?" I waved my arm, encompassing the common, the bandstand, the hot dog wagon. "I mean, do you know you're in Salem?"

"I didn't. The other lady. Stacia. She told me."

And she left you here? Alone?

"Well, you can't just sit here. It'll be dark soon. Come on with me. We'll figure out something." I stood up, motioned for her to follow and pointed toward Winter Street. "I live right over there."

She stood, then abruptly sat again. "I don't know you," she said.

"You don't know anybody," I reasoned, "and you can't just sit here all night. It isn't safe."

"Well, okay. I guess. I'll just have to trust you."

Hey. I'm the one taking a chance here.

I led the way through the iron gate and across Washington Square to Winter Street, trying to figure out what I was supposed to do with the woman once I got her home. *Stranger danger* buzzed around in my head. She didn't appear to be armed so I figured Aunt Ibby and I would be safe for the moment. But I'd call Pete as soon as I got home. I glanced around almost furtively when we passed the big stone Civil War memorial on the corner. Was there somebody behind it? Were we being followed? What if the woman was being followed? I shook away the feeling and turned to her.

"Here's my house," I said as we approached the front steps. "Look, there's our cat, O'Ryan, peeking out at us. Do you like cats?"

We climbed the granite steps together and the woman stood close to the tall, narrow window on the left side of the door. She bent down, looking closely at the big yellow striped cat on the other side of the glass. "I think maybe I do. He looks friendly."

"He's a good boy," I said, unlocking and pushing the door open. O'Ryan greeted me in the foyer with the usual happy purrs and ankle rubbing. "O'Ryan," I said, "this is—um—our guest." The cat cocked his head to one side, seeming to assess the situation.

"Would it be all right if I pat him?" she asked.

"Sure." I watched as she extended her left hand, stroking his head. No rings. He leaned into her hand, half closing his eyes. "I think you do like cats," I told her, "and this cat likes you too." I stepped through the arched doorway into my aunt's living room. "Hello. Aunt Ibby, are you here?"

"I'm in the kitchen, dear," came the answering call. O'Ryan dashed ahead of us while our nameless guest took a step back.

"Come along," I ordered. "Come and meet my aunt. Are you hungry?"

"I am," she said. "Stacia bought me some popcorn. But I gave most of it to the pigeons."

"I can smell something cooking already." I took her elbow and steered her ahead of me. "I'm bringing a guest, Aunt Ibby," I called.

We passed the entrance to the dining room and arrived in the kitchen. My aunt wiped her hands on her red and white apron with "Kiss the Cook" emblazoned across the front, and extended her hand to my companion. "Welcome," she said, then frowned. "Maralee, aren't you going to introduce me to your friend?" Not waiting for my answer, she pumped the woman's hand and went on.

"I'm Isobel Russell. Most folks call me Ibby. What's your name?"

Of course, the question brought a new flood of tears.

"Oh dear. Whatever is wrong?" Aunt Ibby looked at me, then back at the woman who was by then sobbing great heaving sobs. "Here, child. Sit down. Maralee, get your friend a glass of water." My "friend" did as she was told. So did I. Aunt Ibby has that effect on people. The woman sat, sipped the water, and the sobs were soon replaced with hiccups.

"She seems to have lost her memory. She's been sitting on the common all day. It was starting to get dark." I spread my arms apart helplessly. "I couldn't very well just leave her there."

"Of course you couldn't." She patted the woman's hand. "You can stay right here with us, dear. Dinner will be ready in about half an hour. Lovely roast lamb and peas and mashed potatoes. Do you like mint jelly with your lamb?"

That brought a smile. "Yes. I mean, I think I do."

"I have to call Pete," I said. "Maybe someone has reported her missing." I turned to face the woman. "My friend is a policeman. He might be able to help you find your family."

She nodded. "The food smells very good," she said. "May I please use your bathroom?"

My aunt pointed to the little powder room off the kitchen. "Of course." She turned to me when the door closed. "You say she's been sitting on the common all day? Of course the poor thing needs to go to the bathroom."

As soon as she'd left the room I called Pete. He picked up right away, which was good. He doesn't always. "Pete," I said. "The darnedest thing happened today."

"Are you all right?"

"Yes. I'm fine. Why?"

"I don't know. Whenever there's a suspicious death around here, it seems like you get yourself involved somehow."

"Oh, that," I said. "The dead man in Collins Cove? No. This is about a woman I found on the common. She seems to have lost her memory. Doesn't even know her name and has no ID. Do you have any recent missing persons bulletins? She's around thirty I'd say. Brown hair. Blue eyes. About my height and weight."

"You *found* her on the common? And you brought her home with you?"

"Well, yeah. I couldn't very well just leave her there. It's getting dark and Stacia had gone home."

"Stacia? What's she got to do with it?"

I heard the toilet flush in the powder room, and quickly rattled off the story about seeing the woman in the morning with Stacia and again on my way home. "So what should I do about her?"

"It's not real wise to bring a stranger into your house, Lee," he scolded. "Listen. I'm at my sister's house right now. Stacia lives just around the corner. I'll check missing persons with headquarters, then I'll go over to Stacia's and see what she has to say. After that I'll come to your place and see about finding the lady a space at the women's shelter."

I remembered that Stacia's little pink house was only

about a block away from Marie and Donnie's place. (Yes, Pete's sister and brother-in-law are named Donnie and Marie.) "Okay," I said. "See you in a while." Our name-less guest had reappeared and I realized that spending the day with Stacia's pigeon friends can have messy and smelly results.

"Look here," I said to her. "You and I are about the same size, and frankly, you have bird poop on your clothes and in your hair. Come on upstairs while dinner's cook-ing and take a shower and change. We'll put your clothes in the washer while you eat. My boyfriend, Pete Mon-dello, is coming over. Remember I told you about him? He's a policeman. I'm sure he can help."

She looked scared and hesitant, and I couldn't blame her. She didn't know who we were and here I was telling her to take her clothes off in a strange house. "That's a good idea, Maralee," my aunt said. "Nothing like a hot shower and a shampoo to make a person feel better. Then a full tummy to finish the job. Hurry back. I'm going to put rolls in the oven now, and there's peach pie with ice cream for dessert."

It was probably the menu that convinced the woman to trust us, but whatever her reasoning was, she followed me back through Aunt Ibby's living room and up two flights of stairs with O'Ryan leading the way. The orange door on the third-floor landing opens onto my kitchen. Aunt Ibby had surprised me with this apartment of my own just a couple of years earlier. The door is orange because ac-cording to my best friend, River North, the color attracts beneficial feng shui. (It would be even more propitious if it was the outer front door of the house, but Aunt Ibby insists that orange doesn't quite fit with the nineteenth-century exterior of the place.) River is the host of the station's super-popular late-night show and is kind of an expert on all things magic and mystical. Besides all that, she's a witch.

I explained the feng shui thing, but our guest's blank stare told me she had no idea what I was talking about. "Never mind that," I said. "Let's pick out something for you to wear. I led her to my bedroom, opened the closet, and sized up her figure. "How about these jeans and this blue cotton blouse? Looks pretty with your eyes." She nodded, her expression shy and a little bit frightened. "Thank you," she almost whispered. I added a pair of panties and one of those soft sports bras that fit everybody. She accepted the clothes, holding them out in front of her, avoiding touching her own soiled outfit. I showed her the way down the short hall to the bathroom. "Help yourself to shampoo and deodorant and stuff. Just put your dirty things in the laundry chute. It'll drop them straight down to the laundry room." I closed the door behind her, hurried back to the kitchen, sat at the table, and called Pete again.

"So far, so good," I told him. "Aunt Ibby convinced her to stay for dinner. She's in the shower now. Anything new on your end?"

"Seems that Stacia phoned in about the lady on the common and we sent an officer to check on her, but she was gone when he got there." Pete's cop voice was suddenly activated. "It must have been just after you—um—'found' her." Nothing matching your description from missing persons though. She's a Jane Doe."

"Okay. If she doesn't mind maybe we can call her Jane for now," I said. "Dinner smells good. Roast lamb. If you're coming over now, maybe we should join her and Aunt Ibby and eat here. You'll be able to ask Jane Doe questions and you won't have to bring takeout."

"Good thinking, Lee." Normal voice back. "I'll stop by Stacia's place and see if she has any details, then I'll be right along. Love you."

"Love you too." O'Ryan had taken his seat on the windowsill behind my chair, resuming his intense study of the outside world—where, as far as I could see, nothing much was happening. I glanced at my vintage eye-rolling, tail-switching Kit-Cat clock. Time for the seven o'clock news. I turned on the kitchen TV, positive that there'd be a news update. I was right. Phil Archer, the station's oldest anchor, recapped what was known so far about the man who'd been found—recently drowned and apparently bound—on a narrow Salem beach.

"The artist's sketch, aired earlier on this station, has yielded a possible identification of the victim," Phil intoned, using his best big network voice. "No name has been released. Salem authorities have shared photographs, fingerprints, and other details from the medical examiner's office with state, local, and national law enforcement agencies. The medical examiner is waiting for further forensic findings." The artist's sketch I'd seen before appeared on the screen. "Here's a likeness of John Doe, the man found at Collins Cove. If you know or have seen this man, please call the number at the bottom of your screen."

He went to commercial for the Salem Trolley. I reached for a pen. The popular trolley tour of the city might be a likely sponsor for *Ranger Rob's Rodeo*. I jotted down the phone number. A timid voice came from across the room.

"Who was that man?" Jane Doe stood in the hallway, barefoot and looking really cute in my jeans and blouse. Her wet hair was pulled into a ponytail and her face, free from makeup, was flushed.

"Who? Oh, Phil Archer. He's the afternoon anchor at WICH-TV."

"No. The man in the picture. The drawing. The announcer called him John Doe."

CHAPTER 4

The question was a surprise. "I don't know," I stammered. "I mean, that's just a name the police use for a man they haven't identified yet. Like, until we know your real name, they'd call you 'Jane Doe.' Why? Did you recognize him? The man in the picture?"

She stepped into the kitchen, moving closer to the TV where the red trolley rolled past the House of the Seven Gables. "Yes. No. Maybe." She buried her face in her hands for a brief moment, then tossed her head, the wet ponytail spraying droplets of water. "I have no idea. I don't even know who I am. I barely recognized myself in your bathroom mirror. The picture though—something about it—seemed familiar. What happened to the man? Why is he on the news anyway?"

Oh boy. Suppose it's somebody she knows. If I tell her he's dead, will that traumatize her further? I clicked off the television. "I'm not exactly sure," I fibbed. "They're trying to figure out who he is. There'll probably be more about it on the late news. We'll catch it then. But right now let's find you some shoes and go downstairs and get some dinner." At the word "dinner" O'Ryan scooted out through his cat door. I headed across the kitchen to my bedroom and motioned for Jane Doe to follow me. "What size shoes do you wear? I think your feet are smaller than mine."

She shrugged, smiling. "I don't know. I left my shoes on the bathroom floor. Shall I go look? They're pretty messed up."

"Pigeon poop?"

"I guess."

"Never mind. I'm pretty sure we'll find something." I opened the closet door, displaying my kind of impressive floor-to-ceiling shoe rack. I really like shoes—and boots. A lot.

The blue eyes widened. "Wow." She pointed. "Are those Manolo Blahniks?"

"Yeah." Modest shrug. *The woman knows labels.* "Those were kind of an extravagance. They were marked down though."

She pointed to my favorite tie-dye platform sneakers. "Jimmy Choo?"

"Uh-huh," I admitted. "End-of-season sale at Neiman's. Whoever you are, you know shoes."

"I guess I do, don't I?" She looked pleased.

"I admit I have a little Imelda Marcos in me. I think maybe you do too. But honestly, most of these aren't top-shelf brands. I pulled a pair of pale blue Sketchers from the rack. "These are a little tight for me. Try them."

She sat on the edge of the bed and slipped them on. "Perfect," she said.

"Good. You can keep them. Now let's go downstairs and get you some food. We'll take the back stairs." I led the way down the short hall leading to my living room, stopping at the bathroom. "I'll take your shoes down to Aunt Ibby. She has every cleaning product known to man in her laundry room. I'll bet she can save them." I picked up the studded tan suede ballerina flats which I figured may or may not have been Donald J. Pliners. Hard to tell. Jane Doe was right. They were a mess. "Yuck," I said. "You must have walked in some nasty stuff." I wrapped the shoes in a towel and we proceeded through my living room and down the two-flight twisty staircase to the first floor back hall. I tapped on Aunt Ibby's kitchen door, just opposite the laundry room. O'Ryan appeared almost immediately through his cat door, and sniffed at Jane Doe's blue Sketchers. My shoes on her feet. Must have been confusing to his sensitive pink nose. "We're here," I called, ducking into the neat, narrow, white-painted space with its washer, dryer, and ironing board, hurriedly tossing the towel-wrapped shoes onto the folding table, "and we're hungry."

The lock clicked and my aunt pulled open the door. "Welcome. The front doorbell just this minute chimed. It must be Pete. Will you let him in, Maralee?" She smiled at my companion. "You look so pretty in blue," she said, then frowned. "Oh dear. I don't know what to call you."

"You can call me Jane if you want to," she said. "For Jane Doe, you know."

The doorbell chimed "The Impossible Dream" once more and I hurried to let Pete in. O'Ryan, who as usual had raced me to the door, purred loudly with his nose pressed against the window. I pulled the door open and stepped into Pete's arms, returning his enthusiastic kiss. I would have purred too if I knew how.

With the cat running ahead of us, we took our time strolling through the living room. "How's she doing?" Pete whispered. "Has she remembered anything yet?"

"Not exactly," I whispered back. "She seemed to recognize the artist's drawing of John Doe though. At least it looked familiar to her. She doesn't know yet that he's dead."

"Interesting. Thanks for the heads-up." He wore his impossible-to-read cop face. We arrived in the kitchen. "Hello, Ms. Russell." Pete gave my aunt a side-hug. He loves her, but he still couldn't make himself use her first name. He turned and offered his hand to Jane Doe. "How do you do. Detective Pete Mondello. I understand you have a problem. Maybe I can help."

She shook his hand, smiling briefly. "Thank you. I hope so. I'm—well I guess, for now at least. I'm Jane Doe."

"Pleased to meet you, Jane." He returned the smile— in a cop-face sort of way.

"Maralee, would you set the table?" my aunt asked. "I think we'll eat here in the kitchen. It's more cozy than the dining room, don't you think? We'll use the Franciscan ivy-pattern china. I already have the serving pieces. Pete? Jane? Why don't you two sit at the table and we'll be all ready in just a few minutes." She aimed a broad wink in my direction.

I got it. She was leaving Pete and Jane Doe alone together at the table so that Pete could begin digging up facts, putting pieces together.

The two faced one another across the round oak table,

Jane facing in my direction, Pete with his back to me. My aunt busied herself at the stove and I ducked into the short passage between the kitchen and the dining room where assorted china sets were displayed in glass-fronted cabinets on either wall. I selected four plates and four bowls from the ivy Franciscan Ware—my favorite pattern—trying to keep my ears open at the same time. The conversation at the round oak table was muted. I could pick up a word here and there—"Stacia." "Salem." "Vacation." Too disjointed to make any sense to me. Aunt Ibby, at stove-side, had the better listening post by far. I returned to the kitchen, put the china on a nearby counter, and collected the appropriate silverware from its designated drawer.

"Jane, this must be very difficult for you." Pete used his sympathetic-cop voice. "I can't even imagine not being able to remember loved ones, home, pets . . ."

The woman sat up straight. "Pets," she exclaimed. "A cat. I think maybe I have a cat."

I approached the table, began arranging the place settings. "I thought so," I said. "You petted O'Ryan the very moment you first saw him." As if to reinforce my statement, O'Ryan said "Mmurrp," and moved close to Jane's chair.

"That's a good start," Pete said. "Tell us what you remember about your cat."

She shook her head. "I'm sorry. I just thought—never mind. I probably don't have one anyway."

"Don't worry about it," Pete said. "These things come back slowly sometimes. Lee said that the artist's sketch of an—uh—unidentified man looked familiar to you."

"Yes. It did. Quite familiar." She squeezed her eyes shut. "I can almost see him in my mind."

"Do you see him doing anything special? Can you see anything in the background when you visualize the man?"

Her eyes flew open. "No," she said. "No. I don't see anything around him."

"Don't worry about it," Pete said again. "Do you mind if I snap a photo of you with my phone? I'd like to send it over to headquarters. Maybe it will connect with someone."

"I don't mind," she said. "Should I smile?"

"Any way you're comfortable," he said. She smiled. He took several shots, tapped a number into his phone and, satisfied, tucked it back into his pocket.

"Are we ready for dinner?" Aunt Ibby approached the table, carrying an oval platter with the roast, which smelled wonderfully of rosemary and garlic, placing it in front of Pete along with a carving knife. "Maralee, will you serve the potatoes and peas while Pete carves?"

"Of course." I faced the glass-fronted cabinet above the counter while I transferred the vegetables from their pans to the serving bowls. I looked back and forth from the food to the reflection of the people at the table. Jane Doe's reflection faced me. Our eyes met.

Sometimes, when I look at reflective surfaces—any reflective surface—a mirror, a silver tray, an automobile hubcap, a glass-fronted kitchen cabinet—I see things other people don't see. I've learned that I am what's known as a "scryer." My friend River North calls me a "gazer." Whatever this gift or talent or curse is, it usually shows me things I don't want to see. This was one of those moments.

First came the flashing lights, then the swirling colors that always precede the damned things. There in the glass I saw the man, his eyes wide and frightened, mouth open in a silent scream. These visions don't usually have sound, but I knew the man was screaming. In water up to his neck, his head thrashed back and forth. I couldn't see his hands. His mouth was still open when his head sank beneath the water.

Was this the sight that had robbed Jane Doe of her memory?

CHAPTER 5

The vision disappeared as quickly as it had come. Once again, I saw a hazy reflection of Aunt Ibby's friendly kitchen superimposed on the Jadeite bowls and Bennington custard cups neatly stacked on the shelves behind the glass, but the image of the man in the water remained imprinted on my mind. Did Jane Doe witness the actual happening? Did she actually hear the scream that I'd only glimpsed in a square of ordinary window glass? The thought was chilling.

"Maralee? Are you ready with the vegetables?"

"Coming right up," I answered, glad for the interruption, placing the steaming bowls of bright green peas and fluffy mashed potatoes onto a tole serving tray, carrying it to the table. Pete completed his near-professional meat-carving job while my aunt placed a full gravy boat and a silver bowl of sparkling mint jelly onto the table.

Aunt Ibby took her usual seat—one of the things we like about round tables, there's no "head of the table" position. I sat beside Pete. Jane, seated beside my aunt, placed a linen napkin in her lap. "Everything looks so pretty and smells so good," she said. "Thank you for inviting me."

The meal was like many others I'd enjoyed with family and friends at this same table. I'd expected that maybe Pete would pursue questioning Jane Doe, but he kept the conversation light. Aunt Ibby pried a little bit—asking Jane if she preferred coffee or tea, and Jane answered immediately, "Coffee, I'm quite sure. Yes. Coffee." One more fact, but a minor one.

Aunt Ibby pressed on, still on the subject of food. "I'll start the coffee and pop the peach pie into the microwave for a second or two just to heat it up before I put the ice cream on top. Do you like pie, Jane?"

"I'm pretty sure I do." This line of questions would get us nowhere. I decided to try a different angle.

"Jane. Do you remember where you slept last night?"

She frowned, then scrunched her eyes together with an exaggerated look of concentration. "I had pajamas on," she said, opening her eyes. "Pink ones, I think."

I tried again, thinking about my own unwelcome visions. "Can you *visualize* the room you slept in?"

The eyes scrunched up again, then flew wide-open. "I can kind of see it, but it doesn't mean anything." She shrugged. "I've never seen it before."

"What do you say, Pete?" my aunt asked. "Do you think it will be all right if Jane spends tonight with us?" She looked at her watch. "It's a little late for you to make other arrangements, isn't it? Besides, she's a very nice girl." She nodded affirmatively at her own statement. "I'm sure of it."

Pete's cop face was firmly in place, so I couldn't tell what he thought about Jane's niceness or lack of it. He reached into his jacket pocket and pulled out his phone, glanced at it, and stood. "Excuse me. I need to take this call." He stepped out into the back hall, closing the door firmly behind him. O'Ryan, in a display of typical feline curiosity, followed him. It's an old house, and not particularly soundproof. I could detect a buzz of conversation from the hall, but couldn't make out the words. If I'd been alone in the kitchen, I definitely would have had my ear to the door. Instead, Jane and I made polite comments about food while my aunt retrieved the warm pie from the microwave and selected a carton of vanilla ice cream from the freezer.

Pete reappeared just as pie and coffee were served. "Chief says we should get the woman examined by a doctor to be sure this memory problem isn't caused by an injury. Then to answer your question, Ms. Russell, if she checks out okay she can stay here for tonight. No beds available at the shelter. Also, it seems that we already have an ID on John Doe. The manager of the Hawthorne Hotel recognized the artist's drawing. The man was registered there. Coincidentally, his name *is* actually John. John Sawtelle from Brookline—just outside Boston." He sat once again, leaning forward, facing Jane Doe. "Does any of that sound familiar to you, Jane?"

"Not exactly." The voice was soft, hesitant. "The man in the picture looked familiar to me. I already told Lee that—but you know, that bedroom Lee asked me to visualize—now that you mention it, it looked like a hotel bedroom, not a real person's room, you know? So, is this John Sawtelle someone I know? Did I stay at the same hotel?"

"We think it's possible that you were at the Hawthorne Hotel at the same time John Sawtelle was registered there. After dinner I'll take you down to the station, where we can scan your fingerprints. Doc Egan is in his office tonight and he'll look you over. If you don't need any medical treatment we'll come straight back here."

Jane looked as though she was about to cry again. Aunt Ibby quickly changed the subject. "A lot of people stay at the Hawthorne," she said. "It doesn't mean you know that poor man, and Doctor Egan used to be our family doctor before he became medical examiner. If you do have an injury, he'll fix you up just fine, and I'll bet the fingerprints will tell us your name and you'll remember everything." She reached over and patted Jane's hand. "Later tonight a couple of my girlfriends are coming over to watch one of our favorite shows. I'd love for you to meet them."

"The Angels?" Pete asked, not bothering to hide his smile.

The "Angels"—Aunt Ibby, Betsy Leavitt, and Louisa Abney-Babcock fancy themselves amateur sleuths, with ambitions toward becoming "real detectives." They actually do have certain detecting skills among them, which have proven useful to law enforcement in the past. Between Betsy's looks—she's still modeling professionally at sixty-something; Louisa's important contacts—she has enormous wealth and a pedigree back to the *Mayflower* and beyond; and my aunt's research ability and high-tech aptitude, they have access to people, places, and secrets the FBI and CIA might envy.

"Right," Aunt Ibby said. "I'm sure you'd like my friends, Jane, and I know they'd love to meet you. We get together sometimes to have a little wine and watch the newest

episode of *Midsomer Murders*. Maralee joins us sometimes, don't you, dear?"

"I do," I admitted.

*If anyone can pry Jane Doe's secrets out of her, those
three can do it.*

Pete must have had the same thought. "That's a good
idea, Ms. Russell. It'll be good for Jane to have some
company around her."

The pie and ice cream finished, I stood and began to
clear the table. Jane Doe had already started to stack the
dessert plates and forks neatly. *Does that mean she's well
brought-up, or has she worked as a waitress?* "More coffee, anyone?" I asked. Jane and my aunt both nodded.
Pete paused and fiddled with his phone. I refilled our
cups and returned to my seat, realizing that my invisible
field-reporter hat was once again firmly in place. How
could I frame a question that might jog her memory, but
still sound sympathetic to her situation? And what if my
recent terrifying vision had shown me exactly what Jane
had seen? That might very well be a memory we don't
want to jog. For a long moment we three sipped our coffee in silence while O'Ryan, from across the room, regarded Jane with undisguised cat-interest.

"I do hope you'll be able to join us this evening, Jane,"
my aunt said. "Betsy and Louisa are such interesting
women, and besides . . ." She dropped her voice and
looked from side to side as though someone might be listening. "The reason we get together for TV-mystery-
watching every week is because we share a common
interest in solving mysteries. *Real* mysteries. Isn't that
right, Maralee?"

I had to agree. "Right," I said.

Aunt Ibby warmed to the subject. "Someday we hope

to form our own detective agency, but for now we're what they call 'amateur sleuths.' Maybe, just *maybe* we can help you get some answers to your own mystery—for instance, why were you sitting on a bench in the common, not even knowing your own name?"

Jane's eyes suddenly opened wide. "Emily," she said. "I think maybe my name is Emily."

CHAPTER 6

"Emily." Pete tucked his phone into his pocket. "That's good. You're beginning to remember things bit by bit, like the cat and the pink pajamas and now your name. That's *really* good."

"Transient global amnesia," my aunt, wearing her wise-old-owl face, declared. "Mark my words."

"What?" Pete, Jane, and I all answered at once.

"*Mirage*, 1965," my movie-buff aunt declared. "Gregory Peck played an accountant with transient global amnesia. Great old black-and-white movie. He remembered things bit by bit, just like Jane does."

Jane/Emily tapped her temple. "Gregory Peck played an accountant?"

"In *Mirage* he did," Aunt Ibby said. "Maybe you've seen it?"

"I don't think so. It's just something about him being an accountant that seems familiar."

That seemed encouraging. "See? You're remembering things faster and faster," my optimistic aunt pointed out. "Not just the cat and the hotel room and the pink pajamas, but certain words mean something to you. I'll bet by tomorrow your mystery will be solved, just like Gregory's"

"Let's get started then," Pete said. "Do you have a sweater, Jane—er, Emily? It's getting chilly outside."

"You can keep calling me Jane if you want to. I'm not positive about the Emily thing. Anyway, I have a pink sweater. I put it in the laundry."

"It's a lovely cashmere sweater," Aunt Ibby said, "but it badly needs dry cleaning. I'm sure Maralee can lend her one for the evening. We can get the sweater cleaned, but I don't know what to do about the shoes. They're a total mess. They're suede, you know, and they have lots of little metal studs on them. They've picked up all kinds of mucky stuff."

"I'll run up and get her a sweater." I ducked into the front hall, avoiding even a glance at the damned mirror, hurried upstairs, grabbed a white cardigan, and zoomed back down to where the others waited. "Here you go." I handed the sweater to Jane, who once again wore a frightened look. "It's going to be all right," I told her. "You'll be back here with us in no time."

"Could you come with me?" Her voice was thin, tiny. I looked over at Pete, thought about the pile of work in my briefcase, and didn't answer.

"It might make it a little easier for her, Lee. You can come along if you want to."

What could I say? I was the one who'd brought her

home. "I'll come with you, Jane. You'll see. We'll be back here in no time."

"Ms. Russell, if you don't mind," Pete said, "I'd like to take those shoes along with us to the station."

"Of course." My aunt hurried back toward the kitchen and returned quickly with the shoes in a ziplock bag. "They're pretty nasty, and they were beginning to smell bad," she apologized, "but here they are."

It wasn't exactly "in no time," but things did move quickly when we got to the police station. The finger-printing was interesting. They don't use the fingers-on-the-ink-pad method anymore. They use a scanner. Faster and much less messy. While the tech studied the results of the scan, Pete looked over his shoulder and Jane stood behind Pete, seemingly studying the lettering on a door marked "Forensics." Doc Egan stepped out of his office a few doors away and greeted me. "Hello there, Lee. Seems as though you turn up like a bright new penny under some pretty dark circumstances. You reporting on the Sawtelle matter?"

I shook my head. "Nope. Not reporting on anything. I'm here for moral support for—um—Jane Doe." I pointed to Jane. "I guess you're going to see if you can figure out what happened to her memory."

"Just checking for head trauma. She a friend of yours?"

"Not exactly. I kind of found her on the common and brought her home to Aunt Ibby."

He didn't even look surprised. "She followed me home can I keep her, huh?"

"Pretty much. She seems like a good person. She's frightened. It must be terrifying to not even remember your own name."

"We'll see if we can eliminate a blow to the head anyway, then we'll take it from there."

"Aunt Ibby says it's transient global amnesia."

He smiled. "Has Ibby been watching *General Hospital*?"

"Gregory Peck," I said.

He nodded as though my answer made sense and moved toward where Pete and Jane stood, his hand outstretched. "How do you do, young lady. I'm Doctor Egan. Let's see if we can figure out what's going on with you."

Jane Doe took a step back. Once again, she asked, "Can you come with me, Lee?"

Could I? Do I even want to? I threw a questioning look in Pete's direction.

"What do you say, Doc?" he asked. "It's all right with me."

"If it will make you feel better, Lee may certainly join us. This won't take long, and I promise it won't hurt a bit. Step into my office." He led us down a short hall and opened the door marked MEDICAL EXAMINER while Pete, with the plastic-wrapped shoes, walked toward the door marked EVIDENCE ROOM.

The doctor's statement had been true. It didn't take long and didn't appear to hurt. He took her blood pressure and temperature with some pretty fancy-looking equipment, took her pulse the old-fashioned way, fingers on her wrist, checking his watch. He ran his hands over her skull, pressed her temples and behind her ears. "I don't see any bruising." He shone a flashlight into her eyes one at a time, then used a different light to look into her ears, all the while asking questions. "Are you dizzy at all? Is your vision clouded? Any ringing in your ears? Headache? Can you remember anything at all?"

Jane told him about the few things she'd told us, about the cat and the pajamas and the name Emily. "Sometimes it's just a word that seems to mean something to me," she said. "This whole thing is so weird and strange. I don't like it."

Doc has a good bedside manner. I remembered how kind and caring he'd always been with me and Aunt Ibby anytime we'd consulted him. Jane's vital signs and answers to questions apparently meant she didn't have a head injury, and after about fifteen minutes we were back in the hall where Pete waited.

"All clear?" he asked.

"I think we can rule out head trauma as a cause of the problem for now," the doctor reported, "and since she's beginning to remember a few things, it's probably a temporary condition." He shook Jane's hand again. "I think you'll be fine, young lady. However, if you develop a headache, blurred vision, ringing in your ears, we'll set you up for some scans. Don't you hesitate to call if you need me. Ibby has my private number." He winked at me. "Tell your aunt her diagnosis is quite possibly correct." He shook his head. "Gregory Peck, indeed."

"The doctor says it's a temporary condition. That's a relief. But if I didn't hit my head, what made my memory disappear?"

You saw a man being murdered.

Getting her memory back was going to be traumatic for sure. I put on a happy face. "Aunt Ibby will be anxious to know what Doc Egan said. Can we leave now, Pete?"

"No problem," he said. "I'll drop you two off and come back here to tie up some loose ends." We three climbed back into Pete's car and headed for home.

As we rounded the corner to Washington Square, Jane Doe pressed her face against the window. "That's the Salem Common," she said. She pointed. "And that's where you found me, Lee." Stacia's bench was barely visible in the dim glow of streetlamps. We turned onto Winter Street and Pete parked in front of the house.

"Look, Jane," I said. "There's O'Ryan in the window waiting for us."

"Just like before," she said. "It seems like a long time ago." It seemed that way to me too.

I unlocked the front door. O'Ryan gave us each an enthusiastic greeting. Aunt Ibby was right behind him in the foyer, concern in her voice. "What did the doctor say? Are you all right, Jane?" We gave her the good news about Jane's condition and I repeated Doc's confirmation of her movie-inspired diagnosis.

"Good. Then that's settled. Maralee, why don't you show Jane the second-floor guest room. Fix her up with pajamas and toothbrush and such. The girls will be here at around nine thirty. We'll meet in the living room."

I knew I had some serious work to do on my presentation for Mr. Doan, and stopping to watch a TV show certainly hadn't been in my plan. He'd be expecting some sort of proposal to share with the sales force by noon tomorrow. But between Pete's "Keep an eye on her" and my aunt's confidence in the Angels' mystery-solving abilities, I'd have to rearrange my priorities.

"No problem," I said, in as agreeable a tone as I could manage. "May I use your office for a while this evening, Aunt Ibby? I have a little homework to do. Your printer is better than mine, and I'd like to use your spiral-binding machine." I wouldn't have the artwork until tomorrow sometime, but I knew from experience that a spiral-bound report along with a promise of a PowerPoint presentation to come—even if the project wasn't completely thought out—would make a good impression on Bruce Doan.

"A spiral binder? My goodness. You must have a very complete home office, Ms. Russell. I'd love to see it."

"I'd love to show it off." My aunt beamed. "Follow me." With O'Ryan in the lead, we followed her to the spacious office just off the living room. The door stood open as usual, and she switched on the overhead light.

Aunt Ibby's office is worth showing off. Gorgeous cherry furniture—desk, bookcases, file cabinets, tables and chairs, with space for the three-screen computer, top-of-the-line copier, fax machine, phone, iPad, scanner, the spiral binder, paper cutter, and a few more sleekly designed gadgets I've never figured out—and books—lots of books.

Jane was clearly impressed. "Oh, wow! This is amazing. She moved into the room, peering closely at the computer screens. "Are you using QuickBooks?"

"Yes. Took a class at the library to learn it. Do you use it too?"

"I don't know," Jane admitted, "but I guess I must. Maybe I'm beginning to remember some more things."

Another fact about Jane Doe's past.

"That's wonderful," I said, hoping it really was. "I'm sure you're going to be fine," I added, hoping she really would be. "Let's go upstairs and get you settled." The second-floor guest room is very pretty—lots of pink—with a comfortable bed, an adjoining bathroom, and a good-sized wall-hung television. We climbed the front staircase and I opened the guest room door. "Oh, I love pink," she said, noting the very feminine décor. I remembered her comment about pink pajamas. "I'll run upstairs and grab some pj's and toothbrush and comb and stuff for you. Be right back." I really did run up the next flight, remembering the "keep an eye on her" admonition, even though I didn't know what I was supposed to be watching for.

I have a good selection of pajamas—many styles and colors—ranging from basic to sexy. I selected a pair of plain cotton tailored pale pink ones with white piping and single breast pocket, and a pair of fuzzy pink slippers, and put them into a reusable shopping bag from Shaw's. Every time I have my teeth cleaned my dentist gives me one of those neat plastic zippered pouches with toothbrush, sample-size toothpaste, and dental floss. I grabbed one of those along with a comb that came with a gift pack from Ulta, and stuck them into the bag. I added a few paperback mysteries, a pen, and a brand-new composition book, still in its Staples bag, in case she wanted to make notes about memories as they occurred to her, and started back down the stairs. We'd figure out her wardrobe for tomorrow later. Her own clothes could probably be washed and dried by then anyway. I knocked on the still-open guest room door—not wanting to startle the poor woman, figuring that her nerves must have been pretty well frayed by then.

The television set had been turned on. I heard Howard Templeton's voice. I didn't have to look at the screen to know what she'd been watching. Jane Doe stood quietly in front of a window facing north on Winter Street. She'd pulled the sheer curtains aside. "I brought you a few things," I said, putting the bag down on a flowered chintz upholstered chair.

She let the curtains fall back into place, turning to face

me. "I saw it on the news. About that poor man—John Sawtelle—being murdered," she said. "Maybe I actually *do* know him—and what if somebody out there is looking for *me*? Following *me*?"

Keep an eye on her. The words assumed new meaning. *What if somebody* is *looking for her?*

"Don't worry," I said, struggling to sound convincing. "You're safe with us. We have a good alarm system. Pete will be here soon and I'll ask him to stay the night."

"Okay, Lee," she said in a soft, almost little-girl voice. "If you say so. I don't know what else I can do."

"You'll be fine." *Did that sound a little too hearty?* I toned it down a notch. "I have to do a little work for my job. You can stay here and rest until Aunt Ibby's friends arrive, or if you want to, you can come on downstairs with me."

"I don't think I asked you," she said, her voice returning to normal pitch. "What do you do for work?"

I pointed to the TV where a commercial for Stowaway Sweets showed yummy chocolate fudge. "I work at WICH-TV. Program director."

"Really? That sounds exciting. You're so pretty though, I should think you'd be on a show where everybody could see you."

"Thanks. I used to be a reporter. This—uh—promotion is recent. I'm just getting started." I launched into an abbreviated version of my plans for a morning kids' show starring a cowboy and a girl clown. "I'm thinking of a rodeo set. Split-rail fence. A bull chute where guests would run out onto the stage, maybe some circus props too. It's still all a bit up in the air." I had no idea whether any of it made sense to the woman.

"That must be an exciting job," she said. "I guess I'll

come downstairs with you if you don't mind. I promise I won't say a word." She made a zipper motion across her lips. "Quiet as a little mouse."

"I'll grab my briefcase and we'll go to my aunt's office."

Once again, I trotted up the one flight, opened the orange door, and picked up purse and briefcase. Jane Doe waited for me in the hall outside the guest room, O'Ryan seated at her feet. "I see you have company," I said.

"He's very good company." She bent to pat his head. "Good boy. I hope if I *do* have a cat somewhere, that somebody is taking care of him. Or her."

I'd thought of the same thing, but hesitated to mention it. "Cats are very resourceful," I told her. "Really clever. I'm sure it won't be long before we learn who you are and where your cat—if there is one—might be." We went downstairs again, and into the living room. "Aunt Ibby, "I called. "We're back. We'll be in your office."

She popped her head around the corner from the kitchen. "I'll let you know when the girls arrive. Meanwhile, I've put your things in the washing machine, Jane—all except your sweater."

"Thanks so much. You're very kind."

"Nonsense. No trouble at all. But those shoes! What on earth have you been walking in?"

Jane gave a smile and a helpless little shrug. "Beats me," she said, and followed me into the office.

CHAPTER 7

As good as her word, Jane sat mouse-quiet, but alert and interested while I worked. I made a few corrections on my hastily composed proposal for *Ranger Rob's Rodeo*, added a space between paragraphs to make the double-spaced pages look like more than they were, edited and cropped color photos of Katie and Rob, inserting them where appropriate. I'd just printed out a title sheet in crisp black Bodoni bold when Jane broke the silence.

"Do you have any eight-and-a-half-by-eleven clear poly cover sheets?"

"I wouldn't be a bit surprised if we do," I said. "Why?"

"I just thought if you made sort of a collage with those photos and your floor plan and that bull chute thing you were talking about, and maybe some black-and-white photos of the cowboy and the clown when they worked here years ago—then printed your title on it and used it under plastic for the cover of your proposal, then spiral-bound it, it would look more polished. Professional, you know?"

Jane Doe knows something about preparing proposals.

Before long, after raiding Aunt Ibby's office supply cabinet, Jane and I—working together—had produced a dozen copies of what I'd call a polished and professional-looking presentation of a pretty hastily formed idea. As soon as I got Dakota's artwork and mounted copies of it on foam board, this thing would look as though we'd worked on it for weeks.

We returned Aunt Ibby's office to its original state of perfection and carried two neat stacks of our newly minted presentations up to my place. We were on our way back down the stairs when a hum of conversation and a few bursts of laughter announced that the Angels had arrived. We hurried back through the living room and into the kitchen. Aunt Ibby introduced Jane to the two as "Jane Doe," so I knew she had told Betsy and Louisa about the woman's sad predicament.

"We're going to do everything we can to help you find your identity, my dear," Louisa assured her.

"You bet," said Betsy as she uncorked a cold bottle of rosé and headed for the living room. "Don't you worry. Say, can I call you Janie?"

That met with a smile, a shrug, and a "why not?" With Aunt Ibby bearing a tray of wineglasses while I carried the wicker snack basket, it appeared that the evening was off to a good start.

We had a good fifteen minutes to spare before the start

of *Midsomer Murders*, and the Angels lost no time in beginning their own unique style of investigation into Jane
Doe's real life.

"You appear to be a well-brought-up young person of
culture." Louisa spoke firmly. "Obvious good breeding."

Betsy giggled. "She's not a horse, Louisa."

"Of course she's not, but it works the same way. Mark
my words, she comes from a distinguished bloodline."

"Girls, you're talking about Jane as though she's not
here," my aunt scolded. "Jane, do you have any thoughts
at all about family? Parents? Siblings? A home?"

Jane closed her eyes, sipped her wine, and put a
chocolate-dipped pretzel into her mouth, chewing thoughtfully. The room grew silent. We all watched. Waited. Her
eyes popped open. Lilacs," she said. "There are lilac
bushes in the yard. They smell wonderful." She closed
her eyes again, squeezing them tightly this time, her face
scrunched up, forehead creased with the effort. "And I
think—there's that cat again. It's black with a white front.
How pretty."

"A tuxedo cat," Louisa said with an affirmative nod.

"Good job, Janie." Betsy clapped her hands together.
"Anything else?"

"You've made a good start on remembering things,
Jane," I said. "Do you think closing your eyes is helpful?"

She reached for another chocolate-dipped pretzel, then
smiled. "Not especially. I think maybe it's the chocolate
and the wine."

"They always work for me," Louisa said. "And fortunately, we have a good supply of both." This brought a
chorus of laughter from the Angels *and* their new friend
Jane. This was going better than I'd expected. The begin-

ning credits for *Midsomer Murders* rolled. O'Ryan climbed into my lap, and talk of cats, lilacs, and chocolate ceased. The story line involved a real estate agent getting murdered in front of a crowd of people attending the unveiling of a collection of doll houses.

There was a fundraising break midway through the murders. "More chocolate? More wine?" Betsy suggested.

"Sure. Why not?" Jane, smiling, held up her glass. "This is a good show. I don't think I've ever watched it before."

"We find it instructive," my aunt said. "We like the way the detectives deduce without a lot of violence. We watch *Father Brown* mysteries too. Perhaps you'll join us for that."

"I hope I can," Jane said. "I'll have to see what Detective Mondello says about it, and also there's a chance my memory will come back soon and I'll go back to wherever I belong. And mostly I hope you'll all still like me when I get back to being whoever I am."

There was a chorus of "Of course we will," and once again, all eyes returned to the TV screen. O'Ryan abandoned my lap and streaked toward the kitchen. "I think Pete's back," I whispered. "I'll let him in." I followed the cat, who'd already scooted out the cat door when I got there. I peeked out the window and saw Pete's headlights as he pulled into the driveway from the Oliver Street side of the house. O'Ryan and I were both on the back steps to greet him.

"How's she doing?" he asked, after properly kissing me hello and patting the top of O'Ryan's head. "Remembering anything?"

"A black-and-white cat and some lilac bushes," I reported. "The Angels are grilling her gently."

"The manager at the hotel recognized her photo," he said. "She apparently occupied the room adjoining John Sawtelle's."

"Didn't they have her name?"

"Nope. Sawtelle booked both rooms in advance with a company credit card. He apparently headed up a big real estate company in Brookline."

Real estate? Like the Midsomer Murders *dollhouse guy?*

Pete continued. "He was supposed to leave today. The manager opened both rooms for us. Suitcases, personal stuff was all still there. And, by the way, the door between the rooms was locked from both sides." We entered the kitchen and Pete motioned for me to sit in one of the captain's chairs. He sat in another. "It doesn't look like there was anything romantic going on between Jane and Sawtelle. Maybe she's some kind of business associate."

"What are you planning to do with Jane?" I wondered. "She's getting along wonderfully well with the Angels—all three of them. They call her 'Janie.'"

"I told you. She can spend the night. I'll be here to keep an eye on things. Maybe we'll learn more tomorrow. Then we'll see."

"Do you think she saw what happened to John Doe—Sawtelle?"

"Wouldn't be surprised."

I thought of my vision. "Neither would I."

I got the raised-eyebrow cop-face look, but no comment on my observation, which probably sounded a little creepy since I had no basis in fact to support it. Pete knows all about my being a scryer, but avoids what he calls "hocus-pocus" whenever possible. The moment passed.

"Everybody's in the living room drinking wine, eating chocolate, and watching *Midsomer Murders*," I said. "Want to join them?"

"Let's go." With a guiding hand at my elbow, he steered me back toward the living room, where all was dark and silent except for the glowing TV screen, British-accented crime-solvers, and the occasional dainty crunch of a chocolate-dipped pretzel.

CHAPTER 8

We each kept our seats in the living room after the end of the program. After my aunt turned off the set and substituted coffee mugs for the wineglasses, there was a brief discussion among the Angels about a new sleuthing technique used on the show, along with some excitement about the trick of killing someone in full view of a crowd at a dollhouse show. Jane, Pete, and I refrained from contributing to the conversation. Pete, because it's his job to listen, me because I'd missed part of the show, and Jane—I didn't know. She'd shown bright interest in what the other women had to say though, looking from one to the other as they spoke.

When the critique of the show was over, attention turned to Pete. "Have the police learned anything new about the case since you left us?" my aunt wanted to know.

"We have." Pete's voice was solemn. "We know the identity of the man found at Collins Cove this morning." He focused his eyes on Jane Doe. "His name is John Sawtelle. Ring any bells with anybody?"

We all faced the woman, watching her expression. After what seemed like a very long minute, she leaned forward, facing Pete. "I saw it on TV. John Doe's name is really John. Wouldn't it be funny if mine is really Janie?"

"It's not familiar to you at all, Jane?" Pete asked. "John Sawtelle?" He spoke the name carefully, pronouncing each syllable. He's—was—the CEO of High Water Realty in Brookline."

"Brookline? That does ring a bell. But does it mean anything? I mean, it's just a city in Massachusetts, right? Maybe everybody knows that and it's nothing special to me."

"Are you planning to give Janie's pictures to the papers and the TV stations?" Betsy asked. "I mean, what if Janie here saw John being murdered? What if there are bad guys looking for her? If they figure out who she is, wouldn't she be in danger?"

Pete nodded. "Yes. It's possible that she would. So for the time being we're not releasing Jane Doe's picture. We'll continue to monitor missing persons reports and we've contacted Sawtelle's main office. Jane, we believe the people there can tell us who you are. If you agree, I'd like to arrange for a female officer to drive you to Brookline tomorrow to find out if they can identify you, tell us where you live. It's only an hour or so drive from here. Maybe if you go home—wherever that is—you'll remember what it is you've blocked out."

"It might be something bad, Janie," I said, thinking of

my vision, "but it's surely important for you to remember who you are."

"I agree," Jane said. "Sure. I'll do what you think is best, Pete. Is it all right if I call you Pete?"

"Yes," he said. "And I have a feeling we'll all be able to call you by your own name before long."

I was already planning ahead for Janie's journey to Brookline. Her own clothes would be ready by morning, except for her sweater. She'd need another sweater or a jacket and a handbag though, and some different shoes. "Do you plan to have the officer pick Jane up from here in the morning, Pete? If you do, we're going to have to get her organized tonight."

"Organized? Oh yeah. Clothes and stuff."

"Don't worry. We'll fix her up with whatever she needs," I promised. "Her own clothes are already in the dryer."

Janie smiled in my direction. "I'm so lucky that I met you, Lee."

Pete's phone buzzed. "Excuse me," he said, and stepped out into the front hall. No one spoke. Aunt Ibby, always unerringly polite, turned the TV set back on so we wouldn't appear to be listening to Pete's call—which, of course, we were.

"It must be nearly time for the news," she said, changing the channel to WICH-TV. "Let's see what Buck Covington has to say tonight."

"Doesn't matter what he says," Betsy offered. "I just like looking at him."

Buck Covington is the station's incredibly handsome nightly news anchor. His ratings are amazingly high for a local news show—probably because, like Betsy, a lot of women (and not a few men) in the audience just like looking at him. Buck provides not only excellent eye candy, but has the rare ability to read the teleprompter flawlessly all the time, never ever fluffing a word or a line. Mr. Doan says that otherwise the man is "dumb as a brick." My friend River North thinks otherwise and the two have become the station's "glamour couple."

I'd expected that Buck would talk about the police identifying the murdered man—John Sawtelle—and I was right. An actual photo of the man had replaced the artist's pastel rendering. I watched Jane's face as Buck read off the facts known about the victim—the name of his business, the fact that he left a wife and one child, that according to his associates he had no known enemies. There was no mention of a companion accompanying him to Salem. Jane watched the screen with apparent interest, but without any indication of recognition.

Pete came back into the living room and sat beside me on the love seat. "Something new," he whispered. I could tell by the way my aunt leaned forward in her chair, her head turned away from the TV and toward Pete, that she'd heard the whispered words—or maybe had read his lips. Not much gets by Aunt Ibby. Buck had gone to commercial, so she muted the sound.

"Something new going on, Pete?" she asked, her tone polite, her expression innocent, her intent undoubtedly devious.

He folded his arms and shook his head. "Might as well tell you, I suppose. The media will have it soon enough. Forensics says that John Sawtelle definitely drowned, but not in salt water. He was already dead when the body was dumped onto the beach." He looked directly at Jane Doe as he spoke. Janie's expression did not change. No flash of recognition. No gasp of discovery. Nothing.

"So he was drowned somewhere else then? But in fresh water?" Louisa asked.

"They're still analyzing the water in his lungs," Pete said with another glance in Janie's direction. By this time *I* was totally concentrating on watching her face. Still nothing.

"So he was killed in a pond or a river or a lake, right?" Betsy tossed her Farah Fawcett–like hair, pointing a manicured finger in Pete's direction. "So now we have to figure out *where* he was drowned."

"What if it was a bathtub or a swimming pool?" Louisa suggested.

"If it's not someplace with plumbing though, it has to be someplace fairly secluded," Aunt Ibby reasoned. "He must have struggled, and if his mouth wasn't bound up like his hands, he probably yelled for help."

He did. I saw his mouth open. He screamed.

I watched Janie's face. Interest. Nothing more.

"We need to find out how they sneaked his body into the water at Collins Cove," Louisa said.

"Wait a minute, ladies." Pete held up both hands. "What's this 'we' all about? This is strictly a police matter."

"Oh, Pete, dear, don't you worry. We won't get in your way one single bit, will we, Angels?" Aunt Ibby wore her very sweetest smile. "And we'll come straight to you with every clue we discover, won't we, girls?" That pronouncement was greeted with enthusiastic agreement from the other two. I made no comment. Neither did Jane Doe, who looked from one to the other of the Angels, her expression registering—what? Curiosity maybe. Nothing more.

Pete launched into his speech about the importance of citizens letting the professionals handle dealing with crime and criminals. "Citizens should 'see something, say something.' That's helpful. Amateurs sneaking around, putting themselves at risk is *not* helpful."

"Of course. That's what I said. Every little thing we see or hear, we'll come straight to you." My aunt crossed her heart. "Promise."

Pete wore his exasperated-cop face. "Lee. Try to talk some sense into these women while I get Jane's escort for tomorrow set up. Mind if I go upstairs and use your computer?"

"Go right ahead. I'll be up shortly," I said, knowing full well that "talking sense" to the Angels was a waste of time. They were on a mission and wouldn't be deterred by any words of mine. "First, let's see about getting Janie here settled into the guest room. She's had quite a day. Aunt Ibby, will you check on Janie's clothes?"

"I'm sure everything is dry. I'll be right back." She hurried out the back door, returning within minutes with Jane's blouse and skirt on hangers, undies neatly folded. "Here you go, dear. She handed the clothing to the woman. "Maralee will lend you shoes and a sweater, I'm sure."

"Of course." I stood, motioning for Jane Doe to join me. "Ready for bed, Janie?"

"Sure," she said, looking around at the others in the room. "Thank you, everybody. Good night."

To a chorus of good-night wishes, she followed me to the foyer, pausing in front of the hall tree. The tall antique mahogany piece with its handy lift-up storage seat, well-placed coat hooks, and ornate carving surrounding the full-length mirror, has stood in the same place for as long as I can remember. It is, I suppose, a useful, interesting, and decorative piece of furniture. Aunt Ibby likes to check her appearance in the tall beveled mirror before she answers the door.

I try hard to avoid *ever* looking into that mirror, but since Janie stood right in front of it, the flashing lights and swirling colors were impossible to ignore. I saw *two* Janies back-to-back. One, wearing a blue blouse and jeans, faced me. The other, the one in the mirror, had her back to me. She wore a white blouse, beige skirt, and a pink cashmere sweater. As I watched, she reached into the pocket of the sweater and pulled out a key fob.

CHAPTER 9

"Janie," I said in as casual a tone of voice as I could manage while seeing double images, "do you remember having a car?"

She moved away from the mirror and toward the staircase. That was good. It was easier to address jeans-and-blue-shirt Janie. "A car?" She climbed the first step, then paused, looking at me. "A car. Yes, I think so. At least I know to drive. I'm sure of that." She held out both hands, as though she was gripping an imaginary steering wheel. She reached down with her right. "Stick shift." The words were almost whispered, as she made the quick hand movement indicating shifting from park to first gear. The motion was a familiar one to me.

"Me too." I watched her face. "My husband was a race car driver. He taught me. I love cars. Pete calls me a gearhead. Who taught you?"

"Daddy," she said, and continued climbing the stairs. "Daddy taught me to drive his car."

"That's nice." I spoke softly, following her, hoping she'd keep talking, remember more. "Not many people these days know how."

Abruptly, she stopped climbing. I nearly bumped into her. "I remembered that!" She turned and faced me again, her voice excited. "I remember my daddy."

I reached out, wanting to hug her, to share her joy in the memory, but stopped, afraid I might interrupt this new flow of information about her past. "What kind of car was it?" I kept my tone conversational.

The answer came promptly. "A 2015 Jeep Renegade. Black. Way more fun than automatic shift I had."

My inner gearhead emerged. "Six-speed manual transmission? Two-point-four liter engine?"

"Right." With a pleasant nod she resumed climbing the stairs toward the second-floor guest room.

"That's good, Janie," I told her as I pushed open the door to the pink room and turned on the overhead light. "The remote for the TV is on the bedside table and there are plenty of books and magazines on the window seat. Have a good rest and I'll see you in the morning."

"Good night, Lee," she said. "And thank you so much. I . . . I don't know what I would have done without you."

"You're going to be fine," I assured her. "You're already beginning to remember things. Tomorrow will be better. Good night." I pulled the door closed and started up the stairs. Pete had used the back stairs, so I pulled the keys from my bag and unlocked the orange door. I thought of the key fob I'd seen in Janie's hand in the mirror and wondered if that key would start the Jeep Renegade, or some other vehicle.

Pete looked up from my laptop. "I'll be through in a minute here. Did you get Jane Doe settled in for the night?"

"I think so. She remembered a few more things just since you left. She remembers her dad and she knows how to drive. Stick shift."

"No kidding. That's great. Maybe by tomorrow she'll be able to help us with something useful."

"I hope so. It must be awful. Not remembering. Not even your own name." I suppressed a shudder. "Poor Janie. I think I'll change into my jammies too. Be right back."

"Uh-huh," he said, returning to whatever he had going on the laptop.

I grabbed my Donald Duck–print pj's and headed down the hall to the bathroom. I hit the start button on the Mr. Coffee on the way out of the kitchen, planning to keep Pete awake for a while so I could try a little more prying. He'd seemed a little more generous with "cop talk" lately, since I was no longer a field reporter. I planned to take advantage of that.

When I returned to the kitchen—showered, moisturized, and pajamaed—Pete had closed up the laptop and was on his phone. "Okay, thanks for the heads-up." He put the phone back into his pocket. "Well. I'll be damned," he said. "St. Peter's Church."

"Saint Peter's Church?" I echoed. "What about it?" I pulled a couple of mugs from the cabinet, poured us each a cup of coffee, and pulled out the chair opposite his. "What's going on?"

"Darndest thing," he said. "Seems Sister Judith from St Peter's called the station this morning to report that someone had left a car in the small lot behind the church, with the doors unlocked and a handbag in the front seat.

She wanted the department to know she'd taken the hand-bag inside for safekeeping in case the owner called us."

"That was wise," I said. "So did someone call about it?"

"No." He took a thoughtful sip of his coffee. "No. No, they didn't. But when an officer went by the church this afternoon to follow up on the call, the vehicle was still there, so he checked the registration."

"And?"

"It's registered to John Sawtelle."

I tried to smother a gasp. "Don't tell me it's a Jeep Renegade."

He frowned. "No. What makes you think that? It's a white 2020 Audi Q8. We've already towed it."

"What about the handbag? Any ID in it?"

"Yep. License. Credit cards. Cell phone. All belonging to one Emily Jean Hemenway. The key to the Audi was in it too."

"Emily," I repeated. "Our Jane Doe?"

"Definitely. Good thing we printed her earlier. We have no official ID on her yet, but our Jane Doe's prints are all over the Audi."

"So you think Janie drove John Sawtelle's car into the lot behind the church this morning."

"That's what we think."

"But she doesn't remember doing that."

"Looks that way." He glanced around the kitchen. "Got any cookies or anything?"

"Girl Scout. Are you going to try to question her about it right now?" I got a package of Samoas from the Red Riding Hood cookie jar. "One or two?"

"Two, please." He glanced at Kit-Cat. It was past eleven. "Questioning her can wait until morning, I think. Why did you think the vehicle was a Jeep Renegade?"

"That's what she learned to drive a stick on. I guess it must be her dad's." I slid three cookies onto a paper plate. Two for Pete and one for me. "Or hers."

"Her memory is coming back pretty fast," he said. "She could be a big help to us in figuring out what happened to John Sawtelle."

I thought again of the screaming man in my vision. "She might remember some things she'd rather forget," I said. "After all, *something* made her lose her memory."

"You're right. But according to Doc Egan, she's going to remember it all fairly soon, for better or for worse." He bit into a cookie. "Whatever she saw, I'm betting it will lead us to a killer."

"I hope so," I agreed. "I hate the idea that somebody mean enough to tie a man's hands and throw him into the water to drown is walking around free in Salem."

"I guess you realize that this has changed our plans to have Sergeant Rouse take Jane Doe—I mean Emily Hemenway—to Brookline," he said. "There are some serious questions that need to be answered—memory loss or not. Your newfound friend is now a possible witness or maybe even a suspect in a murder investigation. She'll be riding with Rouse to the station, not home to Daddy, whoever he is."

Detective Sergeant Joyce Rouse is a high school classmate of mine, and a genuinely nice person. I was glad she'd be the officer accompanying Janie. "Speaking of the daddy, you'd think by now somebody would be wondering where she is," I said. "Still no missing persons reports?"

"Nope. There weren't any on Sawtelle either."

"That seems odd to me."

"Not really," he said. "Sawtelle and whoever was in

the adjoining room—quite possibly Jane Doe—had reservations for two nights. We've contacted Sawtelle's family, of course, regarding his death. We expect the body will be released fairly soon."

"Did you ask them about Jane Doe?"

"No." He frowned. "We don't know for sure what that connection might be. Business, pleasure, or nothing at all. An older man traveling with a young woman? Well, it could be awkward."

It sure could.

In the morning I was the first one up for a change, anticipating a busy day—on so many levels. First, of course, was the mysterious young woman one floor below us. Was she an innocent bystander who might have witnessed a murder? Was she a business associate of the victim? Possibly a girlfriend? Or did she have something to do with his death? Or all of the above? Besides that, I had a whale of a job to do at WICH-TV without a clear idea of how I was going to accomplish all that needed to be done in the time frame I'd been given. I started the coffee, poured O'Ryan's breakfast kibble into his red bowl, then hurried down the short hall to the bathroom, trying not to disturb the sleeping man and cat on my bed.

I returned to get dressed for the day while Pete headed for the shower. "I'll get Janie up and take her downstairs to Aunt Ibby's for some breakfast," I told him. "I guess you'll need to come downstairs and tell her about the Audi and that we know her real name before Joyce Rouse gets here."

"I'll be there in twenty minutes or so," he promised, pouring himself a mug of coffee. "You look nice."

"Thanks," I said. I'd picked a pale yellow silk shantung pants suit, aiming for a businesslike but casual look for my foray into simultaneous set designing and program directing. "I'm not sure whether I'll be sitting at my desk making plans, or running around on the set arranging props, or trying to build a bull chute out of closet poles."

"I have no idea what you just said, but I'm sure you can handle it." He gave me a quick kiss. "See you downstairs. O'Ryan has already left."

"I don't suppose Janie can have her own handbag back."

That brought only a head shake and an exasperated eye roll. I picked up the sweater and the small cross-body Brighton handbag I'd selected to lend to Janie along with a pair of Gianni Bini tan flats, and stepped out into the upstairs hall and looked over the railing. I could see part of the second floor landing, including the door to the pink guest room. It was slightly ajar.

What if Jane Doe is gone? What if she's remembered what happened to John Sawtelle and has run away?

I ran down the stairs, tapped on the door, and without waiting for an answer, pushed it open. The bed was made. The TV was off. The pajamas I'd loaned her were neatly folded on the flower-print boudoir chair. "Janie?" I called. My voice sounded like a croak. I tried again. "Janie, are you here?"

CHAPTER 10

I had never before in my life been so happy to hear the sound of a toilet flushing.

"I'm in the bathroom, Lee," came the welcome voice. "Be right out."

"Okay," I said, hoping the panic I'd felt a moment ago didn't show in my voice. I put the sweater and handbag on the bed and the shoes on the floor, wondering as I did so if they'd give Janie's handbag with all her stuff in it back to her anytime soon. I'd been pretty sure they wouldn't, so I'd put a comb, lip gloss, tissues, and an in-expensive watch I'd won at a church raffle along with few dollars into the cross-body bag I'd selected for her. "I've brought some shoes and a sweater and stuff for you."

"Thanks, Lee." The bathroom door opened and she stepped into the room, smiling, attractive in her own clothing. She sat on the edge of the bed and slipped on the shoes. "These feel fine. You've been so generous." She put the watch onto her wrist. "So kind."

"You're very welcome. I'm so pleased that we can help. Did you sleep well?"

"I did. I'd probably still be in bed if O'Ryan hadn't scratched on my door. I guess you must have sent him. Smart cat."

"Yes, he is," I agreed. *Was he checking to be sure she was still here?* "But visiting you was his own idea."

"Oh, that's sweet." She picked up the handbag and tossed the sweater over her shoulders. "I guess it's about time for me to take a ride with the lady officer, right?"

"Um—yes, but there's been a change of plans. Pete will explain. Let's go downstairs to Aunt Ibby's and have a bite of breakfast."

"All right." Her voice was hesitant. "Is anything wrong?"

"Pete will explain," I said again, opened the door and stepped into the hall, really glad that the explaining wasn't up to me. Janie followed me silently down the front staircase. I didn't dare to look at the hall tree mirror. O'Ryan waited for us at the arched entrance to Aunt Ibby's living room, then turned and bolted for the kitchen as soon as we'd both reached the foyer.

"Aunt Ibby, it's Janie and me," I called, although I was sure the cat had already alerted her.

"Good morning, girls." She stood next to the open oven door and waved to us with oven-mitted hands. "You're just in time for date scones," she said, deftly moving the pan from stove to counter. "Nigel's mother's recipe." Nigel St. John is my aunt's Scotland Yard gentleman friend who occasionally visits Salem. "Coffee's ready. Help yourselves. Where's Pete?"

"He'll be down shortly," I said.

"Your kitchen always smells wonderful, Ms. Russell." Janie sat, hands folded in her lap while I poured coffee for both of us.

"Do you bake, Janie?" my aunt asked, transferring scones to a napkin-lined basket.

"Yes," she said. "I mean, I think so. The smell of your scones seems familiar to me. Like some kind of biscuits maybe."

"Good. See? It's all coming back to you, isn't it?" She slid a few scones onto a plate. "Just as the doctor said it would. All these need is butter. Lots of butter. Oops. There goes O'Ryan. Pete must be on his way downstairs."

She was right. About Pete *and* the butter. Pete joined us at the table. So did Aunt Ibby. It was while the four of us partook of excellent coffee with real cream and Nigel's mother's fabulous English date scones that Pete broke the news to Jane Doe that she was about to be questioned in regard to the murder.

She took the news remarkably well, considering what she'd already been through in the past twenty-four hours. "So I'm going back to the police station this morning instead of—where was it you thought people might know me? Know me as Emily, if that's my real name?"

"Brookline," he told her. "Mr. Sawtelle's real estate offices are in Brookline. We may not need to go there after all."

"Do I get to stay here then? In Salem? Here?" She looked from my aunt to me and back to Pete.

"Not up to me," Pete said. "Hopefully your memory will return and you'll be able to give us some help in the Sawtelle matter."

Janie/Emily broke off a piece of her scone, buttered it thoughtfully. "Hope so," she said. "This is delicious. When do we leave?"

"Detective Sergeant Rouse will be along soon," he said, checking his watch. "She'll transport you to the station. I'll be along later."

I realized then that he hadn't told her about the Audi they'd found behind the church, or about her handbag with ID in it that identified her as Emily Hemenway, or about her fingerprints on the steering wheel. I guessed that she'd be in for some intense questioning by police experts when she arrived at the station, and I also guessed that Pete would be going to wherever that Audi was being stored—and was undoubtedly being gone over with the proverbial fine-tooth comb.

We'd finished breakfast when Joyce Rouse arrived to pick up her charge. I was glad there were no handcuffs or Miranda rights involved when I said a hesitant "so long" to Janie. Pete hurried away shortly after that. Aunt Ibby had library duty on her schedule, and I was free to get started on my own busy day as program director. Without a minute's hesitation I decided that there'd be no walk across the common on the way to or from work. I grabbed my briefcase with the hastily prepared presentations Janie and I had produced, backed my beautiful but impractical Corvette convertible onto Oliver Street, turned on the radio, and hummed along with Taylor Swift all the way to Derby Street and WICH-TV. It was a new day and I was darned glad of it.

I was greeted by Rhonda as though I'd been gone for a week. "Jeez, Lee, everyone around here is looking for you!" She pulled out a sheaf of those little pink "while you were out" memos Mr. Doan still favors. "Doan wants to know where the plan for the morning show is and for you to see him as soon as you got here. The cowboy wants to know if it's okay to bring a horse on set like he used to in the old days. Marty says they got the wrong color blue for the bull chute. Scott wants to know if your boyfriend told you anything new about the dead guy they found on the beach." She put the memos down on her desk and added, "Francine says she wishes you still had your old job because the new guy talks too much."

"Gee, I got real popular all of a sudden, didn't I?" I patted the briefcase. "Mr. Doan first. I have the goods right here. And about the horse, there are a lot more rules about animal performers than there used to be. Can you check with somebody and find out if we need special permits or anything? It will be cool if he can do it. The kids will love it." I headed for the office manager's door. "I'll see Marty later and try to dodge Scott. Nothing I can do about the new guy." I tapped on the boss's door.

I was barely inside the office when the barrage of questions began. "What about it, Lee? Where's my info about the new show? What's taking so long? We need to get moving on this right away. When do I get something to show to sponsors?"

"Right now, sir." I opened the briefcase and fanned the copies of the presentation across his desk. "I'll have an artist's rendering of the set for you later today, and a Power-Point when I get it all together, but here's some ammunition for the sales force." I could tell from his expression that Janie's ideas for the cover had made a fast and positive impression. The spiral-bound poly covers almost glowed in the light from his desk lamp and the collage of photos and sketches and graphs looked totally professional from where I stood, awaiting his judgment as he perused the pages.

After what seemed like a long time, he looked up, favoring me with a rare smile. "Good job, Ms. Barrett," he declared. "I knew all along that I'd made a very wise decision with your promotion to program director."

I realized I'd been holding my breath. Hey, maybe he was right. Maybe being program director was going to be okay. "Well, sir," I said, "I'm pleased that you're pleased. If you'll excuse me now, I have to see a woman about some blue paint."

CHAPTER 11

By the time I'd caught up with Marty, she'd already straightened out the blue paint dilemma. "I just called the paint store guy and opened that gallon of paint right in front of him. Durn fool couldn't tell the difference between sapphire blue, Olympic blue, and cornflower. Durn fool."

"So we've got the right color now?"

"Of course. Olympic blue. A fresh new gallon all ready for your bull chute. When are we going to get started on building the thing? Chester is a good enough wood butcher to make it. He can hardly wait to get at it." Chester is the night watchman/security guard. Apparently, he was ready to don yet another hat. Mr. Doan would be pleased, and I assured Marty that as far as I was concerned, construction of the bull chute could begin as soon as the measurements of the space involved were verified.

"I have some good photos of the real thing in my office, and I expect to see Dakota with the floorplan today."

Rhonda, efficient as usual, already had the information regarding Ranger Rob's horse, Prince Valiant, performing on the show. "There's the federal Animal Welfare Act," she reported, "that says that the animal must be provided 'humane care and treatment,' so there's no problem there. Also, because Rob owns his own stable, he already has all the necessary state and local permits. He even has a veterinarian on retainer. The horse is good to go." We exchanged high fives.

I managed to avoid Scott Palmer for most of the morning. He finally tracked me down by knocking at the window of my office—the window that faces the newsroom. He made that little two-fingers-and-a thumb hand gesture beside his ear that means "call me." I nodded and gave him a see-ya-later wave and ignored the request. Anyway, Dakota Berman had just arrived at Rhonda's desk and he was on his way downstairs. I could hardly wait to see what he had to show me. I wasn't disappointed. Who knew that an artist's rendering of a simple stage set could be not only accurate, but quite beautiful in its simplicity and stylistic rendering?

"Oh, Dakota. It's perfect. Mr. Doan will be amazed. He'll probably want to frame it for his office. No, for his living room." I almost hugged the shy young artist. "I'm going to make a few copies and mount them on foam board for the sales team, and we'll get started right away on the actual construction. Just leave your invoice with Rhonda, or if you still want to trade for commercial time, she'll take care of it."

"Yep." He grinned. "We're all set. She's already got

me penciled in. *Ranger Rob's Rodeo* is going to be a sure hit."

"Hope so," I said, "and thanks for this." I held the drawing up, admiring it once again. "I can hardly wait for Mr. Doan to see it."

We said our goodbyes and I was right behind him when he left. I hurried back upstairs, anxious to show off Dakota's work. Rhonda, behind the reception desk as usual, was doing something that for her was quite unusual. She was watching, and listening to, the large television set on the wall behind her. Most days she turns down the sound and pays no attention to the programming.

Phil Archer used his network announcer voice and his most serious TV anchor face. On the screen the image of a white 2020 Audi Q8 loomed large, the Massachusetts license plate plainly visible through the chain-link fence of an impound lot. "A reliable source has informed WICH-TV that a 2020 Audi now situated in a police impound lot is in fact registered to a John Sawtelle of Brookline, Massachusetts. A person by that name was found deceased yesterday morning at Collins Cove beach. Foul play is indicated in that death. Police have not yet released information on whether this vehicle is involved in that matter. Stay tuned to this station for updates."

Rhonda pointed to the screen. "You know about this?"

I shrugged. Tried to look disinterested. "Yeah. I heard something." I wondered who the reliable source might be, since the police apparently hadn't chosen to talk about it yet. Maybe Sister Judith told somebody. Pete hadn't even mentioned it in front of Aunt Ibby or Janie. Was I the only person he'd confided in this morning?

"Pete tell you about it?"

I pretended I hadn't heard the question. "Is Mr. Doan in his office? I'm dying to show him this." I held up Dakota's artwork. "Isn't it great?"

"Wow. Yes, it is. He's in. Wait a sec. I'll buzz him and tell him you're here. He's been on and off the phone all morning." She tapped on her console. "Go right on in."

I knocked, then walked in, the drawing under one arm. "I have something to show you," I announced. "I think you're going to like it."

I was right about that. He loved it. I was hardly surprised when he said. "You know, that might look good in a frame in the lobby."

"I think so too," I said. "Dakota is an amazing artist. I'll get copies made for the sales guys and potential sponsors."

"Good thinking. And why haven't we used this Dakota fellow more often? You need to stay on top of these things, Ms. Barrett." He handed the illustration back to me. "Get it framed when you're through with it."

"Yes, sir." I scooted back through the reception area, glad to see that Rhonda was on the phone so that I didn't have to face any questions about the Audi. I had questions about that myself. A horrible thought occurred to me: Pete might think *I'd* been the reliable source who'd leaked the news about the Audi—just when he'd begun to trust me a little more with occasional tidbits of what was happening in his world.

I hurried back to the newsroom. I was going to have to talk to Scott Palmer after all. He'd probably know where the leak came from. I knew the darned whistleblower wasn't me, so I needed to know who else had the early-morning information? If Scott had discovered it on his own, he would have done a flashy stand-up in front of the impound fence, with all the bells and whistles and breaking news banners. But he hadn't, so the reliable source was being kept under wraps for some good reason.

I dropped the precious drawing off on my desk, then made my way to the glass-doored entry to the newsroom. Scott was at his desk, headphones in place, his eyes on the computer screen. I sat quietly in the chair beside his desk. He held up on finger in wait-a-minute mode. I waited.

After a minute or so, he took off the headphones. "Hey, Moon. What's up?"

"Scott, I need a favor," I said, cringing inwardly as I spoke the words. "I hope you can help."

He smiled. I knew it was because I'd put myself in the dreaded "I owe you one" position. I try to avoid that because he never fails to collect on favors done.

"I need to know if you know who the 'reliable source' was on the Audi story."

He leaned back in his better-than-mine office chair. "To answer your question, of course I do. Is that all?"

"No. Will you tell me who it was?"

"Why do you need to know?"

I sighed. How much of my personal business did I have to give up? "Because I knew about it early this morning and I didn't tell a soul. I don't want—um—anybody to think it was me."

He twirled a pencil with two fingers. I never have been able to do that, but he does it all the time. Annoying. "You think the boyfriend will figure you ratted him out? Doesn't trust you yet, huh?"

"Of course that's not why," I stammered, knowing that it was exactly what I was concerned about. "I'd like to know who it was, that's all. That kind of information shouldn't be on the air until the police think it's safe to release it."

"Uh-huh. It's important to you, right?"

Uh-oh. Looks like I'm going to owe him big-time for this one.

"Yep." I waited.

He twirled the pencil, turning his chair to face me directly. He dropped his voice and glanced around the room. "Lot guy," he said.

"Lot guy?"

"Right. I have him on sort of a 'retainer,' you know? He calls if any cars show up that look interesting. Like with bloodstains, or significant dents like from a hit-and-run. This one still had fingerprint stuff all over the wheel and dash. I passed it on to Phil. I can't rat *my* source out."

Relief. "Thanks, Scott," I said.

"My pleasure. But now you owe me—big-time."

CHAPTER 12

With my mind pretty much at ease about the whistle-blower question, and with confidence kicked into high gear by Mr. Doan's enthusiastic approval of the kids' show project, I moved on to the next item on my to-do list: foam-board-mounted copies of Dakota's artwork to be produced quickly. I carried the precious original out to the parking lot, placed it carefully onto the passenger seat of the Vette and headed for the nearest Staples store. It's a pleasant ride, past the sprawling Essex County University campus and the nearby heavily wooded Conant River Conservation Area. Salem isn't a really big city, a little less than twenty square miles, but Aunt Ibby says that more than half of it is under water—counting ocean, lakes, and marshes.

They're beginning to know me at the copy center of the big office supply store. Mr. Doan hasn't seen fit to invest in up-to-the-minute office machines for the station, so I've become accustomed to using either Aunt Ibby's excellent copier at home or the even bigger ones at Staples when I need quality work. I shopped around the store while Dakota's art was copied, mounted, and wrapped—ready to go in what seemed like no time—then headed back to the station.

I'd only been on the road for a few minutes when my opportunity to pay Scott Palmer that big-time debt presented itself. Just between County U and the nearby conservation area, I saw maybe half a dozen Salem PD vehicles pulling into the road leading to the river. One of them was marked CRIME SCENE. I texted Scott in a hurry. "Something's going on at the Conant River Loring Avenue entrance. Lots of cops."

I drove the rest of the way back to the station a little faster than usual. I'd barely reached Derby Street when I saw the WICH-TV's second-string mobile unit, a converted Volkswagen bus with Old Jim—the second-string driver—at the wheel, streak by me going in the opposite direction. Scott was on the way to what might be a crime scene. I figured we were even, and it hadn't escaped me that Pete was looking for a fresh-water crime scene in the John Sawtelle murder case. I wished for a long moment that it was me chasing a breaking news story.

I delivered the mounted copies to Rhonda's desk—reserving one for myself—along with the original with a request that she check out the frame stores and get it framed to suit Doan's décor. "Just saw Scott tearing down Derby Street," I said innocently. "Did he say what's going on?"

"Beats me." She propped the drawing against an artificial flower arrangement of purple iris. "He didn't even check with me before he grabbed Old Jim and took off."

"Guess we'll find out soon enough," I said. I still had plenty of time left to check out the progress on the *Ranger Rob's Rodeo* stage-set-to-be.

Chester, the newly designated official station carpenter, had already completed one of the three-tiered bleacher stands where Ranger Rob's in-studio "little buckaroos" would be seated. When I arrived on the set, he'd begun making chalk marks on the floor where the planned bull chute would be. "Wow, Chester," I said, "you're making great progress."

"Thanks, miss." Wide smile. "I love messing around with wood. This is fun for me."

"Glad to hear it."

Chester had a few questions about what my concept for the set was. I showed him Dakota's drawing, and together we pored over it, Chester using his tape measure more than once on the nearly empty floor. "Sometimes artists get carried away with making pretty pictures. Carpenters have to make things fit." He scribbled figures on a piece of scrap wood with a stubby oval-shaped pencil. "But," he declared finally, tapping the drawing gently, "this guy knows what he's doing."

"So do you," I said and headed for my office, pleased by how well my day was going, but wildly curious about Scott's day. And Pete's. And Janie's. I turned on my office TV set. It didn't take long for me to learn how Scott had fared. His field report rated a "Breaking News" banner, interrupting right smack in the middle of Wanda the Weather Girl's morning advisory.

Scott had positioned himself in front of a low split-rail

fence with a worn and weathered "No Trespassing" sign
on it. A little beyond the fence was a Salem PD van with
all lights flashing, blocking a narrow dirt road. Scott pointed
out several more official vehicles a distance away, where
yellow plastic tape was festooned between trees and
bushes. He told the audience that this property bordered
on a portion of the Conant River.

"Although there's been no official confirmation that
this site may be associated with the death of real estate
executive John Sawtelle, whose lifeless body was discovered yesterday morning on Collins Cove beach, the appearance of so many police vehicles indicates the possibility
that such is the case. Sawtelle's death has been ruled a
homicide." He walked the length of the fence, where there
was a gated opening that appeared to be wide enough for
a car to pass, but it too was blocked by yellow tape. "I've
hiked in this park many times," he said, "but as you can
see, right now there's a large area that's off-limits." He
lifted one foot and looked regretfully at the mud-soaked
boot. "It's not a good day for walking here anyway."

Uh-oh. I think those are his new Tecovas.

He pointed to a tiny glimpse of blue water between the
trees. "John Sawtelle was a waterfront property real estate agent, specializing in ocean- and lakefront properties. It is unclear why he would have had any interest in
this government-administered conservation area."

Scott had done a little homework, probably googled
Sawtelle's office on his way to the site. Everybody in Salem knew that the Conant River Conservation Area was
not for sale. Why would a waterfront real estate agent
possibly have any interest in it?

Scott wound up the segment with some general information about the conservation site, which I suspected he

was reading from an off-camera sign, and closed with a request that anyone with information on unusual activity in the area notify police. Old Jim took a wide shot of the area while the number flashed on screen. Another mobile unit that looked to me like one of Boston's WBZ-TV's fancy rigs had just pulled up. Scott had scooped the big boys. All in all, I decided, he'd done a darned good job. I returned my attention to clowns, cowboys, and carpenters, trying to focus on doing a good job myself.

With a copy of the proposal I'd so hurriedly prepared for Mr. Doan spread open on my desk, along with a pen and a new yellow legal pad, I thought about the task I'd set out for myself and began to make notes, remembering those long-ago shows featuring Ranger Rob and Katie the Clown that had so delighted me as a child.

Was the patter between them scripted? They often gave good advice about safety and being polite and washing your hands and taking care of pets, and other life lessons. The two of them did it in such a funny, kid-friendly way that the little buckaroos never knew they were being lectured. They'd had guests too. I'd need to line up crossing guards and firemen and cops and veterinarians. I'd need circus people too, like maybe a juggler or an acrobat. We'd have Rob's sweet palomino, Prince Valiant, of course, but what about puppies and kittens and bunnies? I put down the pen and thought about the many times Aunt Ibby had said, "Be careful, Maralee, don't bite off more than you can chew."

Maybe I've done exactly that.

I didn't have much time to mourn over my probable shortcomings as a program director. A flurry of activity in the newsroom behind the glass wall provided a welcome distraction. Scott had returned and had gathered several

members of the news staff around him. His wild hand
gestures and animated expression showed his excitement.
Having been that excited about a story a few times myself, it looked to me like he was lobbying for an investigative reporter shot on the late news, and I was pretty
sure he'd get it. If he did, I figured my debt for the information about the lot guy was paid in full—in spite of the
muddied Tecovas. Anyway, Scott's boots didn't look half
as bad as Janie's shoes.

A chilling thought occurred to me.

Maybe Janie had walked a little closer to the river.

CHAPTER 13

I didn't expect to hear anything from Pete that afternoon. I knew that if Scott was right about the commotion at the Conant River being related to John Sawtelle's murder, Pete would be deeply involved in the investigation. So I was surprised to see his name pop up on my phone.

"Hi. What's going on?" I asked.

"Hi, yourself. I just want to give you a heads-up on what's happening with your friend Emily Hemenway before the press gets hold of it. It's not good."

"Why? What's happened?" *Is it about the shoes?*

"You know about her fingerprints being on the wheel of Sawtelle's car."

"Of course."

"It appears that she may have driven the Audi away from the crime scene. Not only that, but the sediment on her shoes tells us that she walked around on foot close to where Sawtelle apparently was drowned."

"Do you think whoever killed him could have followed her? A speeding Audi doesn't have the quietest engine in the world."

"We think that whoever Sawtelle was meeting there came by boat."

"By boat?"

"Right," he said. "There's a steep drop-off at the edge of the property. Plenty of water for a small power boat. We think they got there—and left there—by boat. They could have seen the Audi leaving, but they had no way to follow it."

"So no one would have seen them entering the property by the road. Even if there were cameras," I reasoned. "But anyone around could have seen the Audi arriving."

"That's right."

"But Janie—I mean Emily—doesn't remember anything about being there?"

"Maybe she does and maybe she doesn't. Chief thinks she's faking the amnesia thing."

"Does this mean she's a suspect? That you believe she could have killed Sawtelle?"

Little sigh. "If the chief thinks she's the one, we'll be building a case against her. I'm just telling you what the evidence points to. I didn't want you to see it on the news or read it in the paper. We're going to have to hold her for questioning."

"Okay. I understand. But I don't think she's faking. Don't worry. I won't say anything about it around here."

"I know you won't. Hey, did you know that Palmer has a snitch at the impound lot? That's how the station got tipped off about the Audi in the first place."

"Yeah. He told me," I said, relieved that Pete had never thought it was me, and ashamed that I'd thought for a minute he might have. "But I'm the one who gave him the tip about the Conant River. I spotted the SPD action there on my way back to the station from Staples."

"He was the first press there. He owes you one for that. Do you miss the reporter job a lot?"

"Sometimes," I admitted. "But being a program director is turning out to be quite a challenge."

"Wish I could see you tonight and hear all about it," he said, "but Chief's got a bunch of us tied up here until late. I'll call you if I get a chance."

"Is Janie going to be arrested?"

"I don't know. We've contacted her parents. They're on their way here."

"Good. Seeing them might jog her memory. Is it okay if I tell Aunt Ibby and the Angels what's going on? They've become quite fond of her."

Short pause with audible sigh. "I suppose so. It'll be public soon anyway. But I sure don't want to think that your aunt and her girlfriends intend to get involved in an active investigation."

"I'm sure they'll behave."

"Hope so. Love you. Bye."

I still hadn't told Pete about my vision, and I didn't plan to unless I felt that he needed to know what I'd seen. He's very uncomfortable about the whole scryer thing. But if the vision was correct, Janie *had* been there on the marshy ground near the river, and she *had* witnessed John Sawtelle's last terrifying minutes. The big question—was she somehow responsible for his dying?

The only people who know about this strange "gift" of mine are Aunt Ibby, Pete, and River North. River is the only one who actually likes talking about it. I checked my watch. I knew River's schedule pretty well since I'd worked that late-show time slot myself when I'd first come to WICH-TV. It was early afternoon. She'd be awake. I called her.

River answered right away. "I've been thinking about you," she said. "Is everything okay?"

"Most things are okay," I said, "but I've had a couple of visions lately . . ."

"Got it. I'm just making some lunch. Why don't you come over to my place and we'll talk about the visions—maybe even see what the cards have to say."

"On my way," I said. I put the yellow pad in my top desk drawer and the stage-set drawing in the file cabinet and headed for the parking lot. River lives a short drive from the station, with several friends, all coven members, on Brown Street. I parked the Vette in front of the old house—easy to identify because of the bright orange front door—and climbed the two steps to a small porch. We call it a "stoop" in Salem. River greeted me with a familiar patchouli-scented hug. Her off-the-air appearance is very different from the glamourous star she is on *Tarot Time*. Her long black hair was arranged in two fat braids and she wore no makeup on her perfect oval face. A blue-and-white-checked cobbler's apron covered white shorts and T-shirt.

"If you had ruby slippers you'd look like Dorothy," I said.

She laughed and took both of my hands, pulling me inside. "Come on in. I baked a couple of loaves of anadama bread this morning. Can you smell it?"

I took a deep breath. "Your house always smells wonderful, whether it's bread or homemade soup or incense or sage or whatever magical potion you and your friends are cooking up. I'm so glad to see you."

I followed her to a small dining room with a round table in the center. The silk-covered box where she keeps the tarot deck was on the table along with an arrangement of crystals on a silver tray. "Pull up a chair," she said. "I've got some hibiscus tea brewing and I'm going to put together some nice chickpea, avocado, and almond salad sandwiches on anadama bread for us. I'll just be a couple of minutes. Then we'll talk about you." River is vegan and I've learned that her strange—to me—sounding recipes are usually pretty tasty. I did once draw the line at edamame and mung bean fettuccini though.

"Sounds good," I said and pulled up a chair as directed. I didn't have any particular questions for River—just needed to talk to my friend about the many things going on in my life. Looking to the beautiful tarot cards for advice might be helpful too. In the years I've known River, I've become a believer. Pete still calls it "hocus-pocus," but he often listens to River's advice anyway.

She reappeared within the promised few minutes bearing a tray laden with beautiful thick sandwiches and clear glass cups of pretty pink tea. "There now." She sat opposite me. "Tell me everything." So I did. Between bites of sandwich and sips of tea I gave her a synopsis of what had been going on with Janie, how I'd met her on the common and taken her home to Aunt Ibby, interspersed with snatches of information about my transition from field reporter to program director. I told her about the Angels too, and how they'd all become fond of Janie. She nodded understanding, smiled in the appropriate places, expressed surprise a few times. I could tell that—like the good friend she is—she was listening intently to every word. When I got to the part about the visions, she leaned forward, listening, eyes wide, one hand on the tarot box.

"You think that you saw the man, Sawtelle, in the water, screaming, and that the horror of watching him dying that terrible way was what caused the woman's amnesia?"

"Yes."

"That certainly seems possible," she said. "And now you say the police believe she was there. That she really *could* have seen it happening."

"Even worse," I said. "They believe she was involved."

River tapped the tarot box with one finger. "Because of the Audi with her prints in it. And you saw her with the keys to that car in your hall mirror."

"Right. I asked her if she could drive and she told me she drives a stick shift. That her dad taught her. She's remembering things like that little by little."

"You say Chief Whaley thinks she's faking the amnesia. What does Pete think?"

I shrugged. "He's just following where the evidence leads."

"How about your aunt? Does she believe the woman?"

"Oh yes. She thinks it's transient global amnesia. She saw it in an old movie."

"Of course." River piled our empty plates and cups onto the tray. "I'll just dump this stuff in the kitchen and we'll see what the cards have to say about all of it."

I could hardly wait.

CHAPTER 14

River removed the deck of cards from the silk covered box. Placing her hand over the deck, she bowed her head. "May the powers of the stars above and the earth below bless this place and this time and this woman and me, who are with you." She put the card I recognized as the queen of wands, the one she always uses to represent me, on the center of the table. She shuffled the deck expertly, then extended it toward me. Silently, I cut it into three piles and River began to lay the cards on the table in the pattern which had become familiar to me. The first card she turned up was the two of swords.

"Wow," I said. "How do you do that?"

"Do what? I haven't begun the reading."

I tapped the card. "It's Janie, isn't it?" On the card, a lone, blindfolded woman is seated on a bench. She balances two swords on her shoulders. "A girl on a bench? Isn't that what we were just talking about?"

"It could be," River said. "You see she's blindfolded. It can mean she's blind to her situation. And you see the body of water behind her? There are jagged rocks jutting above the surface. But this is your reading. It's about you. Those swords she's holding are balanced right now, but your situation may be precarious. There may be tension in relationships. Those rocks may be in your path, and that new moon over her head is treacherous. Your sense of balance and direction is good though. You can work your way through the situation involving the girl on the bench."

The next card in the pattern was the knight of cups. A knight is riding on a horse. He wears a winged cap and holds a cup. I thought of Ranger Rob and Prince Valiant, but didn't say so. "A handsome man in your life," River said. "Intelligent. Maybe a musician or an artist of some kind. I feel that he can be helpful to you. This knight is the lord of waves and waters, by the way." I nodded.

Makes sense to me.

She turned over the eight of swords. It was upside down and she angled it so I could see the picture "Uh-oh." I said. "The blindfolded girl again?"

"Yes. She's bound with ropes and she stands in a marshy place. But the card is reversed, so you can relax. This card often means a new beginning." River looked into my eyes. "Know anyone in prison?"

"Not exactly," I said, thinking of Janie. "Not yet."

"The person will be released." River turned over another card. The three of wands. "Interesting," she said. The card showed a man looking toward the sea, small boats in the distance. "You're strong, Lee, and sometimes you don't want to ask for help. Another man, possibly a successful businessman, may offer to help in your present situation. You might consider accepting it."

The six of cups offered me help from a childhood acquaintance, and the eight of pentacles referred to learning a new profession. I figured the childhood acquaintance might be Joyce Rouse and the reference to a new profession was obvious. The ten of pentacles showed a happy family with some dogs, telling me to pay attention to family matters, or it might mean the acquiring of property. River wound up the reading with the six of swords, which might mean a trip, and the temperance card, indicating my high ideals, my creative streak, and a warning that I shouldn't try to do everything myself. I was a little disappointed that the knight of swords hadn't shown up. He represents Pete and he appears in my readings fairly often.

She replaced the cards in the box, and reached across the table and took my hands. "Do you think that was helpful at all? Did it answer any questions for you?"

"I think so. Yes. I know it answered a few. I can't seem to get past the blindfolded girl though. In my mind, she's Janie. But, as you said, this was my reading, not hers. What if I'm the blindfolded girl? That changes everything, doesn't it?"

"Maybe not. It's entirely possible that those cards do represent Janie for you, just as the knight of swords means Pete to you, and the queen of cups means your aunt."

Once again, she put her hand on the silk box. "Did you notice that several of the cards indicated that you may need to ask for help sometimes, even when it makes you uncomfortable to do it?"

I had noticed that. She was right. It *is* hard for me to ask. I thought of how asking Scott about the lot guy had been a struggle. "I'll try to stop thinking I can do everything myself. I've already learned that I can't draw a stage set or build a bull chute."

"A bull chute?" She laughed.

"You'll see it pretty soon. An Olympic-blue bull chute. No kidding. Thanks, River. And thanks for the delicious lunch. I'll go back to the station with tummy and attitude both much improved."

"Blessed be, Lee." She stood and walked with me to the door.

"Blessed be, River." I gave her a hug and stepped out onto Brown Street, closing the orange door behind me.

I was thoughtful on the ride back to WICH-TV. She'd given me a lot to think about. Some of the things the cards had revealed had seemed to have quite specific meaning to me. The girl alone on the bench, of course, and the man on a horse that seemed to be Ranger Rob. But would I take a trip? Would Janie be the person in jail? Who is the businessman? I know lots of them. River's readings often take a while to decipher—just like my visions—but they usually eventually make some sort of sense.

But thoughts of knights and queens, swords and cups, were quickly pushed to the back burner as soon as I pulled into my designated space and my phone dinged. It was Rhonda.

"Where are you right now, Lee?" Her tone was urgent.

"In the parking lot. Why?"

"Good that you're here. Come on up right away."

"Be there in a sec," I said. I locked the Vette and jogged toward the studio door, wondering what could be so critical that would involve me. I took the metal stairs two at a time and practically burst through the door to the reception area. "What's going on?"

"Doan's on a tear. Young Howie and Francine are in Rockport covering an art show. Scott and Old Jim are over at the Conant River filming an entomologist who's mucking around in the riverbed looking for evidence. The chief has just called a presser and neither unit is close enough to cover it."

"And I am to do—what?"

"You and Marty are going to do the presser. Marty's already loaded up Chester's truck with your equipment. They'll pick you up at the studio door. Get going."

"I'm doing the field report?"

"Yep. Looks like you're the last man standing."

"What about makeup?"

"Do the best you can on the way over." She handed me a plastic sandwich bag filled with makeup samples. Rhonda is a Mary Kay rep. "Good luck."

"Okay." I tucked the makeup into my hobo bag, headed to the door, then turned back. "What's an ento-mologist?"

"Bug and slime guy," she said. "Beat it."

As promised, Marty and Chester, in a red Ford extra-cab, waited behind Ariel's bench, motor running, back door open. That bench, with its panoramic view of Salem Harbor, was paid for by Ariel's coven. It's a pleasant spot in memory of a most unpleasant witch. "I've got your fa-vorite stick mic, Moon," Marty called. "And Chester here is an excellent wheel man. Hop in. It'll be just like old times."

Chester gets his fourth hat. He'd win the WICH-TV Employee of the Month award. If there was one.

Applying makeup and brushing unruly red curls isn't easy while careening around Salem's narrow streets, but I did the best I could under the circumstances. When we arrived at the Salem Police Department, I saw that the chief's lectern was already set up on the concourse out front, and a mobile unit from the Salem radio station WESX was there. No Boston TV presence so far. Chief Whaley hadn't appeared yet either, so I knew we'd made it on time.

Chester's Ford wasn't set up as a professional mobile unit, so Marty had to do some fancy rigging to get sound, lights, and mic coordinated, but by the time the chief appeared—resplendent in full-dress uniform complete with many medals—she pronounced that we were good to go.

After a little throat-clearing and paper shuffling, the chief began. "Good afternoon, ladies and gentlemen. We have made some progress on the matter of John Sawtelle's death. As you know, it has been determined that foul play was involved. The death has been officially declared a homicide. Mr. Sawtelle's body was discovered earlier this week on Collins Cove beach. The cause of death was drowning." Chief Whaley didn't look up from his prepared statement. "The medical examiner has determined that the drowning did not occur in salt water. Further investigation has indicated that a possible site of Mr. Sawtelle's death was within the boundaries of the Conant River Conservation Area. This is a well-known popular site for hikers, bicyclers, and nature lovers. We are asking for the cooperation of the community, including the media, in observing the posted section of the park while our investigation continues. There will be officers present around the clock, enforcing all no-trespassing notices as well as police barriers. We expect that all involved trails and bike paths will be reopened soon. Meanwhile, your co-operation is appreciated. Thank you." He turned away from the mic, clearly intending to make his usual hasty retreat. The fancy new mobile unit from Boston's WHDH-TV lumbered onto the property.

I found my voice. "Chief Whaley," I shouted. "Do you have any suspects?"

That brought a head shake and a frosty glare. "We've made no arrests."

"Any persons of interest?" The question came from the newly arrived Boston reporter.

"We're talking to some people," the chief mumbled, moving closer to the door.

"Do you expect an arrest soon?" I called after him.

"Yes." He was gone, leaving three reporters to speculate on what we'd just heard.

I faced Marty's camera. "I'm Lee Barrett reporting from the Salem Police Department, where Chief Tom Whaley has just disclosed that persons of interest have been questioned regarding the recent murder of Brookline real estate agent John Sawtelle. Current investigation is centered within the Conant conservation park, where the homicide may have occurred. The public, as well as media, are instructed to strictly observe all no-trespassing warnings on the premises until further notice. Chief Whaley has confirmed that an arrest in the matter is expected soon. WICH-TV will continue to follow this ongoing story. Stay tuned."

Somebody from the station will continue to follow it. Not me.

I helped Marty pack up our gear, then climbed into the back seat. "Good job, Moon," she said. "You miss this, don't you?"

"Yes. No. Maybe a little," I stammered, "but I'm enjoying the program director thing. It's turned out to be more challenging than I'd imagined it might be."

"Really?" The one-word question sounded doubtful.

Chester had pulled into the police station visitors' parking area to turn around. "No worries about her, Marty," he said. "The girl knows what she's doing. A real take-charge woman."

I was about to thank him for his confidence in my newbie director job when I noticed the black 2015 Jeep Renegade. Janie's parents had arrived. I wondered if Pete would be able to tell me what was going on in that department. Was the arrest the chief expected to make soon going to be poor Janie? I thought about the blindfolded girl on the eight of swords card. If it was Janie, River had said the prisoner would be released. A tiny comforting thought amidst a bunch of disturbing ones.

CHAPTER 15

By the time we got to WICH-TV, both Francine's mobile unit and Old Jim's Volkswagen were in their usual spots in the parking lot. Like Cinderella getting out of her pumpkin after the ball, I stepped out of Chester's truck and back to my program director duties. Marty hurried away, announcing that she wanted to do a little editing before our video aired, and Chester was anxious to get back to his carpentry project. It seemed to me that although the three of us had enjoyed our little excursion into the news business, we were each glad to return to our own realities.

I'd only been in my office long enough to dump the contents of my briefcase onto the desk when Scott Palmer tapped on the door. I waved him inside, curious to see if he'd want to talk about whatever it was the bug-and-slime guy had turned up on the riverbank. He sat in the chair opposite my desk, crossing his left leg over his right knee. The Tecovas boots looked as good as new. Fine leather cleans up much better than studded suede, no doubt about that. "So, what's new?" I asked.

"I was going to ask you the same thing." He did that intensive-stare thing he does. When I first met Scott I'd found it kind of sexy. Now it's just annoying. "Saw you on the news. The chief's presser about the Sawtelle thing. You're not gunning for my job, are you?"

"Are you serious? Of course not. You and Howie were both busy and I guess I was the last man standing." I waved at the mess of papers, paint samples, and assorted sticky notes. "I'm already up to my ears in this. Want your job? Hell, no."

He seemed to relax visibly. "I just wondered. Francine talks about you all the time. 'Lee did this and Lee and I did it this way.' I thought maybe you two were planning to get back together."

"We had a good time," I admitted. "But, no. I'm kind of liking what I'm doing now. I think directing Rob and Katie is going to be fun."

"Is it true the singing cowboy is going to bring his horse in here?"

"Prince Valiant? Yes." I pointed to the boots. "Do you ride?"

"Not since I was a kid. You?"

"Same. I used to. Guess you could have used a good horse over there in the muck and mire at the river." I watched his face, hoping he'd tell me what they were searching for.

"Oh yeah. You should have seen that guy. Up to his hips in mud, using a big sifter. Picking up leaves and rocks and crap like it was gold and silver nuggets." He laughed. "Looked like he was enjoying every minute of it."

"Different strokes for different folks," I said. "Did he find whatever treasure he was looking for?"

"Don't know. I'm not sure *he* even knows what he was looking for. But hey, that line you had about the chief expecting an arrest soon is kind of a teaser, isn't it?" The famous Scott Palmer stare again. "Do you know who he's questioning? Want to pay me back for the lot man tip?"

"I figure I paid you back with the Conant River heads-up."

He smiled. "Yeah. You did. Just pushing my luck a little. Do you know who he's questioning though?"

"Who, me? Little kids'-show-program-director me?" I dodged the question. "How should I know? That kind of information is way above my pay grade."

"The cop boyfriend probably knows."

"Pete says it'll be on the news soon." That was true. He'd told me that. "I'll bet you'll hear about it before I will." That statement turned out to be true also. Scott had left my office and I'd barely finished straightening up the mess on my desk when the chyron ran across the bottom of my TV screen. POSSIBLE WITNESS BEING QUESTIONED RE: SAWTELLE MURDER. Did that mean Emily Hemenway—our "Janie"—was being questioned? Next, the "Breaking News" crawl flashed on the screen, followed by a shot of Phil Archer at the anchor desk. My question—Scott's question—was about to be answered on live TV.

"Ladies and gentlemen. WICH-TV has just learned that a woman who may have witnessed the Sawtelle murder is being questioned by Salem police. While the woman's identity is being withheld due to security measures, police have learned that the woman, a forensic accountant, had recently accompanied Sawtelle from Brookline to Salem on a business matter."

What? Janie is a forensic accountant? What does that mean?

Phil immediately answered my unspoken question. "Forensic accounting is frequently used in the investigation of fraud cases. Forensic accountants use both accounting and investigating skills."

I remembered Janie staring at the door marked "Forensics" when we took her to see Dr. Egan and her comment that the word "accountant" seemed familiar when Aunt Ibby told us about the Gregory Peck movie. Did all this mean that Janie/Emily was in Salem investigating a fraud case? I thought of the black Jeep and wondered if seeing her parents had cleared her memory for good. And if it had, was *that* a good thing?

Phil went on to answer even more questions. "John Sawtelle's automobile, a white 2020 Audi, had apparently been driven by the woman while it was in Salem." There was an archive shot of the Audi behind the impound lot fence, followed by a zoom shot of the bug-and-slime guy, as Scott had reported, up to his hips in muck. "Evidence of plant species and other markers found on the vehicle indicate that it was recently present at the Conant River site. Police are also seeking a small boat that may have been present at the site also."

This all sounded like very bad news for Janie. I couldn't shake the image of the bound and blindfolded girl standing in a marsh. Had she actually been present when Sawtelle went to his death? My vision had said that she saw it. Now the evidence the police had collected said so too.

Phil Archer wound up the bulletin with the usual advice to viewers. "If you have any information about the white 2020 Audi or about any recent unusual activity at the Conant River Conservation Area, please call the number at the bottom of your screen and stay tuned to WICH-TV for up-to-the-minute coverage of this breaking story." Regular programming resumed with a promo for the upcoming downtown Salem sidewalk sale, with attractive footage of last year's event with happy shoppers and counters laden with bargains. I muted the sound and returned to my own business at hand.

Marty had found a couple of VCR cassettes of those long-ago kid shows starring Ranger Rob and Katie the Clown, along with her own Panasonic, which still played the relics. She'd also done all the necessary wiring. All I needed to do was pop the cassette into the proper slot and watch for the picture to appear on my TV screen. What a nostalgia rush! I was back in my playroom—now Aunt Ibby's high-tech office—sitting on the floor in my pajamas, watching my favorite morning show. Rob and Katie harmonizing on "Old MacDonald Had a Farm," while their little sidekick, Cactus, pulled a seemingly endless pile of vegetables from his oversized cowboy hat. It still made me laugh, even though the diminutive actor who'd played Cactus had later come to a definitely unfunny end. I made a quick note on the legal pad. *R&K need a sidekick.* I watched the show all the way to the end, hoping no one would come in and catch me laughing at corny jokes and humming along with familiar old songs, catching my breath at the closing outdoor shot where Rob—astride

Freedom, the beautiful palomino that had preceded Prince Valiant—rode into a glorious sunset. All of the commercials were intact, and several of the businesses were still operating in Salem. Ziggy's Donuts was still there. Puleo's Dairy too, and Dube's Seafood, and Bill & Bob's Roast Beef. I noted all of them, with a reminder to give the list to the sales team.

It had been a pretty full day, but the clock told me that I still had time to run down to the studio and check out what was happening on the set before five. Chester wasn't around—probably had to report for some of his other duties—but he'd made some more progress on the bull chute. At first I thought I was alone, but I was pleased and surprised to see Katie sitting on the bottom tier of the still unpainted "peanut gallery" bleachers.

"Hello, Lee," she said. "I was just sitting here thinking about the old days. So happy to be working again. With Rob. This is going to be fun."

I told her about the program I'd just watched and how much I'd enjoyed it. "You guys are going to need a sidekick. Like Cactus. Have you thought about that?"

"We have," she said, "and we've been rehearsing some of the old songs too. Remember when we had the big model train and we rode around in circles on it singing 'The Cannonball Express' at the top of our lungs?" She smiled a wistful smile. "Good times."

"We can do that again. I'm pretty sure one of your main sponsors, Captain Billy, has one of those trains in his shop." That brought a real smile. "It's been a busy day," I said. "I'm going home now."

"I'd better get going too," she said, checking a balloon-shaped watch. "Have to walk the dog."

"I didn't know you had a dog," I said. "How does Percival feel about that?" Percival was a lovely black cat I'd met several times at her house.

"They seem to get along quite well. I haven't had Paco for very long. An old circus friend passed away and there didn't seem to be anybody else to take the sweet old dog." She spread her arms wide apart and smiled a big Katie the Clown smile. "Paco was never actually in a circus, but my friend had trained him as though he could be. I couldn't very well let them put him down, could I?"

"Of course you couldn't." I said good night to Katie and climbed the metal stairs to the reception area.

"Checking out," I told Rhonda. "It's been a busy one. Say, did you ever watch the old Ranger Rob shows from back in the nineties?"

"No, but I've seen a few of the videos."

"Remember Cactus? The little sidekick?"

"I think so. Are you looking to replace him for the new show?"

"Not him, certainly. Too many unpleasant connections there, but they need some kind of a sidekick. Comic relief."

"I'll see what I can come up with," she promised.

"You and I are around the same age," I said. "How come you didn't watch Rob and Katie back then?"

"It conflicted with the Today Show."

"Of course," I said. "See you tomorrow." I hurried downstairs and out to the comfort and privacy of my beloved Vette. I could hardly wait to call Pete to see what he'd share with me about what had gone on today with Emily Hemenway and her parents.

CHAPTER 16

"I wondered when you'd call," he said. "Curiosity driving you crazy?"

"You bet! Did her memory come back? Did she know her parents?"

"The minute they walked in," he said. "You should have seen it. She laughed, then cried, then ran to her dad."

"She remembers everything? About John Sawtelle?"

"That part was not pretty." His voice was sober. "Apparently she witnessed the death. Pretty awful."

I almost said "I know," but bit my tongue. "Is she still in custody?"

"We've released her to her parents, with instructions not to leave Salem. They've already rented a condo. Nice place. Security guard, doorman, the whole works. We were thinking of ankle-braceleting her, but her lawyer convinced the chief that it wasn't necessary."

"Lawyered up already?"

"Big-time Boston lawyer. Listen, I have time to come over for a while if you're going home now. I was going to call you anyway. I need to get in touch with one of your friends."

"Really? Who?"

"The artist. Dakota Berman."

Like Alice said, this got curioser and curioser. I told him I'd be home in ten minutes, hung up, and started the big engine. In nine minutes flat I rolled into the garage. The Buick was missing. O'Ryan met me on the back steps and followed me up the twisty staircase to my place. I unlocked my living room door while the cat used his cat door. He hadn't climbed up onto his favorite zebra-print wing chair, pulling his favorite I've-fallen-asleep-waiting-for-you game. Instead, he'd streaked toward the kitchen and was sitting on the closed laptop I'd left on the counter. "Mmrrup," he said. "Mmrrup mmrrup." I've learned to translate some of his comments but "mmrrup" seems to mean anything he wants it to mean at any given time. For instance, "meh" means the same in cat as it does in English. It's dismissive. Like, if I said "O'Ryan, do you like this dress?" His "meh" would mean "not so much." O'Ryan knows how and when to use it. "Mmrrup" is different.

Whatever he wanted to tell me had something to do with the laptop. He moved aside. Naturally I opened it. "E-mail?" I asked. O'Ryan shook his fuzzy head. "Facebook?" He left the counter and moved to one of the barstools. There was a message from Betsy. *Lee. I got a call from Janie. I gave her my card when we met, so she had my phone number but not yours. Her real name is Emily. She remembers everything and she wants to talk to*

*you. The cops had her phone and gave it back. I didn't
know if I should give her your number. Here's hers so you
can call her.* I copied the number into my phone. Betsy
ended with a P.S. *Call me and tell me what she says!*

I sent Betsy a thumbs-up and was about to make that
call when I thought about what Pete might say about it. "I
think I'll wait until Pete gets here," I told the cat.

"Mmrrup," was the abrupt response. I chose to think
of it as an expression of agreement. We didn't have long
to wait. O'Ryan took off like a yellow streak for his cat
door on his way to greet Pete and I ran into my room to
check hair and makeup. "Meh," I said to the mirror, but
there wasn't time to do much of anything about it. I heard
Pete's key turn in the living room door. He and O'Ryan
arrived in the kitchen together, Pete with a takeout bag
from Subway in one hand, pulled me close with the other,
and delivered an unhurried kiss. "I brought a couple of
subs. Figured you'd have coffee or soda."

I grabbed a couple of cold Pepsis from the refrigerator.
"Okay. Tell me everything. Her memory all came back?
Just like that?"

He took two plates from the cabinet and neatly arranged our subs and chips. I put the food and drinks onto
the table. "That's what happened. She saw her folks and
bingo! It all came out."

"Did she see who did it? Who killed him?"

"Two men. She saw the whole thing. She's not sure if
they saw her or not."

"So it all happened at the Conant River Conservation
Area?"

"It did. Sawtelle was supposed to meet a couple of
men about some waterfront land."

"The Conant land isn't for sale."

"It was a scam. These guys had been billing Sawtelle's real estate company for commissions on a couple of Salem-area sales of high-end waterfront properties. Something seemed fishy about the sales. One property got sold twice. First for eight hundred and fifty thousand, which seemed fair. Then it looked as though the agent had sold the same home to himself for darn near a million and a half. Didn't look right to Sawtelle, so when they offered him some "new to the market" waterfront land, he'd hired Emily's dad—he's a forensic accountant—to come to Salem with him to check it out. Seems the two men were old fishing buddies. At the last minute Mr. Hemenway couldn't make it, so he sent Emily along to investigate. She's a forensic investigator herself. Who knew?"

"So the crooks didn't know Emily was with him?"

"They were supposed to be showing Sawtelle a parcel of land they said the city was selling. They had what looked like authentic paperwork and professional-looking photos. They said they'd meet him there. He drove the Audi to the site they'd described. It was beyond the no-trespassing signs and the ground was so muddy and gross he told Emily to wait in the car. Must have figured he could handle it himself." Pete shook his head. "Poor guy. Emily heard voices getting loud, so she sneaked down toward the water and peeked from behind a tree. She heard Sawtelle yell 'Run!' just before he went under the water."

"She got in the Audi and drove to the church?"

"She's still not too clear about that. Her dad says his mother, Emily's grandmother, lived in Salem, and when Emily was a little girl her grandmother used to take her to St. Peter's Church. He remembers that his mom used to park in that same little lot."

"That would explain the connection. She just got out of the car and walked to the common. It's just down the street from the church." I could picture her doing just that.

"Looks that way."

"So tell me why you want to get in touch with Dakota? What does he have to do with all this?"

"Darndest thing. I told you that Emily got a look at these two dudes."

"Yes."

"Well, we called our artist in to get her description so we could get some sketches circulating. You going to eat your chips?"

I pushed the small bag toward him. "Couldn't he do it?"

"He's not like a real artist, you know? He uses a kit with different face shapes, noses, eyebrows."

"I remember," I said. "Pretty neat. From the examples I've seen, he does a good job."

"Not neat enough for our Emily. He tried for over an hour. She was in tears by the end of it. None of his faces were right, she says. That's why I think we could use Dakota." He finished off my chips and crumpled the bag. "Of course, Chief thinks she's making up the whole story about the two guys. That's why she can't describe them properly."

"She's telling the truth," I said. I felt sure Dakota's talent would be much better than any kit, however accurate it might be. Besides, Dakota could use his pastels or colored pencils and get a real likeness. "Shall I call him now?" Kit-Cat showed seven o'clock. "He's probably home."

"Would you? I called his gallery but got a recording."

"Sure." I scrolled down to "Dakota and Shannon."

Shannon answered. We chatted for a couple of minutes about the soon-to-arrive baby, while Pete fidgeted with the Mr. Coffee, got our favorite "New Hampshire Speedway" coffee mugs down from the shelf, and put our dishes into the dishwasher. "Is Dakota around?" I asked. "I may have a little freelance job for him."

"He's here," she said. "Hang on."

My conversation with Dakota was brief and to the point. I handed the phone over to Pete, who laid out the situation with Emily and the sketches of the two suspects. I could tell from Pete's end of the exchange that Dakota's responses were all positive and that Pete would get back to him with specific time and place for the meeting with Emily.

"That's that," Pete said. "I hope Dakota's artwork will meet with Emily's approval. We need to get this done before the images begin to change in her memory."

"I've heard of that happening," I said. "By the way, I understand that Emily's phone has been returned to her."

"Yep. About an hour ago. The IT guys went all over it. Nothing out-of-the-way there." He frowned. "Hey. How did you know about that?"

"Betsy told me."

"Betsy? Your aunt's friend Betsy? Charlie's Angels Betsy?"

"Of course."

Cop face in place. He practically growled the words. "How did *she* find out? We're not ready to release that information."

I practiced my innocent face. "Emily called her."

"Why?"

"Emily doesn't have my number. Wanted me to call her."

"Did you?" Regular face back in place.

"Not yet. I waited to see what you thought about it."

"It's a good idea. Call her back now and tell her not to be telling people she saw the killer. She's putting herself in danger."

So I did. She picked up right away. "Janie? I mean Emily?"

"Lee? Is that you? Don't worry about calling me Janie. I was getting kind of used to it."

I heard the smile in her voice.

"You sound good. Pete told me that seeing your parents brought everything back."

"It's so good to be with them. I still don't remember everything. Like going from the hotel to that place in the woods—and getting from there to where I met Stacia. Some of that part is a big blur. But I remembered some things I'd much rather forget. I saw the two men who did it, you know. The men who killed poor John."

"I can imagine." *I don't need to imagine. I saw it too.* "Listen, you shouldn't be telling people you can identify those men. Pete says you might be putting yourself in danger."

"Oh, I know. The chief of police himself warned me about that. But I knew it was all right to talk to you and your friends."

"You be careful, Emily. Are you going to be okay? Is there anything I can do for you?"

"You've already done so much. I'm sure I'll be fine. We're going to be staying in Salem for a while—the police don't want me to leave. My parents had to find a condo that would accept pets. And, Lee, I was right about the tuxedo cat after all. He belongs to my parents and his name is Fred Astaire. I was so glad to see him!"

I could hear the happiness in her voice. "I knew you loved cats," I said. "I could tell by the way you took to O'Ryan."

"I do. I hope I can see O'Ryan again soon. I was wondering if it would still be all right for me to join you and your aunt and Betsy and Louisa for the TV shows sometimes."

"I'm sure we'd all love to have you. But don't you need permission? I mean, aren't you sort of in custody?"

"Yes. Maybe you can ask Pete if I can do it."

"He's here. I'll ask him." So I did. He didn't answer right away.

"I'll have to run it by the chief," he said. "He wasn't crazy about letting go of her in the first place. She's quite likely a material witness."

"Emily? Pete says he'll check with Chief Whaley. We'll all keep our fingers crossed. Hopefully they'll get those two men soon. And here's some good news. My artist friend Dakota Berman is going to help you get their likenesses down perfectly."

"You mean *the* Dakota Berman? The artist? Really?"

Sometimes I forget that Dakota has come a long way in the art world since we met. "Yep. That Dakota Berman," I said, then added proudly, "I was maid of honor at his wedding."

"Wow. You're full of surprises. I can hardly wait to see you again. When they let me come to your place I'll return your clothes and things. I got my luggage back from the hotel and my mom brought along some of my stuff from home, so I'm all set for now. Thanks for calling me."

"Good to talk to you. Stay in touch." Pete was tapping his watch in that "Got to go" posture. I said a hasty good-bye to Emily. "You have to go back to work already?"

"Sorry. Yes. I'll ask the chief about letting Emily hang out here, but I wouldn't get her hopes up. I'll call you." Another nice long kiss that I thought might make him change his mind about leaving. It didn't. O'Ryan escorted him downstairs and I called Betsy to let her know I'd talked with Emily. She agreed that all of the Angels would welcome Janie—she was used to the name—to the TV-watching sessions. I told her about Chief Whaley's reluctance to even let her go with her parents and repeated Pete's warning about keeping quiet about Emily remembering the murder.

"Tom Whaley? That's no problem. I'll call him right now."

"You know the chief?"

"He's one of my very special friends." Soft giggle. "I just love me a man in uniform."

CHAPTER 17

O'Ryan didn't come back upstairs so I figured Aunt Ibby must be home. Changing into pajamas and visiting with aunt and cat seemed like a fine idea. I hurried through shower and shampoo, pulled on soft cozy leopard-print pj's with well-worn flip-flops, and padded out my kitchen door and down the front stairs to the foyer. Avoiding looking at the hall tree mirror, I cut through my aunt's living room, following the sound of music coming from her kitchen radio. "It's me," I called. "You busy?"

"Come on out here," she answered. "I heard Pete leaving and O'Ryan dropped in, so I thought you might be along shortly." She sat at the round oak table where a dozen or so books lay, some open, other volumes in piles of two or three.

"Doing homework?" I asked. It's not unusual for her to bring library projects home. Sometimes she likes to gather together books on a certain theme for a special display, or perhaps an upcoming holiday or civic event might rate particular focus.

"Sort of," she said, waving a hand at the books. "Doing a little studying on Janie's case. I mean Emily, of course. I guess you know she's regained her memory."

"Good news travels fast," I said, wondering whether she'd received her information from Betsy, Emily herself, or if the police chief was one of her "special friends" too. "Are you looking up transient global amnesia?"

"Yes, but also I pulled a few books on Massachusetts wetlands, a brochure on waterfront real estate, and one on what it takes to get a detective's license around here." She patted a slim book at the top of one of the stacks. "We're serious about forming our own agency, you know. You'd be the logical one of us to apply for it."

I held up both hands. "Not me! I've got enough trouble with the job I already have. You and Betsy and Louisa each have more spare time than I do."

"I know. But you already have some of the qualifications. You've completed a couple of years of criminal justice classes and you've worked as an investigative reporter." It was true. Pete had encouraged me to take the online classes, and I was close to receiving my bachelor's degree. I'd enjoyed learning and it had given me a better understanding of his job. "You'd be good at it, Maralee," she declared.

"Pete tells me that all the time," I said. "It's never been one of my ambitions. Never."

"Hmmm." She smiled a sly little smile. "Since you came home to Salem from Florida, it seems to me you've become involved in more than one situation that required you to do quite a bit of detecting."

"Pure coincidence," I protested. "It's a Salem thing. Strange things just happen to happen here."

"True enough," she agreed. "Do you happen to know what line of work Janie is in? Louisa didn't know."

"Why don't you see if she has a Facebook page?" I suggested, reluctant to share the information Pete had given me about the woman being a forensic accountant.

"We did. It's been taken down. Her Twitter account as well."

"It's all for her protection, Aunt Ibby. Maybe it'd be a good idea to let the police handle it."

The police chief doesn't believe her story.

That reminder caused me to rethink. "On the other hand," I added, "maybe a little amateur sleuthing isn't totally out of line."

"Good. Glad you're with us on this." She pushed a colorful brochure in my direction. "Here's an advertising piece about waterfront properties for sale in our area. It's got information on some gorgeous homes, and phone numbers for the various agencies that handle them. Maybe there's something there. Maybe not."

I picked it up, not opening the slick pages. I recognized the magnificent porticoed mansion on the cover as one I'd often driven past on nearby Gloucester's scenic— and pricey—back shore road. "The wetlands books look interesting. Is that your project?"

"It is. You'd be amazed at how much the various things growing in a wetland area can tell us about who's been there and sometimes—what they were doing there."

It clicked. "Janie's shoes?"

A vigorous affirmative nod. "Janie's shoes."

"The police have already figured that out." I thought it was wise to share that much information, picturing in my mind the three Angels at midnight with hip boots and flashlights sneaking around behind the police tapes. "You don't need to investigate the shoes." I frowned. "Anyway, you don't have them."

She couldn't hide her disappointment. "I saved the towel they were wrapped in. There was still some sediment attached to it. I've already identified a trace of broom sedge and maybe even some reed grass. Looked promising under the microscope."

"I didn't know we had a microscope."

"We do now," she said. "Everyone agreed it's a necessary item for our investigations. We all pitched in for it."

I had no ready response for that so I changed the subject. "We're going to be looking for an actor to play a sidekick for Rob and Katie on the morning kids' show. Something like the role Cactus used to play on the old show. Any ideas on where we should advertise?"

She gave a well-bred sniff. "I hope the actor will be a person of much better character than the dreadful man who played Cactus. Are you looking for a man or a woman?"

"Doesn't matter a bit."

"In the old days it would have been *Variety*, but for your purposes I think the websites or newsletters from the schools and colleges that have acting classes would suffice. Like the Tabby for instance, or Emerson College in Boston."

"Exactly what I was thinking," I agreed. "The Tabby first, of course." The Tabitha Trumbull Academy for the Arts boasted a highly regarded student acting division. At least one former student was now working in Hollywood, and Emerson was my own alma mater. "I bet we'll have our sidekick within a week."

*   *   *

I was wrong. We did not have our sidekick within a week. At least not within the first six days of a week. We'd done a couple of dozen interviews. There were one or two near misses. Mr. Doan was becoming impatient. Chester had finished the set, and the bull chute was splendid with several coats of Olympic-blue high-gloss paint. Still, Rob and Katie hadn't found what they wanted— needed—in any of the candidates so far. Captain Billy had already recorded commercials. The sales team had sold enough thirty-second spots to support the show for the first three months. Tentative scripts were ready for rehearsal.

It was the last day of the week when Katie brought Paco into the studio. "I hope it's okay," she said. "We have an appointment for his shots this afternoon. His vet is just down the street and this will save me having to go all the way home to get him." She patted the black dog, who wore a red and white polka-dot ruffled collar.

"Oh, Katie. He's so cute! What kind of dog is he?" I put out my hand and Paco nuzzled my palm.

She smiled. "He's what the vet calls a 'mixed breed.' There's surely some black lab in there, and maybe a tad of pit bull. He has a black tongue, like a chow." She waved a hand. "Whatever he is, he's really smart and very well behaved. He does anything I tell him to."

"Anything?" I said.

"Just about. I told you he was a circus dog, didn't I?"

Within ten minutes we had our sidekick. The Amazing Paco. I was relieved. Mr. Doan was happy. The sales force ordered a quick video of Paco jumping through a hoop, dancing on his hind legs, counting to ten with both barks and paw-taps. The animal was truly amazing. Re-

hearsals proceeded with a new enthusiasm. It was beginning to look as though we had a programming hit on our
hands.

During the same week, Dakota met with Emily and
after several hours, emerged with detailed portraits of the
two men Emily claimed were present at the scene of John
Sawtelle's terrible death. Emily proclaimed Dakota's drawings were spot-on accurate. Copies were distributed on
police all-points bulletins. Television stations, including
ours, displayed them with some regularity every day. One
man, a brown-eyed blond with a crew cut, resembled an
aging California beachboy, and the other with longish
brown hair and a graying beard looked like a kindly high
school English teacher. Actually he reminded me of a
kindly high school English teacher *I'd* had in high school.
Nothing particularly sinister looking about either of them.
John Sawtelle's records had made reference to a Salem
real estate company called Waterview, but didn't include
names. The address of the company turned out to be a
parcel service mail box. Not much to go on there.

At the house on Winter Street, the Angels were in full
investigational mode. Meetings had progressed from occasional get-togethers for wine and snacks, British television mysteries, and gentle gossip fests to frequent evening
gatherings around the kitchen table, complete with more
library books, online chats, and some businesslike reports
from each Angel regarding individual progress. I didn't
attend the actual meetings, just popped in occasionally to
say hello. I was impressed with their diligence, but didn't
see any solutions to the mystery yet.

It turned out that Betsy may have worked her magic on
the chief after all, because Emily got permission to come

to our house for the weekly airing of *Midsomer Murders*. I had no intention of missing that meeting.

The condo Emily currently shared with her parents was just across the common on Washington Square, so it was a very short ride to our house. Emily arrived at the appointed time in a shiny, almost-new SPD patrol car, driven by my old friend and high school classmate, Detective Sergeant Joyce Rouse. Joyce escorted her to the front door, stopped long enough to exchange a few words with me, and promised to return at ten thirty, which allowed enough time for a little visiting before and after the show.

Emily gave me a hug and handed me a canvas bag. "Here are your clothes and shoes and handbag and everything. I can't thank you enough for all you've done for me." I put the bag on the front stairs and took her hand. "Come on. They're all in the kitchen dying to see you." The Angels rushed to greet her and immediately peppered her with questions.

"Is it true that you remember *everything*?"

"I know a good lawyer. Do you need one?"

"Is that dress a Dolce and Gabbana?"

Answers were: yes, she remembers almost everything; no, thank you, she has one; and yes, the short-sleeved black shift with the amazing jungle graphic was a D & G.

We all returned to the living room, Aunt Ibby in the lead, bearing a snack-laden tray, followed by Louisa with wine and glasses. There was still time before the show was to begin, and the Angels each caught Emily up on their own investigations. Aunt Ibby shared a condensed version of the wetlands information she'd gathered. Emily expressed genuine interest, asking questions—especially about water depths and saltwater intrusion.

Betsy had involved herself with the real estate aspect of the matter, collecting pages of sales of waterfront properties in greater Salem. She'd telephoned an impressive number of buyers and sellers of the most expensive properties and had recorded the names and business addresses of the listing and selling agents.

Louisa had occupied herself by following the money trail. Hitchhiking on Betsy's project, Louisa had found several of the high-priced properties that had been resold within a month of the original sale. She'd tried to match up agent names with subsequent sales, but so far hadn't found any matches.

I really had nothing to offer so far. I yielded the floor to Emily.

"Thanks to Lee's friend Dakota Berman, the police now know what the killers look like," she said. "Thank you, Lee."

I mumbled something appropriate and the Angels each voiced their approval. They all knew Dakota and all three owned at least one of his paintings. I treasure one of his early gravestone rubbings.

"It's wonderful that now you're able to help the police," Betsy said.

"I hope I'm being helpful," Emily said. "I talk to them nearly every day. I have to get permission to go anywhere." She sighed. "The days seem very long. I'm bored. Even Fred Astaire seems bored. My dad is really sad about John Sawtelle dying like that, so he's kind of quiet. They were good friends. I guess they used to go fishing together when they were young. It's a good thing I like my parents. It's like being quarantined with them."

"Now that you've remembered your past, what about your job?" Louisa wanted to know. "Can you work from where you're living now?"

Emily nodded. "Yes. That's no problem. I guess by now you all know that I'm a forensic accountant," she said. "That means that I can do a little more than figure out your taxes. My dad and I work together for clients who have more than the usual problems with finances. They come to us when they suspect that something illegal might be going on. Things like theft, fraud, or figures that just plain don't add up. That's the reason I came to Salem in the first place. It's how I happened to meet John Sawtelle. My dad was supposed to make the trip, but he had a conflict so he sent me along to handle it." She shrugged. "It didn't appear to be overcomplicated. I believed it was just an honest mistake in calculating. We were here to simply check up on some real estate deals that didn't look quite right and to check out a possible new listing for John's agency."

"Did you figure out what was wrong?" Aunt Ibby asked. "It must have been significant if it led to murder."

Emily frowned. "Mr. Sawtelle went over the figures with me several times. There were some discrepancies. I remember him saying there was something more going on there, but he couldn't quite put his finger on it. He said the new listing was just too good to be true but was definitely worth checking out."

"Did he give you any idea what it was he couldn't put his finger on?" I asked.

"Not really. He thought maybe the men were planning to offer him a good deal on some prime property to make up for messing with the commission figures. The truth is, my dad and I and John Sawtelle's office are still working on that. I'll tell you this much. It's much bigger than we thought. Uh-oh. Look." She pointed to the screen. "Here comes *Midsomer Murders.*"

All eyes turned to the TV. Conversation halted as we focused our attention on the cozy villages of Midsomer County, awaiting whatever darkly humorous events might take place this time in the otherwise peaceful English countryside. But I couldn't quite shake the dark, not so humorous events that were taking place right here in Salem.

CHAPTER 18

Our TV watching, wine and snack enjoying, investigation conversation, girl-talk evening ended all too soon as far as I was concerned. The Midsomer murder of the week had been titled "Baited Breath" and concerned a giant fish. Definitely a waterfront locale. Coincidence? At precisely ten thirty, the doorbell chimed "The Impossible Dream." Detective Sergeant Joyce Rouse had arrived to pick up her reluctant-to-leave charge.

I had so many questions I would have liked to ask. What did Emily mean by "it was much bigger than we thought?" What was much bigger? How had her talent as a forensic accountant helped the police? So many questions still unanswered. I could feel the imaginary investigative reporter hat sitting firmly on my head. But Joyce was firm too. Girl-cop face and voice in place, she rushed

Emily out the door and into the back seat of the cruiser with only a hasty "Good night, ladies."

I should try to stay focused the way Joyce does.

The after-the-show talk among the Angels buzzed around me as we trooped back into the kitchen for coffee. My inner Nancy Drew refused to be quiet. I needed to get some prints of Dakota's renderings of the killers. I'd have to look up "forensic accounting." I'd never even heard of it until very recently. What about all that flora and fauna lurking in the muck behind the yellow police tape? *How much information will Pete share with me?*

Can I concentrate on my program director job and work on the Emily matter at the same time?

"Sure you can," inner Nancy shouted. "Just do it!" I decided to begin right away. Why not?

"Louisa," I said, "Will you e-mail me a copy of your list of the high-end real estate sales you've been tracking?"

"Of course. Maybe you can make more sense of it than I did."

"Worth a try," I said, and promptly asked Betsy to share her list of phone numbers for buyers and sellers of those choice properties, and requested my aunt's file on Salem's wetlands. I excused myself from the Angels meeting. They were on second cups of coffee and a new round of cookies, but hey, none of them had a day job.

O'Ryan followed me into the front hall. Once again avoiding the mirror, I picked up the bag Emily had left and together cat and I climbed the stairs to home. I didn't expect a visit from Pete, but he usually calls to say good night and I was pretty sure he'd be just a bit curious about what went on with the Angels and Emily. I put the canvas bag on what my aunt calls a "boudoir chair," selected a pair of comfy flannel pajamas from the bureau, and with phone in hand, headed for the bathroom. O'Ryan followed, but gentleman cat that he is, waited outside the door.

I tossed dirty clothes down the laundry chute, and putting the phone within easy reach, sudsed, shampooed, rinsed, and toweled dry. I'd just pulled on the pj's when the phone buzzed.

"Hi, Pete."

"Hi. How'd TV night go?"

"It was fun," I said. "Everybody had a good time. We all wished Emily could have stayed longer though."

"Actually, she's lucky she got permission to stay that long. I was surprised that the chief okayed it."

Thanks be to special friendships!

"She really appreciated it," I told him. "I could tell by the way she interacted with the Angels. But Joyce was exactly on time, both dropping her off and picking her up."

"So tell me how it went," he said. "Did you all talk about Sawtelle's murder?"

"No. Not really. The Angels each talked about what they'd been working on. Louisa and Betsy seem to be mostly involved in the various real estate aspects. Aunt Ibby is studying up on wetlands. We were all interested in hearing about Emily's job. I'd never heard of a forensic accountant before."

"We had a class on it once at the police academy," Pete said, "but that was years ago. I had to look it up myself. It turns out that our Emily Hemenway is one smart young lady."

"We knew that when she was just Jane Doe."

"I guess you all believed in her, didn't you?" he said, "but the chief and I and Rouse, we have to look at the evidence. Your Emily isn't out of the woods yet."

"Out of the woods. That's ironic isn't it? She was literally in the woods when she witnessed a murder so awful that it erased her memory." I felt sad as I spoke the words so I tried another subject. "How's chances that you're going to find the killers, now that you have good pictures of them?"

"You mean the *alleged* killers. They *are* good pictures," he said. "Dakota is great at listening to a description from a witness and putting the face on paper. We've already had a few calls on one of them."

"So you already have a name? That's great."

Short laugh. "Several names. No two alike. Looks like either all the callers are mistaken, or the guy has several aliases."

"Can you e-mail me those pictures? For the Angels?"

Tolerant cop voice. "Don't tell me those nice ladies think they might know these creeps."

"They all get around in the world of high-income housing," I said. "It's possible."

"True," he said. "We've got some wanted posters already made up. Want me to stop by when I get out of here and drop some off for you?"

"You know I'd love to see you, but it's late." I knew the poor man had been working night and day on this. "You must be exhausted. How about breakfast tomorrow morning?"

"You have food?" He sounded surprised.

"Nope. But I'll buy breakfast."

"Good deal. Thanks. Love you. I'll pick you up in the morning."

Kit-Cat told me that it *was* late, but inner Nancy was insistent that I stay awake for a while longer. I turned on the kitchen TV with the volume low to keep me company and pulled a fresh package of index cards from the junk drawer. I've always liked using the neat, lined oblongs for organizing my thoughts.

I pulled a few cards from the package and spread them on the table in front of me. O'Ryan watched with interest from the chair opposite mine. On the first one I wrote *Emily says that the real estate matter they were checking on was much bigger than she and Sawtelle had thought.* I added *How?*

Inner Nancy shouted, "If they knew it was a such big deal, why did he leave her alone in that car? Hmmm?"

I don't know.

"Why don't you just ask her?"

To the card, I added *Ask Emily.*

From the TV came the muted sounds of *Danse Macabre*, River's theme music. O'Ryan's ears perked up. He left his chair and trotted to the bedroom. I took the hint. Turning off the kitchen TV, I returned the cards to the junk drawer, carrying the single one I'd written on to my room, placing it on top of the bureau. O'Ryan was already in his TV-watching posture, facing the blank screen. "Okay. Let's watch River in here." I clicked on the television and climbed into bed, fluffing up the pillows, leaving room beside me for the cat.

River announced the late-night film—Stephen King's *The Mist.* She was lovely in red velvet halter top and ruby drop earrings. There were two high-backed wicker chairs at the table where she'd be reading the tarot cards for callers during breaks in the movie. That meant that Buck Covington would be on hand to shuffle the deck.

He often stayed after his nightly newscast and the audiences loved it when he was on camera with River.

I watched the movie for a while, but dozed off before River's first reading. The dream seemed like part of the movie, only I'm in the mist—alone. I'm behind a tree, bare feet wet, flannel pajamas damp. I'm shivering, cold. *I'm hiding here. But why? From what?* I hear something. Voices. I peek out from behind my shielding tree. More mist. I creep closer to the sound. A voice calls "Run!" I turn to run away. I'm running deeper into the mist. I see a light ahead, and a blue fence—no, it's blue bars. I stop running and walk slowly toward the light. I push open the gate and emerge from the bull chute and look toward the bleachers where two people are seated—two men with faces that look like drawings. I'm afraid. I don't know why, but I'm very afraid.

I woke up with something soft touching my face. O'Ryan sat on my chest, his paw gently tapping, tapping. I hugged him. "Oh, thank you, dear cat. I was having a bad dream."

He gave my chin a lick, then wiggled out of my arms and resumed his spot on the pillow next to mine.

The TV was still on. The overhead camera focused on the tarot layout. River had just turned over the two of swords. I watched as the camera zoomed in for a close-up of the blindfolded girl alone on a park bench.

I turned off the TV and tried to go back to sleep, but gave up. Maybe the Angels had sent the lists I'd asked for. I got up, slipped my feet into bunny slippers, returned to the kitchen, and checked my e-mail. O'Ryan, yawning broadly, followed and sat on the windowsill behind me.

"Look at this," I said to the cat, whose eyes were half

shut. "They both sent their lists." I hit the print button and waited for the printer to whirr to life.

"Meh," said O'Ryan. "Meh. Meh. Meh." He hopped down from the sill and headed back to bed.

"Maybe you're right. Maybe they're not important after all," I said. "I'll look them over in the morning." I yawned, gathered up the printed sheets, paper-clipped them together, and followed the cat.

CHAPTER 19

Slanting rays of morning sunshine brightened the apartment as I got ready for my breakfast date with Pete. O'Ryan had already scooted out the cat door and was undoubtedly breakfasting with Aunt Ibby. By then, in the welcome light of day, I'd already decided that my weird dream belonged in the same category as nutty mirror visions. Undecipherable. I'd seen a shelf full of dream books at the Salem Library. Maybe I'd ask my aunt to bring home one or two volumes so I could figure out this mist-to-bull-chute saga just in case it made some sort of sense to the dream experts. Chalking the two of swords tarot card thing up to mere coincidence, I stuffed the paper-clipped copies into my bag, hurried down the stairs and out onto the front steps to wait for Pete.

His Crown Vic rounded the corner onto Winter Street,

made a U-turn, and pulled up in front of the house. "You hungry?" he asked as I slid into the seat. "I'm starving."

"Looking forward to breakfast, but not starving," I reported. "I loaded up on snacks at the viewing party last night."

"I brought you a few of those posters." He pointed to a brown envelope on my side of the dash. "Enough so you can share them with your aunt and her crew." He leaned across the console for a quick morning kiss, giving me an approving look. "You look especially pretty. Have a good night's sleep?"

"Yes," I fibbed. "Fell asleep before River's first reading." At least that part was true. "Thanks for the posters. I'll be sharing them. I made some copies of the lists Louisa and Betsy shared with us last night." I pulled them out of my bag and put them on the dash. "O'Ryan doesn't think they're important. Maybe you can make some sense out of them."

"Thanks. I'll take a look." He didn't comment on O'Ryan's opinion. He knows I talk to the cat. "Rouse says that Emily had a good time. Talked her ear off on the ride back to the condo."

"I'm glad she had fun. We all enjoyed seeing her again," I said. "She's much happier now that she has her memory back."

"Mostly," he said. "Dakota Berman said that she had a bit of a meltdown while she was trying to describe the two men."

"I don't wonder," I said. "She must have had to visualize the whole scene. It would be like living through it all again. Not easy." We pulled into the small parking area behind our favorite early-morning-breakfast restaurant. It's in a nondescript two-story house on a side street, marked only by a blinking vertical red neon OPEN sign in a front window. Patrons usually include night-shift workers on their way home—and day-shift workers on their way to work. Nurses, taxi drivers, retail store stockers, the occasional kids' hockey team with early morning ice time, cops and firefighters. Good homestyle food and hardly ever any tourists.

The waitress called us by name, indicated the day's specials on a blackboard, led us to our favorite booth at the rear of the room, and poured us each a mug of coffee. We ordered our usual—veggie omelet for me, ham and eggs for Pete. I hesitated for a moment before asking Pete the question that had been on my mind. Inner Nancy prodded. "Ask him." So I did.

"Pete, Emily said that the real estate matter they were investigating here was bigger than she and Sawtelle had thought."

He nodded. "So she claims."

"Is it true?" I asked. "Are those two men part of something really big?"

"Could be. We're working on it."

"That's what Emily said. She and her dad are working on it too. If it's something worth killing over, it must be pretty big," I insisted. "So why did Sawtelle leave Emily alone in that car?"

Our meals were delivered and coffee mugs refilled. "It looks as though he underestimated the danger. He thought he could handle it." Grim laugh. "She says she remembers that he was worried that she'd get her new shoes all wet."

"Those shoes. They had a story to tell all their own, didn't they? Aunt Ibby is studying about identifying things that grow in wetlands."

"It's quite a science. We learned a lot from the samples we had."

"I wonder why Sawtelle agreed to meet in such a desolate place."

"That's easy," Pete said. "Those two had some very convincing paperwork that looked as though the city was prepared to sell a section of waterfront within the conservancy, big enough for a major wetlands plant nursery. They'd told Sawtelle that it was all hush-hush. They said the city council hadn't actually voted on it yet—hadn't even seen the proposal—but for a hefty price he could get in on the ground floor. He went there to see it for himself."

"A wetlands plant nursery?"

"I know." Pete smiled. "I'd never heard of one either. But native plants are big business. People are caring about the environment. You see native plants replacing lawns all over the place. Plants that have been fending for themselves in wetlands for centuries are super-hardy and don't need a lot of attention."

"That makes perfect sense to me," I said. "I'll bet that's why my aunt is reading everything she can get her hands on about them. She's always been into growing things. Just look at our backyard."

"My sister Marie knows about it. She sent away for some special stuff to make a butterfly garden."

"Did it work? Did it attract butterflies?" I wondered.

"Worked great. One of her boys did a project on it and took second place in the school science fair."

"So a native plant nursery might be a big moneymaker for somebody."

"Apparently Sawtelle thought so. We found blueprints, maps, ground studies, all very official looking, in the Audi's glove box. A piece of property like that could be very valuable to the right buyer. Emily told us she thinks the men had agreed to arrange a good deal on the property as soon as it became available in order to make up for the so called 'mistakes' they'd made on previous deals—the ones Emily was there to investigate. Of course they wanted a hefty down payment for the privilege of being on the ground floor."

"Emily told us that Sawtelle thought the deal was too good to be true."

"He was right about that." Pete's smile was wry.

"They were going to cheat him *twice*?"

"Allegedly," Pete insisted.

"Allegedly," I agreed. "He must have figured it out and called them on it and they had to get rid of him."

"That how you see it?"

"Of course. How else could it have happened?"

"I don't know yet." Cop voice. "We'll see where the evidence leads us."

I could tell he wasn't ready yet to talk with me about Emily's part in all this. He looked uncomfortable. "About the two guys being involved in something big," I began. "I guess it must extend past Salem."

"Big enough so that it could reach a federal grand jury someday," he said. "It looks like those two guys, whoever they are, may be part of something that extends *way* beyond Salem. We think they're one cog in a very big wheel."

"Is that why you're being so careful of Emily? Because she saw them? Because she was even investigating them?" I felt suddenly afraid for my new friend.

"That's one reason," he said.

"What other reason could there be? You don't think she's somehow involved with those two creeps, do you?"

"That's not my call, Lee." Reasonable cop voice. "I just look at evidence. That's my job."

I leaned back in my seat. "I know that. I'm worried about her though. I'm glad you're keeping tabs on her—whatever your reasons."

"I'm glad you understand. Now tell me about you. How's the new show coming along?"

I told him about the Amazing Paco, the circus dog. "We went through a week of interviews for a sidekick for Ranger Rob and Katie when the perfect sidekick was right under our noses. Paco is truly amazing. He obeys commands, does all kinds of tricks. The kids are going to love him."

Our waitress arrived with the check and put it in front of Pete. Remembering my promise, I reached for it. "My turn," I said.

Pete held up both hands and laughed. "No objection here. It's good to have a woman who can afford me."

I laughed too. "My pleasure."

"I have tonight off," he said. "Fried clams at Dube's? We can go dutch."

"Deal," I said.

We walked together to the front counter and I poked my credit card into the terminal. Actually, Pete had no idea how much I could afford. We'd never discussed each other's finances. Between my parents' estate and Johnny's insurance, and the wise counsel of Aunt Ibby's shrewd financial advisors, I'm what some people would consider a wealthy woman. I'm also a quite thrifty one. I knew I'd have to tell him about the money eventually. But with everything going on, now was definitely not the time.

CHAPTER 20

As soon as I'd checked in with Rhonda I hurried down to the studio to see how things were progressing on the *Ranger Rob's Rodeo* set.

A dress rehearsal was already in progress when I arrived. It was obvious to me that the warmth and good humor between the two stars was the kind that the camera would capture. I sat on the top tier of the built-for-kids bleachers. My knees were practically up to my chin as I squeezed long legs into the space provided. The repartee between them was funny-silly and just the kind of dialogue kids love. Rob picked up his guitar and launched into "The Farmer in the Dell" while Katie pantomimed a confused farmer picking giant cardboard carrots. Rob did a couple of fancy figure-eight rope twirls with his lariat. Then Katie put two fingers to her mouth and let loose with the piercing kind of whistle most girls can't do. Paco came charging out of the bull chute, wearing a red and white ruff around his neck and make-believe bull horns on his head.

I knew we had a hit.

I'd already started a list of possible guests who might fit into the show's format—people who would hold the interest of preschoolers and had something of value to offer. An hour-long show needs to have more going on than songs and dances and cartoons. Wanda the Weather Girl would be a good choice. She'd have to tone down the brief outfits a bit, but I knew she could impart some fun weather facts. I jotted down Joyce Rouse's name too. Maybe she could speak on bike safety while Katie rode around the stage on her clown-tricycle. The recent conversation about plants gave me the idea of inviting a *real* wetlands plant nursery person to visit and perhaps give a lesson on butterfly gardens. I was on a roll.

If only Emily's legal problems could be solved so easily, I thought. Well, at least she was with her parents and she had her own clothes to wear. That reminded me of the clothes she'd returned to me the night before. I'd left them stuffed in the bag on a chair in my room. *Shoot. I'll probably have to re-iron everything.* I hate ironing.

Pete's revelation about the two men being a cog in a very big wheel was troubling. I was glad Emily was being guarded so carefully. Whatever those two were involved in had led to John Sawtelle's murder. People that desperate to cover up whatever it was they were doing wouldn't hesitate to kill again. I thought about the vision I'd seen in the mirror—of that terrified man screaming out a warning from the rising water. "Run," he'd said. And Emily had run. She'd run to the safety of the Audi, then to the safety of the church. She'd walked down the street to the very public safety of the Salem Common. Then she'd come with me to the safety of our house on Winter Street. Now she was safe with her own parents. *Safe for now.*

Did one of the two nameless—or in this case, multi-named—men in Dakota's drawing see her as she fled to the Audi? Just as she'd finally recognized their faces, did they now recognize hers? Maybe she should dye her hair, get some big dark glasses. I shook the silly thought away and got back to my prospective guest list.

It was nearly noon when I'd finished my list, typed it neatly, added a note asking for more suggestions, and made a few copies to share around the station. I turned my TV on just in time to see Phil Archer giving the intro to the noon news show. The BREAKING NEWS banner flashed across the screen almost immediately. POLICE FIND MURDER BOAT. A closeup shot of the partially burned hull of a small cabin cruiser filled the screen.

"The vessel, which was reported stolen late last month, was found this morning washed up on uninhabited Little Misery Island, just off Beverly's West Beach," Phil reported. "Indications are that the vessel may have recently been used to transport the body of John Sawtelle, whose remains were found last week on Collins Cove Beach, according to a police spokesperson. Field reporter Howard Templeton is with George Abbot, the owner of the stolen boat. Howard?"

Young Howie and a white-haired man wearing a Cape Ann Tuna Club hat were posed in front of a Safe Harbor Marina sign. "Tell me, Mr. Abbot," Howie said. "What happened when your boat went missing?"

"Well, Howard, I was down Winter Island way. I'd tied up the boat good and secure, you know? I went over to the bait store—didn't mean to be gone long—and when I got back she was gone." He hung his head. "I loved that old boat. Guess I'll be getting a new one."

"Was it insured?" Howie asked.

"Oh sure," George replied happily. "I've already sent photos to the insurance company."

"You've seen the pictures of the two men the authorities are looking for," Howie said. "Did they look familiar?"

"One of them sort of does." The man spoke hesitantly. "He was hanging around when I tied up my boat. The crew-cut one. Only the guy I saw had black hair and wore sunglasses. But it could have been the same man." Short pause and wrinkled brow. "He wasn't any kind of fisherman or deckhand or anything though."

"How do you know that?" Howie asked.

"Shoes. You don't wear those shiny loafers with little tassels on them on a boat. No sir."

Shoes again.

Howie did a fast wrap-up and tossed it back to the anchor.

"At present no suspects in either the theft of the boat or the killing of Sawtelle have been apprehended," Phil Abbot continued, "although pictures of two persons of interest have been released by police. Stay tuned to WICH-TV for updates on this ongoing story." Dakota's drawings of the two appeared briefly before Phil cut to commercial.

I spun my chair around so that I could look through the glass wall facing the newsroom. Scott Palmer wasn't at his usual desk. I wondered how he'd let young Howie beat him to the murder boat story—unless of course he was on to something better. That's what I'd be trying to do.

Not my problem anymore.

I spun the chair back to its original position. Back to where I belonged.

CHAPTER 21

My new position as program director involved quite a lot more than the building of bleachers and bull chutes. I was still responsible for the production of *Shopping Salem, Saturday Morning Business Hour,* and *Cooking with Wanda the Weather Girl*. The formats were already in place for all three, but they each still needed a tweak here and there. I turned off the TV. Then, trying to ignore the goings-on in the newsroom behind me, I filled out a requisition slip for promo shopping bags bearing the *Shopping Salem* logo, a copy of a Zig Ziglar book on selling for the *Business Hour* guy, and a pink, sequined chef's hat for Wanda.

I'd just begun searching on LinkedIn for a ghost writer for Wanda's forthcoming cookbook, when Scott Palmer tapped at my door. Without looking up from my screen, I waved him in. "Have a seat. I'm busy."

"I can see that. Did you watch my standup?"

"Told you. I'm busy. No time for TV." Curiosity got the best of me. I looked up. "What standup?"

"Moon, you should have been there. Old Jim had a hunch about that boat they found on Little Misery. It was a nice little Starcraft Islander. I mean it was nice before it got burned and wrecked. Jim knows a dealer he thought might have been contacted when the boat was found."

"Of course," I said. "That's the first place they'd check to find the owner. Right?"

"Right. Not only that, they towed the thing right up to the dealer's dock."

"Wow. You got his story."

Big grin. "And pictures. Yep. He saw right away that it had been torched. No accident there. He'd sold the boat to Abbot a few years back. The forward part of the hull was gone so the registration numbers weren't there, but the dealer's metal tag was on the custom seats. Easy ID." Another big grin.

"You said there were pictures. Interesting pictures?" I knew they had to be.

"The dealer had *very* carefully photographed everything in what was left of the cabin."

"OMG! Jim got shots of all those photos?" Knowing Old Jim's skill with a camera—any camera—I was sure he had.

"Yep. I only used a couple of them on the noon program. Saving them for tonight on Covington's show." He was practically wiggling with excitement. I had to smile too. Pulling off a story like that is so much fun.

"You get the 'investigative reporter' spot, right?" I asked.

"Yes!" He gave a fist pump worthy of Tiger Woods.

I didn't reply for a moment, trying to sort out what my reaction should be. I was startled to realize that I wasn't envious, wasn't even nostalgic about the times I'd achieved that pinnacle of field reporting, a feature spot on the evening news.

"I'm happy for you, Scott," I said, meaning it sincerely. "You deserve it. Good job." He looked surprised, and no wonder.

"Gee, thanks, Moon. Say, want to come to lunch with me—help me celebrate?"

"Oh, I don't know." I waved one arm over the stack of papers on my desk. "Like I said, I'm kind of busy here."

"I'm buying," he said.

"Really? Okay. Just a quick lunch though. I have to drop these requisition slips off with Rhonda first."

"Quick lunch is perfect. I'm busy too. How about we grab some burgers at the Village Tavern? We can sit on the patio." Big smile. "Maybe I'll even buy you a beer."

"A Diet Coke will be fine." I gathered up the papers for Rhonda and put the rest into the proper folders. Although I was happy for Scott, he's still not one of my favorite people. I wasn't ready for a long lunch with beers on the Tavern patio. I looked at my watch. It was almost one. "I can only spare an hour."

"We'd better get going then. My car?"

"Sure. Want to invite Old Jim too?"

"He's busy with Marty, doing production for tonight. Let's go." He held the office door open for me and we were on our way. I dropped off the requisition slips with Rhonda, whose left eyebrow was only slightly raised at the sight of me leaving with Scott.

The weather was nice enough for lunch on the patio. I

had Diet Coke. Scott ordered coffee. We both ordered Village Tavern's justly famous burgers. Scott broke a slightly awkward silence. "I took a few pictures of that boat with my phone," he said. "Want to see them?"

Did I ever! "Of course I want to see them."

He moved his chair closer to mine and held the phone where I could see it. "This is inside the hull."

The exposed ribs were charred almost completely black. What had once probably been upholstered bunk mattresses appeared to be melted. The remains of an orange lifejacket was barely recognizable. He'd taken about a dozen shots, some of the exterior and some inside the wreck. He clicked through the still photos rapidly.

"Wait a minute," I said. "Can I see that last one again?"

He obliged. I pointed. "What's that?"

He peered at the picture. Held the phone closer to his eyes. "Looks like part of what's left of a shoe," he said. "See? It's curled up like the witch's shoes in *The Wizard of Oz*."

"That's exactly what I thought of too. Looks like it had a tassel on it." I pointed again.

He squinted at the small screen. "Sure does. I'm pretty sure Jim got a better shot of it." He put the phone back into his pocket. "Thanks, Moon. That got right by me. Abbot said the guy he thought stole his boat wore shoes with tassels."

"I'm sure the police have picked up on it," I said. *And I'll bet it once had the same mucky stuff on it as Emily's shoes did.*

I thanked Scott for the lunch and we made it back to the station a few minutes before two. He was anxious to arrange for a close-up of the tasseled shoe for the evening news and I was right on time for a meeting with Chester about building a circus-themed dog house for Paco.

By five o'clock the top of my desk was cleared. Everything on my daily to-do list had been accomplished. With a feeling of satisfaction, I picked up my hobo bag, locked my office door, and headed upstairs to clock out with Rhonda. I realized that there was yet another plus to my new job. Unlike the edge-of-your-chair, race-out-the-door-at-a-moment's-notice, day-or-night schedule of the TV field reporter, the hours of a program director were generally quite regular. Almost normal. Well, as normal as things could get at a station like WICH-TV. That made me smile.

I wished Rhonda a good evening, then hurried down the metal stairs to the lobby. I found myself humming an off-key version of "Send In the Clowns" as I climbed into the Vette. It had been a good day, and I still had an evening with Pete to look forward to. I pulled out onto Derby Street, heading toward Hawthorne Boulevard. Passing the hotel I glanced toward the common, automatically focusing on the pigeon lady's bench where I'd first seen Emily. Nobody there. I checked my rearview mirror and made the left-hand turn onto Washington Square.

A red Mazda CX-30 was almost on my tail. I frowned, speeding up a little, pulling toward the curb, thinking it might want to pass. Instead, the car dropped back. As I made my turn onto Oliver Street, the Mazda sped past toward the Civil War monument, slowing down and signaling a turn on the corner of Winter Street. There was something familiar about the red car. I'd seen it somewhere else recently. Where?

I'd almost reached our garage when I remembered. That Mazda had been parked directly across the street when Joyce had dropped Emily off on movie night. That solved that. Someone in the neighborhood either had a new Mazda or had a visitor who drove one.

Maybe I should mention it to Pete anyway—just in case it has something to do with Emily.

Aunt Ibby's Buick was missing again. My aunt is a busy woman. O'Ryan met me on the back steps and followed me up the stairs to my apartment.

"I wonder if that Mazda is parked across the street again," I remarked to the cat. "Then I could be pretty sure it belongs in the neighborhood." He didn't reply. None of my windows open onto Winter Street, so I walked down the front staircase to the foyer and looked out the long window beside the door. No red Mazda. I opened the front door and looked up and down the street. Uh-uh. Not there.

I made a mental note to mention this to Pete.

Just in case.

CHAPTER 22

Once back upstairs I found a text from Pete saying he'd pick me up for fried clams at around seven. Good. That gave me time to shower, do something with my hair, and figure out what to wear. Also, I'd empty the bag full of clothing and accessories I'd loaned to Emily. Maybe I'd even do a reluctant tad of ironing.

In terry-cloth robe with hair towel dried, I dumped the contents of the bag onto my bed. O'Ryan, in typical curious cat fashion, immediately stuck his pink nose into the middle of the pile. Blouses and jeans, sweater and pajamas, had all been neatly laundered and folded. Shoes and handbag were polished and plastic bagged along with the new composition book I'd left in the guest room. My watch and a ballpoint pen were in a sandwich bag. I hung up the jeans, put the pajamas and the sweater into the proper bureau drawers and shoes into their allotted spaces in the closet. I put the watch into the secret jewelry compartment in my bureau and put the handbag on its usual hook next to the shoe rack. The blouses could benefit from a quick touch-up with the iron, so I laid them on the bed, instructing O'Ryan that he must not sleep on them. He put on a sulky face, but left the bedroom in favor of his kitchen windowsill. I picked up the bagged composition book, carried it to the kitchen table. Emily probably hadn't had time to use it. I could always use an extra notebook at my office. I slid it into my briefcase.

I'd already decided on white jeans and a navy turtleneck for our date at Dube's. It was nearly six thirty by then, so I dressed, brushed hair, did minimal makeup, and rescued the blouses from the bedroom. "I'm going down to the laundry room," I told O'Ryan. "Want to come with me?"

He made a little trilling purr sound and scooted down the hall to the living room. He'd already used the cat door by the time I got there. I was sure he had no interest in ironing, but would make a beeline for Aunt Ibby's kitchen just opposite the laundry room. The sound of John Denver's "Take Me Home, Country Roads" told me that my aunt was at home. I tossed the blouses onto the ironing board and knocked on her door.

"Come in!" she called. "It's open."

That was a big no-no. Pete has warned her many times to keep her doors locked. She and I had each learned the hard way how important that can be. "It's supposed to be locked," I scolded as I let myself in.

"Oh, I thought it was Betsy and Louisa. They should be here any minute. I opened it for them." She gave me a hug. "You're welcome too, naturally. Betsy called an emergency meeting of the Angels."

"Emergency meeting? What's happened?"

"I don't know. I guess she wants to surprise us. Want to stay and find out for yourself?"

"I can stay a few minutes," I said. "How can I resist an emergency meeting? Did she give you any idea of what it's about?"

"Not exactly. But since they're both working on the real estate aspect of the mystery, it must have to do with buying and selling."

O'Ryan headed for the back hall. "Here they come," my aunt said. "We'll know soon enough what they've discovered."

Cat and aunt were correct. Betsy and Louisa had arrived together in Louisa's Lexus, each of them clearly excited about whatever they'd discovered. Barely exchanging greetings, the two, along with my aunt, pulled out chairs and all began talking at once. I held up both hands. "Whoa," I said. "Slow down, ladies."

"Sorry," Betsy said. "Louisa, you go first."

I remembered that Louisa's project had been checking on recent sales of high-end properties that had been resold at a much higher price within a month of the original sale, while Betsy had collected names and contact numbers of listing agents.

Louisa fanned out several colorful advertising brochures on the table and, in her well-modulated voice, described how she'd personally called people who'd originally sold the properties. Since she moved in the most rarified of the North Shore's moneyed circles, she knew quite a few of those folks, who'd been happy to share the names and business addresses—and in some cases, the business cards—of the selling agents and the buyers involved.

Here Betsy took up the narrative. She stood, and smilingly tossed three sheets of paper onto the table. "Here are the copies of sales of the properties Louisa just described. Got them all from city hall. Oddly enough, though the names are different, the contact numbers of the most recent buyers match the numbers for the selling agents on the original deals. What do you think of that?"

I looked at my watch. Five minutes to seven. "Wow. I hate to leave you all, but I have to," I said with sincere regret. This was going to be one heck of a meeting!

With blouses still un-ironed and leaving what promised to be a fascinating Angels meeting, I dashed out the door and started up the twisty staircase to grab purse and phone and be on time for my date with Pete.

Unlocking the door—I take Pete's advice about locks seriously—I grabbed my hobo bag from the back of the kitchen chair and was about to stuff the phone into its copious insides.

This giant bag is a bit of overkill for dinner at Dube's.

The little cross-body bag I'd loaned to Emily would be perfect. I retrieved it from the closet, transferred wallet, lip gloss, tissues, and a pen, added the phone, and I was good to go when my doorbell chimed "Bless This House," signaling that Pete was downstairs.

O'Ryan, as usual, had beat me to the door to welcome Pete, but quickly returned to Aunt Ibby's kitchen through his cat door just as soon as I'd arrived on the scene. Maybe he didn't want to miss any of Betsy's and Louisa's show-and-tell either.

Pete had noticed Louisa's car in the driveway. "Another Angels meeting already?" he asked as he held the passenger door for me, "What's going on?"

"I left too soon to know exactly," I told him, "but they're all pretty excited about some stuff Louisa and Betsy have dug up on the real estate people involved in whatever Emily and Sawtelle were investigating."

"We're working on that too." His tone was noncommittal as he backed out of the driveway and headed toward Bridge Street.

"I guess Emily is pretty helpful, considering her forensic accounting background and her knowledge of Mr. Sawtelle's business." I tried for noncommittal too. A moment of silence from Pete's side of the car.

"Yep. You look pretty."

"Thank you." We'd merged onto Washington Street by the time I gave up the polite query technique. "I saw some pictures of the burned murder boat today. Did your forensics guys get anything from what was left of it?"

Tolerant smile as we passed the police station and headed for Jefferson Avenue. "Well, you know what they say. A criminal always leaves something at the crime scene and always takes something away. Ready for fried clams?"

"And French fries and coleslaw. Is that shoe tassel something left or something taken away?"

"You spotted that?" He'd just parked outside the restaurant. "Did I ever tell you you'd make a good cop?"

"Fairly often. And my aunt wants me to be a detective. Not interested in either job. But really, that shoe probably belonged to the boat thief, right?"

He took my hand as we approached the front door.

"Smart girl. And you're guessing that the boat thief is our killer, right?"

"Might be," I said. "If he is, he left the shoe at the crime scene. But if there are bugs and slime on it, he took something away too."

Quizzical look. "Bugs and slime?"

"Rhonda's definition of what an entomologist examines," I explained.

"Got it. Did you mention the shoe to the Angels'?" We were seated, declined the menus because we'd already made up our minds, and Pete ordered two light beers.

"No. I haven't mentioned it to anyone but you, and, of course, Scott Palmer."

Slight frown. "Scott Palmer? Why?"

"They were his murder boat photos."

"I guess we'll see them on the news tonight then." He sipped his beer. "Any other observations, Nancy Drew?"

"There is one thing I want to tell you about." I described the red Mazda and told him how I'd noticed it when Emily came to our house, and that I'd felt that maybe it had followed me that afternoon.

When I'd finished, he didn't smile either. "Did you get the license plate number?"

"I didn't. He was too close behind me for me to see it in the rearview mirror, then I turned onto Oliver Street and I saw him turn at Winter Street."

"You didn't tell me about it when you saw it the night Emily was there," he said. "How come?"

Our meals had arrived and I reached for the ketchup. "I thought it belonged to a neighbor, or maybe somebody's guest."

"I don't like thinking somebody is watching you. Or

Emily. If you see it again, call me right away." He reached for my hand. "Hell, Lee. I thought when you got the new job, and didn't have to run around covering crime stories, I wouldn't have to worry about you so much."

"It's probably nothing, Pete."

"Sure. Why not? I worry too much because I love you." He smiled. "Now what's this about your aunt wanting you to be a detective?"

"Don't worry about that," I insisted. "Not going to happen."

CHAPTER 23

We enjoyed one of our favorite seafood meals, and lingered over coffee. When Pete reached for the check, I objected. "We said we were going dutch tonight. Half of that is mine." I opened the purse and reached inside for my wallet. "Hey. What's this?" I'd pulled a colorful business card from the cross-body I'd loaned to Emily. I held the thing up between thumb and forefinger.

"What is it?" Pete asked.

"A business card from a real estate agent. Emily must have left it in here." I peered into the open purse, extracting my wallet. "It's not mine."

"May I see it?"

"Sure." I handed it to him.

"'Alfred J. Pridholm,'" he read aloud. "'Specializing in waterfront properties.' Ever heard of him?"

"Nope. Must be somebody Emily knows. Or, more likely, somebody she was investigating."

"That's what I was thinking," he said. "Mind if I hold on to this?"

"It's all yours," I said. "Did you get a chance to go over those lists I gave you?"

"They didn't add up to anything for me, but I think they're worth studying some more. I handed them over to our forensic accountant to check further. Maybe O'Ryan was right about them though."

"Maybe. Speaking of accounting, how much is my half of the check?"

He slipped the business card into his breast pocket. "Since you bought breakfast, how about I get this one and you do the tip?"

"Good deal," I said, slipping the appropriate bills under my coffee mug. "It's still pretty early. The Angels meeting might still be going on. Want to crash their party and see if they've come up with anything?"

"You said they were talking about real estate people?" He patted his pocket. "People who were involved in whatever Emily was investigating?"

"Yep. Let's go." Like a couple of conspirators plotting a spy mission, we headed home to casually "drop in" on the Angels meeting. We decided to first do a quick drive-by on Winter Street just to see if the Mazda might be there. It wasn't, so we drove around the block to Oliver Street. Louisa's car was still in the driveway and Pete pulled the Crown Vic in beside it.

"Maybe we should have brought ice cream," I whispered as we approached the back steps where O'Ryan waited for us. As soon as I opened the door, the cat darted ahead of us into the hall.

"Too late now," Pete said. "Anyway, if O'Ryan did his usual racing-through-the-cat-door act, they already know we're here." He tapped on the kitchen door. "I hope this is locked."

"Who is it?" my aunt called.

"It's me, Aunt Ibby," I answered. "Pete is here too." We heard the lock click open.

"Come in, come in," she said. "We've been so busy. Wait until you see all we've uncovered."

Louisa, Betsy, and my aunt, beaming like kids who knew they'd aced a final exam, invited us to join them at the round oak table where a manuscript-sized stack of paper was neatly centered.

"Looks like you've been working hard," I said. "What's all this?" I pointed to the paper pile. "A book?"

"No book," Betsy said, "but we've come up with names. Louisa made a list of waterfront properties listed for sale recently, from Portland all the way down to Provincetown. Janie—I mean Emily—had told us about a house that got sold twice. The second time for a much-inflated price. So I researched sales of waterfront homes that fit that pattern."

"You actually found matching names?" Pete asked. "Between the two lists?"

"We've found five," Aunt Ibby reported. She pushed a piece of paper toward where Pete and I sat. "But we haven't been able to actually locate any of them. Very strange. No business addresses on any of their cards."

Pete and I scanned the list and my attention snagged on an entry. One of the names on the list was Alfred Pridholm.

"Good work, Angels!" Pete said. He touched the list.

"You've gone pretty far afield. Portland to Provincetown, you said?"

"Yes, sir." Louisa said. "And we're thinking these swindles may cover even more territory than that."

"Do we know yet exactly what the swindle is?" I asked.

Four pairs of eyes turned toward me. "Of course. Emily had that pretty well figured out in the first place," my aunt said. "It's a very sophisticated scheme. It apparently involves a number of different people who hold different positions in the real estate industry. Isn't that right, Pete?"

"Looks that way. It may involve bogus businesses and financial institutions not just in Salem or even just in Massachusetts," he said, "and if Louisa is right about Portland and Provincetown, we have a lot more investigating to do."

"They must have access to some excellent counterfeiters," Betsy put in. "We think they're using fake IDs, fake licenses, even fake certificates of deposit they used for down payments."

"How does it work?" I asked.

"As near as we can figure it out," Aunt Ibby said, "the scammer sets up a phony buyer with a fake certificate of deposit to buy a fairly high-priced home. Then he creates a sham sale of the property to himself for a much higher price—usually over a million dollars. Then, using that property as collateral, he gets a loan for close to the million-dollar figure. He pays off the smaller loan, keeps the change, then gets another loan for more than a million to refinance the property."

"Do this eight or ten times on five or six properties and

you'll have many millions," Louisa said. "Many, many millions. Do you agree, Pete?"

"I do."

"John Sawtelle must have figured it out," I said. "No wonder you're worried about Emily." I thought again of the red Mazda. Whoever was driving it had seen Emily come into our house and had seen her leave. *Whoever was driving it knows where I live and maybe where I work.* I tried to shake the thought away.

"Do you mind if I copy those names down?" Pete asked, pulling his ever-present notebook and pencil from an inside pocket.

"Of course we don't mind," Aunt Ibby said. "We just hope it will be helpful to Emily."

Louisa muffled a ladylike yawn. I took the hint. "Pete, these women have put in a full evening's work. They must be tired."

He stood. "You're right. Good night, Betsy, Louisa, Ms. Russell. Thanks for your help. We'll keep in touch."

"Good night, Pete," my aunt said, "and I do wish you'd call me Ibby."

"Good night, Ibby," he said obediently. I gave each Angel a hug, and Pete and I left by the kitchen door. O'Ryan stayed behind. I gave my wrinkled blouses a glance as we passed the laundry room. "I need to do a little ironing tomorrow," I said. Pete didn't comment.

"I'm surprised," he said as I unlocked the door.

"About what? That my door is locked?"

"No. I'm surprised by what the Angels have done with the small amount of information they had to work with." He led the way down the short hall from my living room to the kitchen, taking off his jacket as he walked. "They even came up with the same name that's on this card. Alfred Pridholm." He held the card, as I had, between thumb and forefinger, staring at it. "Surprising."

"They are getting pretty good at the detective business, aren't they?" I was proud of my aunt and her friends.

"The detective business? Is that what the chatter about you becoming a detective is about? He draped the jacket over the back of a Lucite chair. "You know something? You could do it."

"They want to form a real detective agency," I said. "But at least one Angel has to be licensed by the state. They've apparently voted me 'most likely to succeed.'"

"You can do it, you know, if you want to. You're about a semester away from your BA in Criminal Justice. That'll give you the foundation you'll need to move forward." Big smile. "Of course, you'd have to put in some time on the police force first."

"Not happening," I said. He was right about the online degree though. I'd been working toward that for a couple of years. I'd begun studying when Pete and I had first started dating seriously. *Time for a subject change.* "Hey. It's time for the late news. I want to see how Scott does with his murder boat story." I reached for the remote on the counter and turned on Buck Covington's late news show. Whenever there's an investigative piece, Buck usually winds up the newscast with it. "Shall I put on some decaf?" I asked. "Scott won't be on until the end."

"Sure. Got any of those Girl Scout cookies left?"

"Samoas and Thin Mints."

"You pick."

I started Mr. Coffee and fished a sleeve of Thin Mints from the Red Riding Hood cookie jar while Pete went into the bedroom and stashed his gun in one of the secret drawers in my bureau. O'Ryan joined us via the kitchen cat door as we sipped and snacked and watched as Scott described Jim's excellent coverage of the charred boat. He'd included some file footage of Little Misery Island to give some perspective on where it had been found, a picture of the beach at Collins Cove and the by-now-familiar shots of Dakota's drawings, along with the well-known reminder to "See something, say something."

"What do you think?" Pete asked. "Did he do a good job?"

"Yes. He did fine."

"You missing having that job? That kind of spotlight on your reporting?" He reached for another cookie.

"I can honestly say I don't," I told him. "I was ready to move on."

"Ready for the detective gig yet?"

"I meant I was ready for cowboys and clowns and trick dogs. That's plenty for me."

CHAPTER 24

We went out for breakfast again since I still hadn't made time for food shopping. This time it was a fast stop at Dunkin'. I resisted the cinnamon doughnuts I really wanted in favor of a bacon, egg, and cheese croissant. Pete ordered the same. I'd save the doughnuts for some special occasion. We went dutch on the tab and I promised myself that I'd stop at Market Basket on the way home from work.

Pete dropped me off in front of our garage, with a kiss and a promise to call me later to let me know what his schedule for the day was going to be. First on his list was a visit with Emily to talk about the names the Angels had found, the card in the purse, and the red Mazda. I was happy in the knowledge that *my* schedule was just a nice, normal, nine-to-five workday.

I checked in with Rhonda a few minutes before nine,

and out of long-standing habit, looked at the whiteboard where she posts daily assignments for reporters and videographers. Howie and Francine were booked for a feature on the ongoing restoration of the replica tall ship *Friendship of Salem* overseen by the National Park Service. Scott and Jim were slated for a boat tour from eight to noon. I pointed to the board. "A boat tour? Why?"

"Pretty cool assignment, huh? A nice day for it. They got picked up next door at Pickering Wharf at eight o'clock. First they go out to Little Misery Island, then to Collins Cove, and finally a cruise-by at Conant Park." Rhonda counted each stop on her fingers. "It's called the Murder Mystery Tour. Typical Salem entrepreneurship at work. They're selling tickets like crazy."

"How come Scott got the plum assignment instead of young Howie?"

She shrugged. "Doan liked what he did on the murder boat piece last night."

"I never got a boat tour assignment," I grumbled, and headed through the metal door toward my new glass-walled office overlooking the newsroom where all the action seemed to be.

It didn't take long for the scene of the action to change. "Hey!" somebody shouted. "There's a horse walking around in the downstairs studio." I reversed direction and ran for the window overlooking the parking lot. I recognized Rob Oberlin's Ford F150 King Ranch Supercrew. The horse trailer behind it bore the logo of the Double R Riding Stable. Ranger Rob had arrived for work astride Prince Valiant.

I clattered my way down the stairs and pushed open the door to the long, darkened room. Even in the dim light, it was easy to spot the big, beautiful, pale-cream-colored Palomino horse with his bright flaxen mane and tail. Prince Valiant, with Rob tall in the saddle, picked his way carefully past the various permanent sets in the room, toward the lighted soundstage where Katie the Clown and Paco the wonder dog waited. I liked what I saw.

I picked my way extra carefully through the studio too, since I was following behind a very large, healthy horse. Katie waved excitedly when she saw me. "Lee! Paco has learned a new trick. Watch this." She clapped her hands once and spoke softly. "Paco. Open the chute."

The dog obediently trotted to the blue gate, stood on his hind legs, lifted the latch with his teeth, then quickly moved aside. Katie clapped again. "Paco. Close the chute."

Paco pushed the gate closed, and with one paw holding it firmly, replaced the latch. He ran to Katie, who slipped a treat from her voluminous pocket and fed it to him.

"That's amazing," I said. "If I'd known Prince Valiant was going be here, I would have brought a treat for him too."

"That's okay," Rob said. "I brought him in today to see how he reacts to the bull chute. He might not like it." He patted the horse's mane. "He might not even fit in there with me on top."

"We should have measured it first," I said. "My bad. Should have thought of that before I gave Chester the plans."

"Might as well find out now," Rob said. He made a *click-click* sound and turned the horse toward backstage. "Katie, want to open that bull chute gate as wide as it gets in case Prince wants out in a hurry?"

"Got it," she said, swinging the gate open and quickly stepping away from the entrance. "Out of the way, everybody." She waved toward where I stood with Marty and Chester. We three retreated to the bleachers, waiting to see how horse and rider might fare—and if the admittedly Mickey Mouse construction of the bull chute would stand up to the test. Katie and Paco joined us.

Some snorting and whinnying went on backstage, but within a minute Prince Valiant, with his best parade high-step, emerged from the blue tunnel with a grinning Rob. "He's not crazy about it"—Rob gave a fancy over-his-head twirl of his lariat—"and I won't ask him to do it every day. Will once in a while be all right, Lee?"

"Of course. Whatever you say. The kids will be excited to see him no matter how he gets onstage."

"It may be better if he does it when it's a special occasion," Marty said, and Katie agreed.

"Like cinnamon doughnuts for breakfast," I said, and they seemed to understand.

Marty and Chester left us to do some blocking, marking x's on the stage floor while Paco chose to explore the corners of the set. Katie stayed with me.

"Lee," she said," there's something I want to tell you, only I don't want you to think I'm being nosy or spying on you or anything." Her voice trailed off.

"What's wrong?" I asked. "I know you're not nosy."

"I get here pretty early in the morning, you know. Clown makeup takes a while, and I never want to rush it." She patted the orange wig and swung her big shoes back and forth.

Where was this going? Did she want to be paid overtime? I waited for her to continue.

"There are usually not many cars in the parking lot when I get here," she said, "so I know most of them. Rhonda gets here early and sometimes Francine's truck is already here. Chester's truck too. So if there's a car I don't recognize, I usually notice it. Especially if it's a pretty one." She paused, looking down at her feet. "This probably doesn't mean anything. I hope you don't think I'm being silly."

"No. Of course not. Go ahead."

"So you remember the day I first brought Paco to work with me?"

That made me smile. "I'll never forget it. You'd found our sidekick."

"Right." She smiled too. "Anyway, that morning I noticed a really nice car parked out there next to the seawall. One I'd like to have myself. There was a man in the driver's seat. I figured he must be one of the salesmen. I haven't met all of them yet."

"Go on."

"After you'd met Paco I took him outside to do his duty, you know? And that cool red car was still there."

A red car? I waited for her to continue.

"There was a man over next to *your* car. I think it might have been the guy I saw in the red car. He saw me looking at him and he turned real fast and faced the water, like he was admiring the view."

"It *is* a nice view, but you were suspicious of the man anyway." I stated it as a fact. I didn't even ask her if the red car was a Mazda.

"Kind of. But the reason I'm telling you this is because I left work right after you did yesterday. And, Lee, when you drove off, I saw that same red car pull out of the Pickering Wharf overflow lot next door. He followed you. I know he did."

"I think you're right, Katie," I said.

"That's not all. When the man was next to your car the first time I saw him, I think he might have put something under the back part. He was kind of bent over, you know, and he was touching the back fender nearest the wall."

"Putting something under my car? Damn! My car is bugged."

"That's what Rob said too, when I told him about it. He said I should tell you."

"Thank you, Katie," I said. "I'm grateful that you did. You said the man saw you looking at him. Do you think he would recognize you? Now I'm worried about you."

"I was wearing one of my clown suits when I walked Paco. When I come in to work or leave, I look like the dowdy old lady I really am," she said. "Hardly anyone recognizes Agnes as Katie."

That was true, even though she's definitely not a dowdy old lady. I worried about her anyway. I worried about me too. I excused myself from the rodeo set, went back to my office, called Pete, and told him exactly what Katie had told me.

CHAPTER 25

"Listen, my love," Pete said. "Drive straight home after work and put your car in the garage. Ask Ibby to put hers in the driveway so I'll have room to see what's going on with the Vette. As soon as I get out of here I'll call you so you can unlock the garage side door for me. Okay? Don't worry. We'll see what's going on."

Our garage is an old-fashioned, freestanding building behind the house, with its sort-of-new Genie automatic door facing onto Oliver Street. There's a regular door on the side of the building opening onto the flagstone path that leads to the garden and the back door.

"I'll run down and unlock it as soon as you call," I promised. The advice about not worrying didn't work for me, but otherwise I was confident that Pete would figure out what was going on. Beyond being worried, the thought of some creep touching my beautiful Vette infuriated me.

All right, call me obsessive about my car. Picturing some strange man reaching under one of those Bimini-blue fenders and planting a foreign object there, I almost felt personally violated. Damned creep!

The rest of that day passed in a blur. Oh, I did everything I was supposed to do. Checked the items off one by one. Called Captain Billy about doing a guest spot on *Ranger Rob's Rodeo* about the newest toys. Had Marty shoot a few teaser spots about the upcoming show. Interviewed a ghost writer for Wanda's cookbook. Had to drive over to PetSmart to pick up a doggie bed for Paco—cringing all the way thinking about the foreign object tracking me. Caught up on some paperwork and managed to avoid Scott Palmer all day long. I was glad when five o'clock arrived. I made a fast trip to Market Basket and checked out via the ten-item line. I compulsively looked at the rearview mirror every minute or so on the ride home, half expecting to see the Mazda, and hated myself for doing it. It was a great relief to pull into my own garage. Aunt Ibby's Buick wasn't there though, so I texted her, asking her to park in the driveway, saying I'd explain tonight. I knew that message would arouse her curiosity. No doubt now she'd be home sooner rather than later.

O'Ryan met me on the back steps with purrs and ankle rubs, which always makes even the worst of days a little better. I put down the grocery bag, picked him up and buried my face in his soft fur. "I love you, big cat," I told him.

I imagined that his answering "Mmmrrrrow" meant "I love you too." I put him down and he followed me up the twisty stairs. He stayed close while I put the groceries away, hung up my jacket, and put my shoes in the closet.

I changed into soft faded jeans, big loose T-shirt, and sneakers, put my cell phone on the kitchen table so I'd be able to grab it the minute Pete called. I could hardly wait for him get there and to take that disgusting thing off of my beautiful car.

I jumped when the phone buzzed. Not Pete though. It was Aunt Ibby. "What's going on, Maralee? I'm on my way home. Library board meeting today. I thought it would never end. Why am I parking in the driveway? Not that I mind, but why?"

I explained as briefly as I could, trying not to frighten her in the process. "Pete will be here in a little while. He asked that you park outside so he'll have room to work on whatever that man put under my car. I don't think it should take very long."

"Maralee, I don't like this one bit. Why would some strange man want to track your comings and goings?" I'd scared her, no doubt. "Do you suppose this has something to do with Emily?"

"Wouldn't be a bit surprised," I told her. "Pete's calling. I'll see you when you get here. Bye."

I was relieved to hear Pete's voice. "I'm almost there. Want to unlock the garage door now?"

"I'll be right down. See you in a minute. Come on, O'Ryan." I hurried back through the living room and down the stairs. "Pete's here." Since the cat usually knows who's coming to which door before anyone else does, he looked confused, but took my word for it and was out the back door and waiting beside the garage when Pete pulled the Crown Vic into the driveway, carefully leaving plenty of room for the big Buick. Perfect timing. I unlocked the side door and clicked on the overhead light.

Pete joined me inside the garage. He wore jeans and a PAL T-shirt and carried a large red toolbox. "You look ready for work," I said, accepting a quick kiss. "I'll be so glad when you get the damned thing off. Will you keep it for evidence?"

"Not exactly," he said.

"Not exactly?" I echoed. A knock at the door behind me interrupted my next question. Aunt Ibby had arrived. "Come on in," I said. "Pete just got here too."

"Am I in time to see you take the gadget off, Pete?" She moved toward the Vette. "Do you know where it is?"

"I have a good idea where it will be," he said. "I need to get a couple more things from my trunk." We watched from the doorway as he retrieved one of those creepers mechanics use to get under a car, and a long-handled mirror, and carried them back to the garage. He opened the toolbox and selected a flashlight. "Let's take a look."

We could have heard the proverbial pin drop as my aunt, O'Ryan, and I stood in a silent row as Pete walked slowly around the Vette, the long-handled mirror in one hand and the flashlight in the other. He passed the mirror along the underside of the car, pausing every so often to lie on the floor and focus the flashlight up under there. He reached the rear left fender, the one Katie had said the man had touched.

"Okay," he said. "There's one here." He pulled on gloves and lay on the creeper, the flashlight in one hand. Within less than a minute he slid back into view with a small black box in his hand. "Here's the little devil. Want to see it before I put it back?"

"Put it back?" My aunt and I spoke together.

"Yes. And I'm going to install another one under the

dash." He held the oblong box toward us. "Not a cheap magnetic one like this though."

"I get it," I said. "The bad guy will know where I am, but so will you."

"Exactly. Whenever this car moves, someone from the department will be on your tail in an unmarked car. I'm betting we'll have this guy within a day. We're checking Emily's dad's Jeep too. I won't be surprised to find one of these babies under it."

"I can see why these people are interested in Emily," I said. "She's actually seen them. She may have witnessed a murder. But why do they care where I am?"

"You were the first person to get to Emily—besides the pigeon lady. And your house is the only place she's been except for the jail and her parents' condo. The only other person besides Emily they think could identify them and could connect them to the real estate scam was John Sawtelle."

"And he's dead." Aunt Ibby finished the thought. "Oh dear. This isn't good at all."

"Don't worry, Ms. Russell—I mean Ibby. We're on it."

"But I'm not on to anything," I protested. "Emily never told me anything about her job or exactly what she and Mr. Sawtelle were doing in Salem in the first place."

He removed a square black device and a roll of electrical tape from the toolbox. "Unlock the doors to the Vette, will you, Lee? I'm going to hard wire this tracker." He got into the driver's seat and pushed the seat back. "They know Emily is confined to home most of the time. But you're easy to keep track of—and they know you have access to Emily."

"Holy cow." That old imaginary light bulb went on over

my head. "So do the Angels. Betsy even has her phone number. Are they following Betsy and Louisa too? And what about Aunt Ibby?"

"Yes," my aunt chimed in. "What about us?"

"There's no indication of that. Hand me that screwdriver, will you, Lee?" He pointed to the toolbox. I gave him the tool he'd indicated. I could tell that he was being extra careful removing the dash. He knows how much I love my car. "I know you both realize this real estate scam is big. Possibly a multi-state operation. The two guys we're looking for may be pretty far down on the list of players. They've probably been told to clean up their mess."

O'Ryan began to meow.

"All right, dear cat," Aunt Ibby said. "I know we're late for happy hour." She opened the side door. My aunt and O'Ryan spend this special time together most evenings. She with wine, he with homemade chicken broth. "I'll leave you two to your spy tactics. O'Ryan and I will be at home."

"This won't take much longer," Pete said. "Twenty minutes or so."

"What about Katie?" I asked. "Whoever put that tracker on here must know she saw him."

"I sent an officer over to talk to Katie this afternoon. She was really helpful. Can you aim the flashlight for a minute while I strip the wire?"

I focused the light where he'd indicated. "Helpful how?"

"Really good description. Looks like the man Katie saw is the blond guy in Dakota's pictures, but with dyed black hair and horn-rimmed glasses."

"I didn't get a good look at the man driving the Mazda," I said, "but he could have had black hair."

"That's okay. Katie got a fairly close look at him. We had Dakota redo his picture to match Katie's description. You'll see the new version on TV and the newspapers by tonight."

"That was fast."

"We need to catch these guys fast. We've had a couple of calls about the other one—the one with the beard. He's apparently a real estate agent. The callers each gave a different name for him though."

"Does either name mean anything?"

"One sure does. It's Alfred Pridholm."

"The card in the purse Emily borrowed," I said. "But she didn't have my purse when the murder happened. Do you think she deliberately put it there for me to find?"

"Exactly when did you give her the purse, Lee?" Pete pushed the dashboard firmly into place and carefully rubbed the surface with a sanitized wipe.

"It was when she was still Janie. Before she remembered anything," I said. "But where did the card come from? She didn't have her own purse until it showed up in the Audi. I gave her jeans and a blouse and underwear."

"What did she do with her own clothes?"

"She put them down the laundry chute in my bathroom."

"Do you suppose she emptied the pockets before she did that?" He closed the door to the Vette. "By the way, did you go to the grocery store?"

"I did. We have food. And yes, she probably emptied them. I know I would, whether I'd lost my memory or not." I could almost see it. "There were pockets in her sweater. I saw her take out a tissue when she was on the common. She probably emptied the pockets and put whatever was there into the purse."

"Like maybe a package of tissues or a stick of gum or a business card."

"Sure. Things like that."

"So she put the card into the purse before she got her memory back." We left the garage and I locked the door. He jiggled the knob. "Allegedly," he added as we walked toward the house.

"Allegedly what?"

"Allegedly got her memory back."

"You're still doubting her story, aren't you?" I felt a little flash of red-haired temper. "Pete, she's obviously telling the truth."

"I just follow the evidence, Lee. That's my job. The business card is evidence."

I repressed a sigh. "Okay. I guess so. I understand." I stopped beside Aunt Ibby's garden and glanced over the fence. "I wonder if we could make a butterfly garden here." I was starting to get really good at subject-changing.

"I'm sure my sister would be glad to help," he said. "Your aunt would probably like it. The plants are pretty. Marie says it attracts hummingbirds too."

"I'll talk to her about it," I said. O'Ryan strolled toward us. "How do you feel about butterflies, O'Ryan?"

"Meh," he said, which I took to mean he didn't care one way or the other and we followed him into the house. Aunt Ibby didn't express much interest in the butterflies either. She was much more concerned with my double-bugged car. "I don't like the idea of someone following you, Maralee. I mean, even if Pete and the other police know where you are, that doesn't mean they can get to you soon enough to protect you from who-knows-what."

"We'll be close by, Ibby," Pete promised. "Wherever the Vette goes, one of us will be right around the corner. I promise."

His words brought a slight smile. "You promise?"

"Of course. You don't think for one minute I'll ever let anything bad happen to her, do you?" He reached for my hand.

"I know that," she said. "Maralee has been my child since she was a baby. I worry."

I wanted to hug them both. In that moment I felt truly loved. "I'll be fine," I told them. "They'll have those two guys by tomorrow."

"Wouldn't be a bit surprised," Pete said. "Meanwhile we're looking over the tapes from that outdated old security camera on the WICH-TV building. If that Mazda was within camera range, we might get the license plate number."

"It's possible, I guess." I wasn't too hopeful about the possibility. Pete was right about the age and condition of the security system—clearly not one of Mr. Doan's top priorities.

"We'll find him." Pete's cop voice was edgy. Stern. I believed him. So I changed subjects again.

"I did a little grocery shopping," I said. "Pete's going to brave my cooking tonight."

"I'm sure it'll be delicious," my aunt said, with conviction.

"I'm sure it will," Pete said, with hope.

CHAPTER 26

While Pete moved the Buick into the garage, I gathered together the items I'd bought for an Italian dinner—angel-hair pasta, a jar of Ragu, a frozen package of mixed vegetables (onions and red and green bell peppers), a bag of salad mix, a fresh loaf of Italian bread, and a frozen Sara Lee strawberry cheesecake. I already had grated Parmesan cheese, Italian dressing, dipping oil for the bread, and a bottle of red wine. A meal not much like Pete's Grandma used to make, but I figured the general effect would be okay.

While I dumped the salad into a pretty bowl, Pete prepared the spaghetti al dente. (It's al dente, Pete's grandma had claimed, when a strand sticks when it's tossed at a wall.) The sauce with seasonings bubbled nicely while the bread warmed and the cheesecake thawed.

The general effect, if I do say so myself, was excellent.

Pete declared that everything was delicious, and I decided that this domestic diva thing wasn't so difficult after all. I made a mental note to buy a copy of Wanda's cookbook when it was ready.

As we relaxed with after-dinner coffee and cheesecake, I told Pete about Scott and Jim's cushy boat tour assignment. "They call it a Murder Mystery Tour. It'll be the feature on the late news, I suppose."

"Let's watch it. You never got an assignment like that, did you?"

"Tell me about it." I chased the last crumb of cheesecake around my plate. "I'll be interested to see what Scott does with it—besides give the tour some free advertising."

While Pete and I lingered over coffee, O'Ryan had already declared bedtime by climbing up onto my bed, turning around three times, and plunking himself down facing the TV. We took the hint. While I straightened up the kitchen and loaded the dishwasher, Pete headed for the shower. He was still in the bathroom when I'd finished my after-dinner chores, so I grabbed white satin pajamas and went downstairs to my second-floor childhood bedroom to use the facilities there.

Aunt Ibby's housekeeper takes charge of keeping everything spic-and-span on the first two floors of the house. I saw that the winter bedspread and draperies had been replaced with lighter, more colorful summery patterns, and I smiled when I spotted my old Ranger Rob and Katie the Clown dolls on the window seat. Aunt Ibby's special touch, I knew. She'd brought them down from the attic because the real-life pair were now in my grown-up world. I crossed the room and picked up the Katie doll. She looked as good as new. So did Rob. I figured they'd probably had a trip to the dry cleaners along with Emily's pink sweater. *I sure do love you, Aunt Ibby.*

Pete was already in bed with O'Ryan, and the TV was on, tuned to *Nightly News with Buck Covington*, when I came back upstairs. Snuggling in between man and cat, I watched handsome Buck as he did his usual flawless job of reading the national news from the teleprompter. When he broke for a My Pillow ad, I told Pete about the dolls. "They look just like they did when I was a kid," I said. "Katie's clown suit and her orange yarn hair and Rob's little checked shirt and blue jeans—even Katie's clown shoes and Rob's boots look the same."

"They must be collectors' items by now," Pete said. "I'll bet you could do an interesting field report about them. You could interview one of the antiques dealers on that *Shopping Salem* show."

"You know, that's not a bad idea—even though I really don't want to be a reporter anymore. Hey look, there's the teaser for Scott's segment."

The thirty-second teaser began with a slow-rolling drone's view of Collins Cove Beach, which made it look much more desolate and lonely than it actually is, followed by clips from the video of Scott in front of the no-trespassing signs at the Conant preserve, winding up with a montage of shots of the charred hull of the ruined Star-craft Islander. The accompanying audio promised "a close-up view of an ongoing investigation into murder from WICH-TV's field reporter, Scott Palmer. Stay tuned."

We stayed tuned. As promised, Buck Covington wound up the newscast, with Scott on hand in person to do commentary. The video began with a shot of the sleek, eighty-foot party boat at the Pickering Wharf, where a crowd of people were lined up for seats on the Murder Mystery

Tour. Old Jim had panned his camera along the line of customers. I'd learned from working with Jim that when he pauses the camera during a standard shot like that—it means he's spotted something worth noting. He paused for a fraction of a second too long on one of those patrons.

"Did you see that?" I sat straight up, dislodging O'Ryan, and pointed to the screen.

"The Viking-looking guy with the red beard and the aviator mirrored sunglasses?" Pete was already out of bed and reaching for his phone. "I sure did."

"The kindly high school English teacher, now with a dyed beard," I said, remembering my impression from the drawing. Even with the beard and glasses, he still looked like my old teacher. "Why would he do something so obvious? It doesn't make sense. I wonder if Scott caught it." I grabbed my own phone from the charger on the bedside table. "Gotta call Marty and get still shots of him."

"The classic case of returning to the scene of the crime," Pete said. "Happens more often than you'd think." He shook his head. "But this one gave him a view of the crime locale, a shot of the body dump site, and a look at where they tried to destroy key evidence. A scene-of-the-crime trifecta. Hard to resist, I guess."

I knew Marty would be on hand at the station. She'd be doing River's show in a few minutes. While the phone rang I returned my attention to the TV, where Scott described the scene he'd shot at the Conant preserve after I'd given him the tip about police presence there. He followed with the Collins Cove piece and a pretty look at Little Misery Island. Old Jim was playing it straight. No more lingering shots, even at the windup pictures of the charred cabin cruiser. If Scott had noticed that one of the wanted perps was aboard the party boat, he didn't mention it.

Marty answered on the second ring. "What's up, Moon?"

"I need some still frames from Scott's shoot on the party boat," I said. "Can you grab me some, of the guy with a red beard and mirrored sunglasses, and send them to me ASAP? It's kind of important."

"No problem. I'll get to it right after *Tarot Time*. You going back to reporting or something?"

"Or something," I said.

Naturally we were both wide awake by then. Pete's phone call took longer than mine had. I overheard him ordering a check of the Pickering Wharf security cameras and any onboard cameras the party boat might have, along with records of reservations booked with credit cards.

"Shall we see what River has going on?" I asked when he'd come back to bed. "Maybe the movie is a good one."

"Might as well," he said. "You know who else must have recognized Red Beard if he watches the news? Dakota Berman. He'd spot that face in a New York minute."

"So would Emily Hemenway," I said. "If she was watching."

River's scary movie du jour was the 1968 hit *Rosemary's Baby*. Always worth watching again. I managed to stay awake right up to the part where the creepy neighbors invite the young couple to dinner. River had just begun a reading, and with O'Ryan snoring gently beside me and Pete already sound asleep, I decided to join them in dreamland and clicked the TV off.

So much for dreamland. I was back in that soggy mist left over from the last scary movie I'd watched on River's show. Still in wet flannel pajamas and bare feet, this time I was in a butterfly garden. At least there were lots of butterflies fluttering in and out of the mist. Again I heard someone shout "Run." I ran. I looked back. The red-bearded man was gaining on me. I tripped over a bucketful of water. Picking it up, I poured water on the advancing man. Of course, like the witch in *The Wizard of Oz*, he melted—nothing left but aviator glasses and one tasseled shoe.

Once again, O'Ryan came to the rescue, waking me by gently tap-tapping on my nose. "Thank you, darling cat," I whispered, hugging him. Had this been an important, symbolic, prophetic dream? Or should I just avoid eating cheesecake late at night?

CHAPTER 27

It was one of those nightmares that lingers until morning.

The smell of coffee brewing and the sound of country music told me that Pete was up. I made the bed and selected jeans, shirt, and shoes, dashed for the bathroom, and prepared myself for the day. Pete, of course, was already dressed, groomed, and gorgeous.

More or less put together, I hurried back to the kitchen, put on one of Aunt Ibby's aprons, and selected the makings of breakfast for Pete and me. My ten items had included orange juice, bacon, eggs, and English muffins. We already had a fresh jar of Aunt Ibby's homemade strawberry jam. Classic and easy breakfast. Pete poured coffee and fried bacon. I scrambled eggs and manned the toaster. While the last muffin browned nicely, I took a hurried peek at my laptop. Had Marty sent the pictures?

She had. "Pete, look at this. It's him, all right. I'll forward these to you."

He looked over my shoulder. "No doubt about it. He's playing a dangerous game. Wonder if he's overconfident or just stupid."

"Probably a little of each," I said.

"If you're not going to use the pictures of Red Beard yourself, are you forwarding them to the news department?" Pete spread a generous blob of jam onto the hot muffin. "Or are you going to give them to Scott Palmer? Or maybe Howard Templeton?"

"We can't be the only people who recognized him. The station has probably already had dozens of calls. The police station too." I thought about his question. "Anyway, it was Scott's shoot. I'll send them to him without comment. He'll figure it out." So that's what I did—before I could talk myself out of it. I wondered why Old Jim hadn't tipped him off before last night's late news. I remembered though, he'd never tipped me off to that lingering camera trick. He'd always let me figure it out for myself. Scott's return text was swift. "Thanks, Moon. Don't know how I missed it."

"We'll let Emily know about the new disguise," Pete said. "Not that she's apt to be out anywhere without a police escort, but just in case."

"In case they might find a way to get to her?" I wondered aloud. "They're getting awfully bold. One of them watching me from a bright red Mazda and the other one deliberately letting himself appear on TV."

"Yeah. You're right. We'll probably add another layer of security around her," he said.

"Me too?"

"Well, I may be spending more nights here, if that's

okay with you." This was followed by the Groucho Marx eyebrow wiggle and silent-movie-villain mustache twirl. "Strictly in the line of duty, you understand."

"Understood, sir," I said. "But seriously, the Angels are going to be asking if Emily can come here for the weekly meeting. Do you think it will be allowed?"

"Maybe. How about if Detective Rouse sits in on the meeting with her? Would the Angels go for that? Having an armed guard in the room?"

"Are you kidding? They'd be thrilled. They'll probably drive poor Joyce nuts with questions about the detective business though."

"She won't mind. The woman loves her job."

"Do you love yours?" I realized I'd never asked him that before.

Thoughtful frown and long pause. "I don't think 'love' is the right word. I like being a cop. I'm good at it. I guess we all like to make a living at something we're good at." He gathered up the dishes and carried them to the dishwasher. "But love it? No. I love you and my parents and my sister and the nephews. That's quite different."

"I know what you mean. I've always liked being in the television industry," I said. "It's been my dream since I was little. You know something? I think this new job—as program director—might get to be my favorite part of the business so far. But do I love it? Nope." I put the remains of our breakfast items back into the refrigerator with a silent reminder to self that if Pete would be staying over more often, I'd need to do some serious food shopping. I gave him a quick impulsive hug. "But I love you."

His return hug could have made us both late for our respective liked-a-lot-but-not-loved jobs. We reluctantly moved apart. I took off my apron, organized the contents

194 *Carol J. Perry*

of my hobo bag, slid my laptop into its case, and together Pete and I climbed down the twisty staircase to the back hall. I glanced into the laundry room and realized that the ironing fairies hadn't appeared. Oh well. O'Ryan had already joined Aunt Ibby, but poked his head through the cat door to acknowledge our presence.

"I think I'll follow you to work." Pete spoke in serious-cop voice. "Just to look around, and to let anyone interested know that you have a friend on the force."

"You're worried about me."

"I'll know exactly where you and the Vette are every minute. I'm just taking a look around."

"Okay. I'm glad you are. See you tonight?"

"Absolutely. I'll call you later." Short pause. "And Lee? Call me if you see anything—anything at all that doesn't look right. Promise?"

"Promise." I unlocked the garage and watched as Pete drove away, knowing that all day long I'd be focused on finding things that didn't look right. I was very much aware of the two GPS devices hidden beneath my beautiful car. I'd be glad when all this was over and both of the damned things were gone. I checked the rearview mirror. Pete was two cars behind me. I looked away from the mirror as soon as I saw the swirling colors and flashing lights in the shiny surface. Driving along on one of Salem's narrow one-way streets is not a good place to take eyes off the road. I'd check out the oncoming vision later. Or not.

I tilted the mirror to one side so that it no longer distracted me with its flashing and swirling. It no longer showed me what was behind me either. When I turned off Derby Street into the WICH-TV parking lot, Pete followed, made a U-turn in the lot, gave a toot of his horn, and continued on his way.

I pulled into my assigned parking space in the far right corner of the lot and, still avoiding the mirror, looked out over the harbor—where everything looked just as it should. I shut off the big engine and glanced around. Francine's truck was in its usual spot. Ranger Rob's Ford truck was there too, sans horse trailer. Both mobile units, the big new one and the converted Volkswagen bus, were in their regular spots. Everything looked right. I checked the dashboard clock. I was a few minutes early. With a re-signed sigh, I tilted the rearview mirror back to where it belonged—and where I was undoubtedly going to see something that didn't look right.

Flashing lights. Swirling colors. Then I saw the Salem Common—at first from a distance—almost like a drone camera video. I saw the whole place—the white arched entrance, the kids' playground, the bandstand. The view narrowed. I saw the woman sitting alone on the bench, just as I'd seen Emily the first time. But now she was blindfolded, like the woman on River's card. The two swords were there too, but this time each one was held by a man. The men's backs were toward me and the swords were pointed at Emily.

Pop. The vision was gone.

I sat there for a moment, still staring at the mirror, which now reflected exactly what it should—the WICH-TV parking lot. Automobiles and trucks in a variety of shapes and shades. Pavement, painted white lines, a glimpse of granite seawall. In the lower left corner of the mirror I saw a flash of color near the ground-level studio door. It was Katie in full clown costume with Paco on his leash. I stopped the mirror gazing, picked up my handbag and laptop from the passenger seat, and got out of the car.

"Hi, Katie." I waved and started across the lot. She waved back and started toward me, her big clown shoes making the act of walking cute and comical. Paco, wearing a bright yellow ruffled collar, trotted along by her side.

The gray sedan seemed to come from nowhere, speeding onto the lot, hurtling straight toward Katie, blocking my vision. I heard her scream, heard Paco howl. The gray car didn't slow down. I ducked between Francine's truck and call-screener Therese Della Monica's little PT Cruiser, watching as it sped past me and back out onto Derby Street. I dropped purse and laptop and ran toward where Katie lay on the ground, Paco standing close beside her, teeth bared.

CHAPTER 28

"Katie!" I yelled, racing across the pavement while hitting 911 on my phone. "Are you all right?" *Such a silly question. Of course she's not all right.* I knelt beside her, relieved when her eyes flicked open, when her hand reached out for Paco, grasping his collar.

"Paco saved me." Her voice was hoarse. "He pushed me out of the way. Is that guy crazy or what? He could have killed me."

I spoke into the phone. "We need an ambulance and a police officer. Hit-and-run." I gave the address. I also gave the gray sedan's license plate number. This time I'd seen it and memorized it. "A gray 1997 Mercury," I told the 911 operator. "Male driver. Red hair and beard."

Katie raised her head, struggled to push herself upright. "Stay still, Katie," I told her. "Let's find out if anything's broken before you try to get up."

She lay down. "Paco saved me," she said again. "I think he may have been hit. Listen. He's whining. Is he okay?" By this time a small crowd had gathered around us and the sound of sirens grew close.

"What happened?"

"Was that a hit-and-run?"

"Look, the little clown is hurt."

"The dog's paw is bleeding."

Paco whimpered softly and held his right front paw awkwardly off the ground. The yellow ruffled collar was steaked with red. Paco the wonder dog was not okay. I heard the studio door open.

"What's going on out here?" It was Chester's voice. "Oh no. Agnes! What happened?" He knelt beside Katie. Paco growled.

"It was a hit-and-run, Chester," I said. "The ambulance is on the way."

"I don't think anything is broken, Chester," Katie said. "I'm all right. Paco saved me. Can somebody take him to his vet? He's hurt."

An ambulance pulled into the lot and the people scattered. Two EMTs ran to Katie's side. "Make room, please." They motioned me and Chester away. We moved. Paco didn't leave his position. "Stretcher and neck brace," one said, gently prodding Katie's arms and legs. and the other quickly produced the needed items. Two police cruisers, lights flashing, sirens blaring, arrived on the now-crowded scene. The first cruiser to arrive was Pete's. He and the uniformed cop from the other one moved quickly, asking questions as they drew closer to where the EMTs had carefully secured Katie on the stretcher.

Ranger Rob appeared, kissed Katie on the forehead, gathered Paco into his arms, assuring the by then immobilized Katie that everything was going to be all right, and carried the dog to his truck.

"Did you see what happened?" Pete was at my side. "I'd just walked into the station when your call came in."

"I saw it all, Pete. It's the bearded guy. He was trying to kill her!"

"Was he the one Katie saw messing with your car?"

I shook my head. "I don't think so. It was the other one. She was wearing the clown suit when she saw him. I suppose blond crewcut told gray beard about her. It's the only way he had to identify her."

"You did a good job, getting the license number," he said. "We'd already found that car abandoned less than a mile from here. It was stolen last night. This guy is taking a lot of risks. He's even willing to kill again to cover up his tracks."

I found all this hard to believe. "All Katie did was see somebody hanging around my car. It's not like she took his picture or anything."

"I know," Pete said. "And other than the dye job, he's not even trying to disguise himself. It's almost as if he's trying to get caught."

"Then why wouldn't he just turn himself in?"

He shrugged. "Don't know, but it happens. Sometimes they do it because getting caught by us is a better fate than what their higher-ups can do to them when they mess up a big operation."

"Do you think that's what he's doing? Trying to get himself captured?"

"It could be that," Pete said, "but in this case I don't think so. He's just too brazen. It's possible that he has such a high opinion of himself that he believes he can outsmart us. Outsmart everyone. Remember the Son of Sam murders? The killer actually sent letters to the newspapers bragging about the crimes."

It was a chilling thought. "Do you think there could be more murders? That the kindly high school English teacher is enjoying his crime spree?"

"Don't worry, babe. We'll get him."

Just about all of the WICH-TV staff had gathered in the parking lot by then, along with some lookie-loos who happened to be passing by. Scott and Old Jim were already in the VW bus. Rhonda ran toward us. "Rob phoned. He says they took Katie to Salem Hospital. Did you see what happened? Is she badly hurt?"

"Paco knocked her out of the way. She was conscious and talking when the ambulance came," I told her. "I don't think she was badly hurt. She was mostly concerned about Paco. His paw was bleeding."

"Rob said he's taking the dog to the vet and then he's going to the hospital to check on Katie," she said. "I'd better round up the crew before Doan figures out that all the help has left the building."

"I'm surprised that he's not out here too," I said.

"He's reading over Katie's contract in case he has to hire another clown to take her place."

"I'd better get going too," Pete said. "I'm going to take a look at that car."

"I guess Rhonda's roundup includes me. Call me when you get a chance, please," I said, while wondering if

Scott and Old Jim would get to the impound lot before Pete did. I was pretty sure I'd get a call from Scott, once he found out that I'd been an eyewitness to attempted murder. I went back and retrieved my purse and laptop, brushed them off, and followed the parade of on- and off-air talent, salespeople, and videographers back to work.

The first thing I did once inside was call Aunt Ibby. I surely didn't want her to find out about what had happened to Katie from anyone but me. I left out the part of darned near being hit myself. I'd tell her that some other time. I promised to keep her informed about Katie's condition and got back to business.

With the rehearsal for *Ranger Rob's Rodeo* scratched, I hurriedly rearranged my planned schedule. The program director gig wasn't turning out to be as orderly as I'd thought it was going to be. I put Chester to work on bookshelves for the *Saturday Morning Business Hour* and phoned Captain Billy to schedule a guest shot on *Shopping Salem*. The bookshelf project reminded me of my quest for a dream book. Perhaps the public library's dream book selection wouldn't be as esoteric as what I might find in some of Salem's witch shops, but mists and butterflies and tasseled shoes seem like fairly ordinary things people might dream about. Well, maybe not the tassels. I was hesitant to share my dreams with Aunt Ibby. She's still uncomfortable with my scrying "gift." I called her back. She promptly agreed to bring home a few books on the subject without asking any questions as to why I wanted them.

Ranger Rob texted me from the hospital to say that Katie seemed to be fine but that her doctor wanted her to stay overnight for observation. "She wants to come straight back to the station and resume rehearsals," he texted, "but I talked her into staying the night."

"Good news," I texted back. "I'll spread the word. How's Paco?"

"Vet says his paw is badly scraped but probably not broken. She's going to keep him overnight for more X-rays and blood work."

I knew Bruce Doan would be delighted to hear that he wouldn't need to replace either clown or dog, so I rode Old Clunky up to the second floor to deliver the good news. Rhonda buzzed Doan's office and told me to go right in. "Is Scott back yet?" I asked.

"On his way," she said. "He says he hit a double on this one."

"What does that mean?" I asked.

"Haven't the slightest," she said. "Scottie likes to talk in riddles sometimes. We'll know soon enough."

"Guess so," I agreed and tapped on the station manager's door. I delivered my happy message, assuring the boss that in all likelihood, Katie and Paco would report for work the following day, then—skipping the elevator—used the metal staircase and returned to my own office.

Ignoring the not-too-big pile of papers on my desk, I swung my chair around so that I faced the newsroom. I didn't see Old Jim, but Scott was back, high-fiving everybody in sight. He caught my eye, put thumb and little finger to his ear and mouthed "Call me."

I didn't hesitate. I hit his private number and watched as he pulled the phone from his pocket. It was almost like Facetime, but bigger and better. "What have you got, Scott? Must be something good."

"We went straight to the impound lot after Katie got hit. I guess you'd figured that. You should have been there, Moon. Your boyfriend was there. He looked plenty busy, investigating both cars."

"Both cars? The gray sedan and what else?"

"A cute little red Mazda. At least what was left of it."

CHAPTER 29

I darn near dropped the phone. *That* Mazda? The one the black-dyed crew-cut beachboy killer was stalking me with? "Did Katie tell you about the red Mazda she saw in our parking lot?" I asked, not sure of how much Scott might know about my connection with that particular car.

"Oh yeah. She figured he might have put a GPS under your Vette. Rob told me about it. Did he? Was your car bugged?"

It still is. "Yep. It was. You say the Mazda is wrecked?"

"Totaled. Your boyfriend has a crew going all over it. My contact guy at the impound yard says they towed it from over near Castle Rock. Looks like somebody drove it right into a bridge abutment. Pretty much tore off the whole right side. He says it looks like there was blood in the front seat. We couldn't get close enough for Jim to get good pictures of it though. The gray Mercury was closer to the fence. A little front-end damage was all I could see on that one. How's Katie?"

"She's going to be all right," I said. "Paco shoved her out of the way. He took a hit but hopefully, no broken bones."

"Glad to hear it. Nice dog. You saw it all, huh?"

"I did. It happened so fast it was like a blur. But I did see that Red Beard was driving."

"What I'd like to know, Moon, is what all this has to do with you." I detected some genuine concern in his voice. "Why does anyone want to bug your car?"

I wish I knew for sure. "Not sure," I said. "We think it must have something to do with my connection to Emily Hemenway."

"The chick that's mixed up with the real estate guy getting killed, right?"

"Yes. Did you know the Mercury was stolen?"

"Yep. We stopped on the way here and interviewed the owner. I did that one live. For the morning news. Did you see it? No? She had a security camera. The cops have already grabbed the tape though. She says it was late last night. She'd already gone to bed. The car was unlocked. The red-bearded dude just walked right up the driveway, got in and jump-started it somehow." He waved to me. "Come on in here. Jim and Marty are editing. Come on. I'll give you a sneak preview. Show you what you're missing by changing jobs."

Changing jobs wasn't exactly my idea. "I'll be right there." I shoved the pile of papers into the top desk drawer and headed for the newsroom.

It was nice to see the welcoming smiles and calls of greeting as I approached Scott's desk. After all, I knew everybody there. I'd been one of them for years—though I'd never rated a desk in that rarified room. I passed a desk—a new-looking shiny one—bearing a brass plaque with Howard Templeton's name on it. Howard wasn't there. Were Howie and Francine off somewhere covering something more important than Scott's two-car bonanza?

"Okay, Scott, time for show-and-tell," I said.

"Sure. A little payback for that still shot of Red Beard you sent over. I totally missed it. Thanks, Moon."

"It's your story. Not mine."

He led the way to the bank of monitors in a corner. Marty and Jim had their heads together in front of a bright screen. Even from halfway across the room I recognized the rear end of the gray Mercury. The view was shot from behind a chain-link fence—a much less terrifying aspect than the same vehicle hurtling past me while I cowered between cars on the WICH-TV lot. I gave myself silent kudos for memorizing that license plate number so fast.

Although as Scott had told me, the only shot of the red Mazda was a glimpse of a badly crumpled right front fender and a shattered rearview mirror barely visible from behind a distant outbuilding. Marty had patched in a dealer's photo of the same model.

Scott had done a voice-over on site, detailing the attack on Katie. There was a brief reference to the Mazda, mentioning only that the car had reportedly been driven recently by one of the murder "persons of interest," and that it was a leased car, registered to a real estate corporation. He hadn't mentioned the alleged bloodstains. I watched as Marty and Jim worked together to select the best visual components to complement the audio. I knew from what I watched on the monitor and from my history of working with both of them, that the end result would be excellent TV. They'd even worked in a publicity shot of Katie in her clown outfit with Paco, and some footage of Red Beard from the Murder Mystery Tour along with Dakota's updated drawing of the crew-cut beachboy with black hair.

"Good work, Scott," I whispered. "You bucking for the shiny new desk over there?" I cocked my head toward Howard Templeton's gleaming new work space.

"Who me? Hell, no. I just want the new mobile unit for Jim and me instead of the old VW bus."

I laughed. "Never happen. Howie's the boss's nephew, remember? By the way, where did he and Francine go today?"

He frowned. "Another plum assignment. They scored an interview with John Sawtelle's widow and his office staff. They went to Brookline this morning." He looked up at the clock over the monitor bank. "Almost noon. They should be back any minute now."

"That should be very interesting," I said. "Maybe they'll find out exactly what Sawtelle and Emily were looking for in Salem."

"Hasn't your new friend Emily told you about that?"

"She told the police what Sawtelle had told her," I said. "There were questions about the figures on some real estate deals on some local waterfront properties Sawtelle's agency represented. Since Emily's dad was originally supposed to make the trip to Salem and Emily was brought in at the last minute, it seems she had just the basic information to work with. I'm sure the police have already interviewed Sawtelle's office staff and Emily's dad about it."

"That's all Emily told you? Same story she gave the police?"

"Of course. It was all about numbers to her. That's what she does. She thought it was something fairly simple—like cheating on commissions. That can amount to a lot of money on the kind of high-priced waterfront properties Sawtelle represented."

"Turned out to be more than that," he said. "Turned out to be worth killing over, huh?"

"So it seems."

"Somebody ought to start checking on all the high-priced waterfront deals they can find," Scott said. "There might be more deals worth killing over."

I thought about the Angels. *Somebody already is.*

"Yep," I agreed, "somebody should. Thanks for the preview. I need to get back to work."

"You sure? You don't want to hang around in here?" He waved an arm, taking in the whole newsroom.

"I don't get paid to hang around. See you later." I fast-walked my way out of there, straight back to my new glass-walled haven. "Moving on," I told myself. "That was then, this is now." I sat at my desk, pulled the abandoned papers out of the top drawer, and started on a new script outline for a *Ranger Rob's Rodeo* show.

I was aware of a little flurry of activity in the newsroom when Howie and Francine returned. I resisted the tiny temptation to go back and get the firsthand scoop on what they'd learned in Brookline. Nope. I'd learn about it later when Phil or Buck introduced it to the viewing public. I didn't pause for lunch but worked my way to the bottom of the to-do pile. Last item in the pile was a grocery list for the once-a-week *Cooking with Wanda the Weather Girl* show. Taping of the show was scheduled for the following day. Wanda usually does her own shopping, but she'd attached a sticky note apology (shaped like a pair of lips) explaining that she had a costume fitting and wouldn't have time to do it.

I didn't mind. I knew I could use some practice in food shopping. I was convinced that there was more to it than making sure the purchases would always qualify for the ten-items-or-less lane. I could tell at a glance that Wanda's list exceeded that number. I stopped at Rhonda's desk and announced my planned shopping trip to Market Basket.

"So, what's Wanda cookin'?" Rhonda wanted to know.

I read the heading on the list. "A prepare-ahead-of-time Sunday brunch."

"Sounds useful," Rhonda said.

"Lots of ingredients." I held up the paper so that she could see the long list. "Looks complicated. Way above my pay grade, I'm afraid."

"Never know till you try," Rhonda said. "You might like it."

Sort of like my new job. I placed the list in my hobo bag, walked down the stairs and out into the welcome sunshine. I crossed the lot, realizing for the first time that there were no skid marks on the pavement. The bearded killer hadn't even attempted to stop. If I hadn't dodged when I did he would have run me over for sure. Unlocking the Vette, I slid quickly into the driver's seat and re-locked the doors. I hesitated looking into the rearview mirror, but knew I had to if I was going to back out of my space safely. *Is walking across the lot and getting into my own car going to be like this forever?*

CHAPTER 30

Armed with Wanda's list, a company credit card, and a few reusable grocery bags marked with the WICH-TV logo, I selected a cart and prepared to shop. I learned right away that Wanda's recipes for baked items require double ingredients because she bakes one ahead of time to show viewers the finished product. The other stuff is for the on-camera demonstration of putting the thing together. It didn't take as long as I thought it might to fill the cart. Eggs, Canadian bacon, mushrooms, green onions, lots of spices—so far it sounded like something Pete would like for breakfast. I finished up with some beautiful red ripe tomatoes, grapefruit, oranges, tangerines, a few packages of frozen spinach, and a lot of grated Parmesan cheese.

Pete likes Parmesan cheese. Maybe Rhonda is right.

Maybe I'll watch Wanda put all this together and I'll try
it myself. Maybe.

I felt quite proud of myself as I wheeled the cart with
three bags full of groceries back to the Vette. Unlocking the
trunk, I carefully deposited my bounty. I closed it, then
pushed the cart into the proper area.

The voice came from a vehicle passing just behind me.

"I'll see you later, sweetheart."

Naturally I turned to see who'd spoken. The beard was
gone. The hair was still red, partially covered with a ball
cap. The eyes were cruel, the smile mocking. The car
sped away.

I ran for the Vette, yanking the phone from my bag.
Once inside, I hit 911.

"One of the men you're looking for just left the Market Basket store on Highland Avenue," I almost shouted.
"Green Toyota. No plates. There's a for-sale sign in the
rear window. He's shaved his beard."

Had I given enough information? The dispatcher got it
right away. "The red-haired one?"

"Yes." I started the Vette, hands shaking, heart pound-
ing. I was still being stalked. And I'd just been threat-
ened. He'd timed everything perfectly. In the few seconds
it took me to get back to my car and start it, he was long
gone. I hadn't even seen which way he'd turned. There
was no way I could have followed him. Wherever my police department tail was, they wouldn't have seen anything out of the way going on. The Vette hadn't moved an
inch.

I called Pete and told him what had just happened.
"The car was stolen from a used car lot about half an hour
ago," Pete said. "The salesman went inside to get dealer

plates for a test drive and the guy took off. He'll ditch that car pretty quick," Pete said. "Are you okay?"

"I'm scared," I admitted. "How long has he been following me? And why? 'I'll see you later,' he said. That's a threat, isn't it?"

He didn't answer the questions. "Can you get time off from work, Lee? I'd like to keep you out of sight until we catch this one."

"Oh, Pete. No. I can't. There are a lot of people depending on me. Heck, I've got a trunk full of groceries for Wanda that need to be delivered right now. I'm in charge of four different programs. Other people's jobs hang on mine. I just can't stay home."

"Okay. How about if I assign an officer to you. Plain clothes. Until this is over."

"Will that help you catch him? He knows where I am all the time because of the GPS. He knows where I am right this minute." I heard my own voice rising in fear and fought to control it. "Would the officer have to ride to work with me?"

"Not if you don't want him—or her—to. I'd follow you to work in the morning. The officer would have his own transportation. Okay?"

"Is Chief Whaley going to be all right with this?" Chief Whaley isn't exactly crazy about me. I'd understand if he wouldn't want to use an officer's valuable time babysitting me.

"He wants to get a killer off the streets. You may be the key to getting that done."

"I don't understand. Why me?"

He didn't, or couldn't, answer that. "Are you going straight to the station now?"

"Yes. I have a trunk full of fresh produce."

"I'm sending Jimmy Marr over right now. Plain clothes. Maybe you can find him something to do where he can keep an eye on you." I knew Officer Marr from some previous messes I'd managed to get myself mixed up in.

"I'll think of something. I'll see you later tonight?"

"Absolutely. I love you."

"Love you too." It's a wonder I didn't cause an accident on the way back to Derby Street. I checked my rearview mirrors every few seconds, while trying to explain on the phone to Rhonda that my "bodyguard" would be there soon and that we'd need to arrange some kind of cover for him.

"This is scary stuff, Lee," she said. "You sure you don't want to just stay home until the cops get this creep?"

I told her the same thing I'd told Pete. Other jobs depended on mine, and anyway I felt safe enough at the station and at home. Coming and going from home to work was the tricky part. Anyway, I'd have police protection all the time.

"Okay then. Maybe we can dress your bodyguard up to be Chester's helper," Rhonda suggested. "A pair of paint-spattered overalls and a hammer in his hand and he'll hardly be noticed."

"I like it," I said. "Will you run it by Doan? I've got to get Wanda's groceries put away."

I parked in my usual space, opened the trunk, and realized that I was actually frightened by the simple act of picking up the grocery bags. Was there someone behind me? I put one of the bags under my arm, very much aware that it contained two dozen eggs, grabbed the other two and whirled around. No one there, of course. I hurried across the lot, punched my code numbers into the pad beside the ground-floor door, and stepped into the familiar cool darkness of the studio.

Wanda's stage kitchen, with its gleaming stainless steel appliances and white cabinets, was straight ahead of me at the end of the long black-walled room. I heard muffled music from the Ranger Rob set on the opposite side. The familiar sights and sounds were welcome. I began to relax.

"Lee? That you?" Wanda popped into view from behind the long quartz-topped counter where the completed food offerings would be displayed. "Got my stuff?"

"Sure do. Three bags full." I scurried down the center aisle, passing the *Saturday Morning Business Hour* set where the newly constructed bookcase stood empty. "Assemble business books," I reminded myself. *Shopping Salem*'s sparse and simple set could use new background draperies. "Have Chester measure for drapes," I told myself as I carefully deposited the bag containing two dozen extra-large eggs on the counter, followed by the other two bags containing less fragile produce and trimmings. "I can hardly wait to see you put all this together."

"Marty says we'll be shooting it early tomorrow morning. If you want to sneak in early—like around seven— you can watch. I'll probably bake the demo one tonight after the I tape the late weather. That's around ten. Of course, the easy way is to just watch the show at the regular time."

Does the woman never sleep? "I'll try to catch you in the morning," I said, realizing as I spoke that maybe Officer Marr wouldn't want to start his babysitting duty that early. I also realized that I needed to do a better job of memorizing the show schedules. I didn't know what time or even what day *Cooking with Wanda the Weather Girl* aired. *Some program director I'm turning out to be.* Wanda spotted my confusion. "Wednesday," she said. "Ten a.m."

"Right," I said. "I'll catch it one way or the other. Got to go find Chester. See you later."

I ducked back into my office to make out a requisition slip for those business books, and rummaged through the desk drawer for the printout of the list the *Saturday Morning Business* guy had e-mailed to me. I'd never even met the man because I most often have Saturdays off. I ran up the metal staircase to give Rhonda the slip for Doan's approval.

"Your police escort arrived," she said. "I sent him down to see Chester about making his plain clothes even plainer. He's nice looking. Is he married?"

"He sure is. I'm looking for Chester too, I need to get some measurements. Know where he is?"

"He's set up a little workshop for himself behind the Ranger Rob set. You can get to it through that bright blue thing."

"Bull chute," I explained.

"Excuse me?"

CHAPTER 31

Two birds with one stone, I thought. Hoping to find both carpenter and cop in one place, I left via the metal staircase, which leads straight down to the studio. Considering my third-floor apartment and all the various flights of stairs at work, I'm pretty sure I'll never need a step class. The studio is right next to the side door exit. I crossed the center aisle and walked carefully in case Prince Valiant had been there, toward the Ranger Rob soundstage. Rob sat by himself on the kid-sized bleachers, strumming on his guitar and looking sort of lost. I knew he was worried about Katie. So was I, not because of her possible injuries, but because she'd been targeted by the same apparent nutjob who was watching me.

"Hi, Rob," I called. "Any news about Katie?"

His face brightened. "I talked to her. She's got a few

aches and pains, but her doctor said she could come home tomorrow. I'm going to stay at her house tonight to take care of Percival."

"Wonderful news," I said. "Is Chester around? I understand he's made himself a little hideaway somewhere around here."

He jerked a thumb toward the bull chute. "He's back there with his new helper."

"Thanks, Rob." I pulled the gate open, stepped into the short blue tunnel and emerged in the gray backstage area. I didn't see anyone. "Chester?" I called. "It's Lee. Where the heck are you?"

"Over here, Lee," came the answer from behind a plastic-covered row of costume racks. I followed the sound of his voice. He'd set up a neat little carpenter's shop back there. It even had that nice smell of new wood. Chester and Officer Marr, each wearing overalls, stood in front of a circular saw. "Got me a new helper here, Lee," he said. "I understand you know each other."

"Yes. We've met before. Good to see you." *Do I call him Officer Marr? Jimmy? What?*

"Hello, Ms. Barrett. I've clued Chester in to my assignment." He stuck out his hand and I shook it.

Chester beamed. "Glad to help the officer out. I'm the security guard here at the station, so all this undercover stuff is right up my alley."

I wasn't sure this was· exactly the way Pete had planned my protection, but expressed my appreciation to both men, and got down to business. "Chester, can you measure for new draperies at the *Shopping Salem* set? As soon as you get the dimensions, I'll order some new ones."

"Sure thing." He stood, selected a tape measure from a toolbox. "Come on, Jimmy. We've got work to do. You need us, Lee, you just holler."

"You bet." I wasn't too worried about my safety within the building. It was my comings and goings that had me scared. The two crazy people who were stalking me were fond of public streets, parking lots, and an assortment of cars. Now that the Mazda had been destroyed, I expected that the crew-cut killer might show up with new wheels any minute. I was happy to take all the police protection I could get.

Back behind my office desk, I texted Pete to tell him that I'd met with Officer Marr and that he'd assumed his role as Chester's helper, and called my aunt to relay the good news about Katie and Paco. I felt safe there in my glass-walled cage. I was in plain sight of a roomful of news people and within a short walk (run?) to Rhonda's reception area.

I realized that I'd become fearful of too many places, too many circumstances. I'd been avoiding Old Clunky because what if I was alone in the elevator and *someone* got in with me on another floor? I wasn't enjoying driving my beautiful Vette anymore because I'd become obsessive about watching the rearview mirrors. I'd even been peeking out the windows at home in case the Mazda had been parked out front.

None of it was fair and it made me angry. How could a couple of real estate swindlers I'd never even met have so completely altered my life? Could my simple act of befriending a woman who was so clearly in distress have set all of this into motion?

For me, it had all started with a sad stranger on the pigeon lady's bench. But where had it begun for Emily? Did it begin when she witnessed John Sawtelle's murder—or had her involvement with the killers begun before then? Chief Whaley seemed to think so. Maybe Emily knew a lot more about those men than she'd admitted.

I don't like the direction these thoughts are taking.

I jumped involuntarily when my phone buzzed. Pete. I relaxed when I saw his name.

"Hi, babe. How're you doing?" he asked.

"Fine." I tried to make it sound convincing.

Serious cop voice. "Something's turned up you should know about. It's better if you hear it from me. Your newshounds will be on it soon enough."

"What is it?" I didn't like the sound of this.

"You know we found that Mazda."

"Of course."

"We found the driver too. He's dead."

I couldn't stop my shocked gasp. "Crew-cut guy? What happened to him?" My nerves ratcheted even higher.

"Somebody shot him, wrapped him completely in plastic, stuffed him in a dumpster behind a big apartment complex on Lafayette Street, and left him there to die."

"That's awful." It was awful. The mental image was awful. Nobody, no matter how rotten, should have to die that way. "Any witnesses? Security films? Anything?"

"Not much. A homeless guy says he checks that dumpster once in a while. He says people moving in or moving out of the apartments throw some really nice things away. He was heading there last night when he saw someone drive up in a gray car and unload stuff from his trunk. He ducked out of sight, thinking it was the apartment super, and beat it out of there. But he came back real early this morning to see what he could find. Unfortunately for him, he found the body."

I swallowed hard. My voice came out as a squeak. "The gray Mercury was stolen last night."

"That's right."

"Do you think that when Red Beard tried to run down Katie this morning, the other one, the crew-cut man, his partner—was already dead?"

"We're leaning that way."

"So next he got a green Toyota, but he's already ditched that, right?" I was thinking out loud. "No way to tell what he'll be driving next."

"We're not sure about it, but right down the street from where the Toyota was recovered, somebody reported their kid's bike stolen from their yard," he said. "A Cannondale. Nearly new. Bright orange."

I almost smiled. "You don't seriously think a wanted murder suspect is riding around Salem on a bright orange bike, do you?"

"It's possible. He took that murder mystery boat tour, remember?"

Pete was right. It seemed as though the man wanted to get caught. I wished they'd hurry up and grant his wish. Meanwhile I had a job to do. "I'm going to have to go over to the curtain store sometime today. Does Officer Marr need to ride with me?"

"Yep. That's what he's there for. I'll come over to your place as soon as I get out of here tonight. I'll bring dinner. Marr will follow you home after work. Call me when you get there, okay?"

I agreed, and returned my attention to program director duties. I turned on the TV monitor. I wanted to see if

Pete had been right about the "newshounds" learning about the body in the dumpster. Howard Templeton was broadcasting on site from the apartment complex where the crew-cut suspect had died. A giant green dumpster in the background was festooned with yellow crime scene tape. Howard was getting better at this. His diction was good and he'd lost the deer-in-the-headlights look he used to get when he first faced the camera. "The name of the dead man has not been released," he said.

I wondered if Officer Marr knew who he was. I turned off the set and hurried back to Chester's hideaway behind the bull chute where the two overall-clad men huddled over Paco's nearly complete dog house. "Back already, Ms. Barrett?" the officer asked. "Everything okay?"

"I'm fine. Did you get those measurements, Chester?" I asked. "I'd like to get over to the curtain store and get them started on the new draperies."

"Sure did." He handed me a piece of lined paper with the *Shopping Salem* set neatly diagrammed with appropriate measurements.

"I'll go along with you, Ms. Barrett," Officer Marr stated. It was not a question.

"Okay. I'll stop by my office, pick up my handbag, and meet you in the parking lot," I said.

"I'll come with you right now." Cop voice. "We'll take my car." There was no question implied there either.

"Okay," I said again. I knew it was okay. Jimmy Marr was taking his job seriously. It made me feel safer, yet somehow—more frightened.

As he'd suggested, still in overalls, he followed me to my office and stood by the door as I picked up my hobo bag, making sure I had the paper Chester had given me. I followed him to the parking lot, where we paused beside the building while he looked all around the lot. I've seen Pete use that same, all-encompassing glance many times. The unmarked car was parked close by, just behind Ariel's bench. He held the passenger door open for me, still watching the surroundings. As he bent to get into the driver's seat, the oversized overalls did not hide the holstered gun.

I didn't have to give him directions to the curtain shop. Everyone in Salem knows where it is. "I'll come in with you," he said as we parked in front of the store. There were only a few customers inside. Marr stood by the door, watching the street while I looked at sample books, discussed fabrics with the clerk, and decided on a cotton/linen blend in a neutral wheat color. Fortunately, the draperies in the proper width were in stock and only needed to be shortened. "We'll get right on this, Ms. Barrett," the clerk said. "You can probably have them sometime tomorrow or the next day at the very latest." I handed over Chester's measurements, along with the station's credit card.

"All done," I told my escort. "And they'll probably be delivered tomorrow or the next day. Perfect!"

He held the door open, looked up and down the street, and watched carefully as I climbed into the car. Once again, although I knew I was safe and protected, I found all this attention frightening. *How much danger am I actually in?* "I heard on the news that they have the name of that poor man they found in a dumpster," I said. "Who was he? Do you know?"

"He had some ID on him, but we're not sure it's legit. The ME fingerprinted the body. We should have a positive ID pretty soon." I could tell by his tone of voice that was all the information about the deceased Mazda driver

I was going to get right now. I settled back in my seat for the silent ride back to WICH-TV. We parted once inside the studio, he going back to Chester's hideaway while I went upstairs to check in with Rhonda. She handed me the book requisition slip signed by Mr. Doan and I turned in the receipt from the curtain store.

Once back in my office I did a little filing and a lot of thinking. The Mazda wouldn't be tailing me anymore, and the crew-cut driver was dead. The thought of that agonizing death brought chills. The other suspect, certainly no longer a kindly schoolteacher in my mind, seemed to be roaming at will around the city. If the Mazda driver had phony ID, it was pretty certain that the other one—he of the green Toyota—had one or more aliases too. I thought of Louisa's assortment of high-end real estate brochures and business cards. She had dozens of those glossy cards from waterfront real estate dealers. Chances are John Sawtelle had stacks of them too. I thought about the card I'd discovered in the purse Emily had borrowed. It was quite likely that the same card had been in the pink sweater pocket when I'd first seen her on the common. Later she'd carried it in the pocket of the jeans I'd loaned to her. Even when she was poor, confused Janie, Emily must have thought there was something special about that particular card. I was willing to bet that the real name—the real identity—of one or the other of the men would turn out to be Alfred J. Pridholm.

CHAPTER 32

While I waited for Louisa to answer her phone, I felt a little bit guilty. Was I doing personal business on company time?

"Why, good afternoon, Lee. How nice to hear from you."

Is it afternoon already? I forgot about lunch again. "Hello, Louisa. I have a quick question for you."

"Glad to help in any way I can, dear. What's your question?"

"When we last met, I noticed that you had quite a collection of business cards. Were all of the names and numbers on those cards included on your printout?"

"Oh no, dear. Many of them seemed irrelevant to the immediate problem. I was concentrating on those real estate agents who represent luxury homes."

"I see. Do you still have those cards?" Fingers crossed.

"I believe so. Would you like to see them? I'll be at Ibby's this evening for a while. We're going to begin watching the next season of *Miss Fisher's Murder Mysteries*. I'll bring them along."

"Thanks ever so much. I'd appreciate it."

I wasn't exactly sure what I expected to find in Louisa's card stash, but I felt strongly that they deserved a look. I unwrapped a granola bar and moved on to the next item on my mental to-do list. I called Salem Hospital to try to get an update on Katie's condition. I was pleased when I was immediately patched through to her room phone. She sounded as cheerful and cute as ever. A real trooper.

"I'm fine, Lee. Don't worry about me. Rob called a little while ago and says that Paco is going to be okay too. He's got a bandage on his leg, and a little walking cast. I've got some tape on my road-rashed arms, but my costume will cover them. We'll be okay. We'll be back to work tomorrow."

"You're so brave, Katie. See you tomorrow." I was pretty sure Officer Marr would include Katie in his bodyguard duties at the station, but what about her comings and goings? I'd ask Pete about that.

Five o'clock rolled around faster than I'd thought it would. Officer Marr tapped at my door at exactly five, overalls exchanged for jeans and navy denim shirt, open at the throat and loose enough to cover a holstered gun. "Ready to roll, Ms. Barrett?"

"Be right with you," I said, hurriedly assembling folders, filing them neatly, alphabetically, in my desk's file drawer. In an overabundance of caution, I locked the drawer. *I'm getting more paranoid every minute.* I picked up my hobo bag and the laptop and sneaked a glance at the newsroom behind the glass. Scott Palmer was at his desk, scribbling on a yellow pad. Marty and Jim had their heads together in front of a small screen, Phil Archer was seated at the news desk, and Wanda the Weather girl, gorgeous in bright yellow hot pants and black and yellow bumblebee-striped crop top, waited in front of the green screen for her spot in the five-o'clock news.

Was I the only person in the building working normal hours? Lucky me. I followed my official police escort to the parking lot. He walked with me to my car, waited while I got in, and started the engine.

"I'll be right behind you," he said.

I backed out slowly, knowing that somewhere, *someone* knew exactly where I was and that I was on the move. I knew too, that Pete had the same information, along with the entire Salem PD. That made me feel a little better. A little.

In the rearview mirror, I saw Officer Marr's vehicle fall into line behind me. But was there another car close by, following? Watching? Knowing?

I turned in on Oliver Street, activating the garage door opener when I got close enough. I pulled in, keeping my distance from the Buick, rolling forward until the suspended yellow tennis ball tapped the windshield. I closed the garage door, pushed open the side door, and waved to the officer, who by then stood beside his car.

"I'm fine from here on in," I called. "Here comes my cat to escort me to the back door." I pointed to O'Ryan, who approached with a jaunty step, whiskers bristling, meowing a greeting.

"You sure?" he answered. "I'll walk you to the door."

"I'm already there." I climbed the two granite steps, waving my key in his direction. "See you in the morning."

Oops. I forgot to ask him about Wanda's seven a.m. cooking prep. "Never mind," I told myself. "I'll watch when they do the taping."

He got back into his car, waved, and continued down Oliver Street. I poked my key into the lock. O'Ryan used his cat door. Stepping into the hall and closing the door behind me felt so good. I was in a place of safety. Like Dorothy, I whispered, "'There's no place like home.'" I deposited laptop and hobo bag on the bottom step of the twisty staircase, passed the laundry room, avoiding even a glance at the ironing board, and tapped on Aunt Ibby's kitchen door as O'Ryan scooted in through his own entrance.

"Coming," called my aunt, and I heard the *click-click* as she released the lock. "I'm baking giant oatmeal cookies. Tabitha's recipe," she announced. "The Angels are coming by later."

"I know," I said. "*Miss Fisher's Murder Mysteries.*" Aunt Ibby is compiling a cookbook, using recipes from Tabitha Trumbull's handwritten pages. Tabitha was the wife of the founder of the long-ago Trumbull's department store—the vintage building now housing the Tabby.

"How'd you know about Miss Fisher?" She wiped her hands on a blue cobbler's apron marked "Crazy Cat Lady" and slid a cookie sheet into the oven.

"I talked to Louisa today," I admitted. "She's going to bring me her collection of real estate agents' business cards."

"We all saw those. Do you think maybe there's some useful information hidden among them?" She wore her wise-old-owl expression. "Something important?"

"Could be." I reached for a cookie on a cooling rack. "Mind if I eat one? I skipped lunch."

She made a disapproving *tsk-tsk* sound, but added, "Help yourself."

"Pete's coming by later. He's bringing dinner."

"He's a very considerate man. How did last night's dinner go?"

"Really well." I told her about my shopping trip for Wanda's groceries. "I'm going to watch her put it all together. She thinks I could do it. Did I tell you she's writing a cookbook too?"

"I'll bet she'll sell a ton of them. Speaking of books," she said. "I've brought home a couple of dream books for you. I left them on the seat on the hall tree."

I thanked her, reminding myself to try to avoid looking into the mirror when I picked up the books. It felt so good to sit in Aunt Ibby's pretty kitchen, eating a big, warm oatmeal cookie and chatting about food and TV mystery shows, I didn't want to think about nightmares and visions and real-life murders. I knew I'd have to tell her about the man in the green Toyota, and about how Pete believed I needed police protection, but I decided it could wait a little longer. Her kitchen TV wasn't turned on, and Salem doesn't have an afternoon newspaper anymore, so it was possible she didn't even know yet about the wrecked red Mazda and the grisly find in the dumpster.

"You look tired, Maralee," she said, changing the subject abruptly—something like the way I'd found myself doing lately. "Is something wrong? Are you feeling well?"

I sighed. I've never been able to put much over on her. "I'm not sick or anything. But it's been a really difficult day. There was a lot going on at work, what with Katie's accident and all." I stood up, brushing cookie crumbs from my lap. "The Angels will be here soon and I'm expecting Pete. We'll talk later. Okay?"

"Of course, dear." The oven bell dinged, signaling that the cookies had reached perfection. Glad I'd left my belongings on the back stairs and could avoid facing the hall tree mirror for a little while, I followed the cat into the hall.

I picked up my gear, climbed a couple of the stairs and looked around for O'Ryan, who usually races ahead of me so that he can pretend to be asleep in the zebra-print wing chair when I enter the living room. "Come on, cat," I said. "Let's go." O'Ryan sat, motionless, facing me. "What is it, boy?" I asked.

He took a few steps toward the back door, then sat again. "Mmmrrupp," he said.

"You want to go back outside?" He sat.

"You want me to go outside with you?"

His quick exit and the fast flapping of the cat door answered the question. I followed. He trotted toward the garage and stopped beside a thick hedge just behind the old structure. If it hadn't been for the flash of bright color, I probably wouldn't have noticed the orange bicycle amidst the greenery.

CHAPTER 33

I froze.
I mean I literally froze in fear. In broad daylight in my own backyard, I stood immobilized. I couldn't move my arms or legs or eyes. I couldn't scream or cry. I'd never felt anything like this before. I was totally, immovably focused on that tiny patch of bright orange metal.

With loud meows and repeated ankle rubs, O'Ryan pulled me back to reality. It was like waking up from a truly hideous nightmare—nothing simple like mists and butterflies. "Good boy," I said to the cat, picking him up, hugging him, and repeating over and over "Good boy. Good boy." As soon as I trusted legs and feet to carry me away from the garage, I turned and moved—still trance-like, but motivated—toward the house.

What did it mean? Had the bike been there when Officer Marr dropped me off after work? Was it possible that it had been left there in the short time I'd been happily eating cookies and chatting with my aunt? If that was true, was the killer still nearby? Had he found his way into the house?" I looked up at my third-floor bay window. Was he standing there, hidden by my potted plants and hanging baskets and my beautiful painted carousel horse—looking down at me with those cruel eyes, that cold smile?

"See you later, sweetheart," he'd said. It had sounded like a threat. And a promise.

I ran the rest of the way along the flagstone path, still clutching O'Ryan in my arms. I realized that in my hurry to follow the cat, I hadn't locked the back door. I stopped on the top step. What if the killer had ducked inside while I stood stone still behind the garage? What about my aunt? I put O'Ryan down and pushed my way into the hall. I didn't tap gently on the kitchen door this time. I pounded on it. I yelled, "Aunt Ibby. It's me!"

I heard the familiar *click-click*. "Good heavens, child. What's wrong?" She pulled the door open. "You're pale as a ghost. Come in. Sit down."

I sat. She handed me a glass of water, then sat beside me, holding my hand. "What is it?"

The words tumbled out. Some of it was out of order, I knew. I told her about the green Toyota and the smiling threat, and about the gray sedan hurtling toward me, about my police escort, and last—about the orange bicycle on our property. On our property at that very moment.

"O'Ryan knew it was there," I said. "He knew exactly where it was. He showed me."

She squeezed my hand. "Your hands are freezing. The bicycle must have been put there very recently. O'Ryan didn't pay any attention to those bushes when I arrived home, and apparently he didn't try to alert you to any-thing when you got here a little while ago."

"I know," I said. "And I didn't lock the back door when I followed the cat." I fought to keep my teeth from chattering. "He could have sneaked in here. That horrible man could be upstairs."

"I see." Her voice was calm. "I think you need to call Pete right away. Let's go now and sit on the front steps until he gets here. We'll be in full view of all the neigh-bors." She picked up her phone from the cat-shaped holder. "I'll call the Angels. Can't have them walking in on who-knows-what. Hello. Betts?"

"Good idea." I wanted to grab my hobo bag from the back hall, but didn't dare. "Right now. Let's go." O'Ryan was already on his way through the living room with my aunt, who was talking very fast on her phone, and me right behind him. "Wait." I stopped short in the arched entrance to the foyer. "I left my phone in my bag. Tell Betsy to call Pete and Louisa. We've got to get out of here."

While I struggled with shaking hands to manage the complicated double lock on the front door, I listened to my aunt give precise, clear instructions to Betsy. "I need you to call Pete. You have his number? Good. Tell him there may be an intruder in the house. Send help right away. We'll be on the Winter Street front steps. And call Louisa."

I wrestled the door open and O'Ryan bolted through. Aunt Ibby and I followed. "Better not lock it," my aunt warned. "Neither of us has keys to get back in." O'Ryan positioned himself on the bottom step. We followed and sat, one of us on each side of the cat. The hair on the back of my neck stood up as I visualized the intruder standing behind the door, watching us through the tall side window. I didn't dare to turn and look. I realized at the same moment that I'd passed the hall tree without looking at the mirror. The welcome sound of sirens interrupted any further thoughts. Aunt Ibby and I both stood. O'Ryan remained seated.

"That was fast," Aunt Ibby said, waving to the approaching vehicle.

"Pete told me there'd always be a cruiser just moments away from the Vette's location," I said. More sirens. More flashing red, white, and blue lights. Pete's car skidded to a halt. He approached us at a dead run. "Lee. What's going on here? Are you all right?"

"Pete, the orange bicycle. It's in our yard. Out behind the garage. Maybe the bearded guy got into the house. Only he doesn't have a beard anymore. He said he'd see me later. O'Ryan found the bike." I knew I was babbling, trying to get it all out at once.

Pete put his hands on my shoulders and pulled me close. "It's okay, Lee. We'll check the house. You didn't touch the bike did you?"

"Touch it? Of course not. I ran into the house to make sure Aunt Ibby was all right."

By then there were four police cars on the usually staid and quiet Winter Street. Neighbors had started to come out of their houses. Pete motioned for two of the officers and directed them through the iron gate and into the yard. He pointed to the front door. "Is that unlocked?"

"Yes," my aunt said. "Neither of us has keys."

"How about the back door. Is that secured?"

Aunt Ibby and I looked at each other. I knew I hadn't stopped to lock it. Had she locked her kitchen door? We both shook our heads. "Looks like everything's unlocked,"

I admitted. "Except the garage and my apartment. All of my keys are in my handbag on the back stairs."

Pete raised an eyebrow, but didn't comment on our mistakes. We already knew how he felt about locking doors. He'd reminded both of us often enough. "Okay. You two please wait in my car. Make yourselves comfortable. Officer Costa will stay with you. We'll do a full search of the premises." He opened the back door of the Crown Vic. He'd left the motor running, the air conditioner turned on. Aunt Ibby and I climbed in. Officer Costa, ramrod straight, stood on the sidewalk beside the car. O'Ryan chose to stay with Pete and trotted beside him as he directed two more officers through the wrought-iron gate to the back of the house. Then Pete and a uniformed officer, with guns drawn, and cat following, entered our house.

We crowded together as close as we could get to the side window, peering out, trying to see—what? Because it was early summer, all of the windows were curtained with sheer draperies. We caught an occasional glimpse of motion behind the fabric, but were we seeing Pete and our protectors, or was a killer watching us? The only window without curtains was the small round one in the attic, just below the triangular peak of the roof. Is that where an intruder would hide, up there in the dim stillness, where cast-off bureaus and trunks and rocking chairs cast weird shadows on bare wood floors? I hate that place with good reason, and never, ever go up there alone.

When my aunt and I are together, we usually keep up a steady stream of conversation. I guess we just find each other interesting. But that day in Pete's car, we barely spoke. Instead, eyes fixed on the front of our lovely old home, we each dealt with our own thoughts and fears. I wasn't actually aware of how much time passed while we waited for the search to end, but it felt like a very long time. Then Pete and the other officers, along with O'Ryan, appeared all at once in a crowd of blue uniforms on the sidewalk beside us. Officer Costa opened the car door and we got out. Pete's smile told me what I wanted to know. They'd found no one inside.

CHAPTER 34

"We searched every inch, every corner, every space and crevice where a human could possibly hide," Pete assured me for about the tenth time. "That man did not enter your house, I promise you." We sat together on the couch in my living room. He frowned and took my hand. "But he did leave that bike behind the garage. It was no coincidence. He wanted you to see it."

I knew that. I also knew I was being cruelly targeted and probably stalked, by what might very well be a madman. I didn't know why, and clearly, neither did Pete. The only connection between me and the once-bearded, once gray-haired stranger was Emily. And the only connection between Emily and me was our random meeting on the Salem Common. It didn't make sense.

"You're keeping a good watch on Emily too, aren't you? I mean, she's in way more danger than I am. Isn't she?" I tried hard to keep my voice level. The past few hours had been terrifying, and I wasn't yet able to relax, even with Pete sitting close beside me.

"Absolutely. Their condo has excellent security, and Joyce Rouse will be tagging along with her and her parents every time they leave the house," he promised. "Besides, the guy's picture is all over the place. Everybody's on the lookout for him. He'll probably try to steal another car and we'll grab him."

"I suppose Chief Whaley won't allow Emily to join Aunt Ibby and the Angels for their weekly TV show," I said. "Too bad. She really enjoyed those get-togethers."

"You might be in for a surprise about that," he said. "Chief isn't actually opposed to letting her go. He figures it might draw this guy out from whatever rock he's hiding under."

"That puts the whole bunch of us in danger." My voice slid up the scale a little more.

Sympathetic, calm cop voice. "I truly believe we'll already have this creep in custody before then. If not, Rouse will be right beside Emily every minute. I'll plan to be here with you. Tell Louisa and Betsy to arrive and leave by cab. We'll tail them home. We'll probably want to beef up the house alarm system you already have here though."

"Aunt Ibby called the alarm people while we were in your car," I said. "They'll be here first thing tomorrow morning."

"Perfect," he said. "We've got a couple of days before your TV mystery show airs. Plenty of time to get everything in place."

His confidence made me feel better, and it surely helped that Pete would spend that night with me, but the terror lingered. My handbag," I recalled suddenly. "He could have taken the keys from my bag."

"I put your bag and your laptop in your bedroom," he said. "Your keys are still there. I checked."

"You've checked everything. I know you have. I'm just being a scaredy cat." I looked around the room. "Cat. Where's the cat? Where's O'Ryan?"

"He was in the bedroom last time I looked. I turned on the TV in there for him. He's watching *Deadliest Catch*." He pulled me closer. "He's had a busy day. He went over every bit of the house with us. Snooped into every corner."

"He's a good boy. He must be hungry. I know I am."

"Oh yeah. I was supposed to bring dinner. Do you still feel like Chinese? Let's order out." He pulled his phone from his pocket. "Want to see if Ibby would like to join us, since the girlfriends won't be coming over?"

"I'll run downstairs and ask her," I said. "I need to pick up a couple of library books she brought home for me anyway. Don't forget to order crab Rangoon in case she does."

"Sure thing." He grinned. "It won't go to waste either way."

"I'll use the front stairs," I said, heading toward my kitchen, "and I'll fill O'Ryan's bowl on the way." I peeked into the bedroom where, as Pete had told me, O'Ryan lay, comfortably sprawled out in the middle of the bed, green eyes focused on the TV screen. The sound of Meow Mix being poured into his red bowl caught his attention and he joined me in the kitchen. I turned off the bedroom lights and TV, filled his water dish, went out into the hall, and started down the stairs. I stopped on the second-floor landing, across from my childhood bedroom, and looked over the railing. From that position I could see the hall tree next to the front door. The library books were on the seat, just as Aunt Ibby had promised. Thankfully, the mirror behaved itself and I picked up the books without any disturbance from that direction. I stepped into Aunt Ibby's living room. "Hello. It's me," I called. "Thanks for the books."

"You're welcome," she answered from her office. "I'm just catching up on a little library paperwork. Come on in." With the two books tucked under my arm, I crossed the room to where the office door stood open, light spilling out onto the oriental rug. I stood in the doorway. "Pete's ordering Chinese for dinner. He wants to know if you'd like to join us."

"I'll bring the wine," she said, "and I'll come up as soon as I finish here. I talked to Louisa. She says she has some banking business to attend to tomorrow not far from WICH-TV, and she'll be glad to drop off those business cards for you."

"Perfect," I said, and avoiding looking at the hall tree, climbed the stairs to the third floor. The only two doors on that landing are my kitchen door and the door to the stairway that leads to the attic. As usual, I avoided looking at that one.

I'd locked my door when I went downstairs, so I knocked. "It's me, Pete," I called.

He opened it right away. "I was just going to come down to wait for the delivery guy," he said. We always use the Winter Street address when we order out. Directions to the back entrance get too complicated. "Is your aunt going to join us?"

"She is. She'll bring the wine."

Pete had already put some bowls, plates, and silverware on the counter. I added three wineglasses, then sat at the table and opened the first book. The topics were neatly laid out alphabetically. "Mist" wasn't listed, but I found "Fog," easily. "Fog conceals things," it told me. "Your vision is blurred. To dream of fog indicates uncertainty—not knowing which way to go in life."

That made sense. The new job. Am I a reporter or a program director? I moved on to "Butterflies." The book told me that a butterfly is a powerful dream symbol, connected to personal transformation. "Just as a caterpillar turns into a butterfly, you may be going through a transformation into something better." *Wow. Another work-related dream.*

Next I looked for "Shoe," remembering the tasseled shoe with its turned-up toe. "The shoe reflects your path and movements in your life. It also tells you to stand your ground. Stand up for yourself." Mixed message there.

Last on my list was the open blue gate. The gate was symbolic of safety and protection. I liked the sound of that. I made a quick check of the other book. The information offered there for each topic was worded a bit differently, but was basically the same, except for the gate explanation. The second book told me that I was close to the beginning of a new journey—a new phase in my life.

That sounds like something more important than a job promotion at a small local TV station, doesn't it?

I heard the beginning chimes of "The Impossible Dream" from my aunt's doorbell. Dinner had arrived. I put both books on my bureau and opened my kitchen door to welcome Pete, Aunt Ibby, and dinner.

All of us, as if by unspoken consent, avoided all talk of murder, waterfront real estate, and orange bicycles. It was a really good evening. It was after nine o'clock when

Pete escorted Aunt Ibby downstairs with a bowl of left-over crab Rangoon. As soon as he returned, I selected cool green nylon pajamas and left for the second-floor bathroom adjoining my childhood bedroom, leaving the upstairs facilities for Pete. We've found this a time-saver whenever he stays the night. Besides, all his shaving stuff is in that bathroom, and I have duplicates of all my makeup and soaps and all the girlie things in both places.

We watched the ten o'clock news on the kitchen TV. I was glad there'd been no media coverage of the flurry of excitement on Winter Street. There was a rehash of the two cars in the impound lot, and the police had released the name of the man who'd been driving the red Mazda—the crew-cut beachboy. Sean Kiley. I didn't recognize the name, but I was willing to bet it would be on one or more of the business cards in Louisa's collection.

"You didn't tell me you'd come up with his name," I said.

"You'd already had a pretty upsetting day. I didn't see any point it bringing it up."

"You were right about that," I agreed. "But does the Mazda driver, that Kiley man, have a record?" I asked.

"Yes. Some petty stuff. None of it recent."

"And the other one? The killer?"

"We believe he may be using his real name. Alfred Pridholm."

I wasn't surprised. "Does he have a record too?"

"Not that we've been able to find."

"An address?"

"The address turned out to be a parcel service mailbox in Peabody."

"But no record," I repeated. "It doesn't seem as though someone could become that evil overnight."

"It happens," he said. "That's one of the things that makes it more difficult to find him. No criminal record. No permanent address. No known patterns of behavior."

"I guess the way he seems to be trying to get caught is helpful." At least I sincerely hoped it was, since Alfred Pridholm seemed to be focusing his attention on me. "If he rode that bike here, he must have walked down Oliver Street to get away. I suppose there are security cameras along the way."

"Yes. He showed up on several of them. He walked toward Bridge Street. We lost him after that."

I yawned and realized how exhausting the day had been. "I'm ready for bed," I said. "Want to join me?"

"That's an offer I can't ever refuse." Eyebrow wiggle. He turned off the TV, took my hand, and led the way to the darkened bedroom. "Guess O'Ryan beat us to it," he said, pointing to the curled-up cat shape at the foot of the bed. "Can't you find someplace else to sleep, old man?" he asked, turning on the overhead light.

O'Ryan's eyes opened wide, but he didn't release his grip on the Katie the Clown doll, clutched protectively in his big paws.

CHAPTER 35

"Where'd he get that?" Pete pointed to the doll.
"I don't know," I said, puzzled. "She was in my room last time I saw her."

"He doesn't want to let go of it," Pete said, puzzled. "A new favorite toy?"

"Oh no." I was horrified. "My Katie? A cat toy? Never." I moved closer to the bed. "He must have followed me when I went down to my old bedroom. The doll is important for some reason, or he wouldn't have swiped it."

I know Pete rolled his eyes at that statement. He knows O'Ryan is special to Aunt Ibby and me, but he has never been able to fully accept the fact that the big yellow-striped boy is far from being an ordinary housecat. "So now are we supposed to guess what he's trying to tell us?"

"Exactly," I said.

"It has something to do with Katie," he said. "The real Katie. Not the doll."

"I think so."

"He's in a protective mode," Pete said, moving closer to the end of the bed. "Or is it a loving mode?"

"I'd say protective." I hoped O'Ryan's claws weren't digging into my doll's delicate rayon clown suit, then felt guilty for the thought.

O'Ryan's green eyes followed Pete's every move. He clutched the doll closer, his pink nose pressed into her orange yarn hair. Pete reached out a tentative finger, touching the doll's shoe. A low but unmistakable growl issued from the cat.

"He's serious," I said. "Katie—the real Katie—is in danger. We've got to do something."

I watched Pete's face. He didn't roll his eyes. "Lee, I can't spare another cop for this case. I'm stretching it as it is."

"Katie needs protection," I said, knowing with all my heart that my words were true.

"Babe, I can't tell the chief that I need another officer to protect a lady clown because my girlfriend's cat says she's in danger."

"I know," I said. "But what can we do? He's already tried to kill her."

"She's safe for now. How long will she be in the hospital?"

"Rob says she'll be released tomorrow. He's staying at her place to take care of Percival," I reported. "She's planning to come straight to work."

"You say this creep has never seen her in her regular clothes? Without the clown makeup?"

"That's right. He probably knows her name though." I was scaring myself. "It wouldn't be too hard to get. She used to be locally famous. He might even know where she lives by now."

All thoughts of sleep were gone. "We have to do something."

Pete was wide awake too. He paced silently from the end of the bed to the doorway and back a couple of times. "That pink guest room still available?"

"Of course."

"If Katie can stay here, and ride to work and back with you, Marr will be able to keep an eye on her along with you, and I'll be here at night." His jaw tightened. "If this guy keeps showing off how smart he thinks he is, he'll trip up very soon and this will all be over."

"I pray you're right," I said. "How about this? I'll call Rob in the morning and tell him about the plan. He'll explain it to Katie."

"You're not going to tell him this was your cat's idea, are you?" Pete almost smiled.

"Nope. He's already worried to death about her. He'll just be glad there *is* a plan." I knew I was right about that. "If anybody can convince her to go along with this, it's Rob."

"Okay then. We'll get up early and get things underway." He patted the pillows. "Bedtime. And look, O'Ryan is giving your doll back to you."

He was right. O'Ryan had relinquished his grip on my clown doll and, with a pink-tongued lick on her painted cheek, picked her up gently by the ruffled collar and plopped her down in the center of the bed.

"Thank you, O'Ryan." I picked up the doll and put her

on top of the bureau. "We'll keep her safe." Turning off the light, I climbed under the covers beside Pete. The cat turned around three times, then lay quietly at the foot of the bed.

In the morning I awoke to Kelly Clarkson's "Break-away" and the smell of brewing coffee. I kissed Pete good morning, fed O'Ryan a can of pâté with tuna and a creamy gravy center, then carried the Katie doll with me to the second-floor bedroom. I put her back beside the Ranger Rob doll, then took my shower and dressed for the day. While Pete was still in the upstairs bathroom, I searched the refrigerator and came up with three English muffins and a jar of strawberry jam. I put out paper plates to save on dish washing. Visions of Wanda's egg scramble casserole danced in my head. *I will definitely watch her put it together. I will learn.*

While we ate our uninspired but pretty-good-tasting breakfast, Pete laid out the plan for the day. "Okay. You call Rob and tell him he *has* to convince Katie to go along with this. I'll call Marr and tell him Katie has been added to the package." We each pulled out our phones.

"And Paco too," I said. "We'll be taking Paco back and forth to work."

Pete lowered his voice and gave a sidelong glance toward O'Ryan, who was enthusiastically enjoying his pâté. "What about you-know-who? How's he going to feel about a d-o-g in the house? And there's another cat involved too, isn't there?"

"Yep. Percival. They've already met and get along just fine," I said. "About the d-o-g, I'm not so sure. I guess we'll find out tonight. I'll tell Aunt Ibby this morning what's going on and make sure it's all right with her. The guest room is always ready, so I'm sure there's no problem there."

I punched in Rob's number.

"Double R Riding Stable," came the familiar baritone voice. "Ranger Rob speaking."

"Good morning, Rob," I said. "Sorry to call so early, but it's important."

"Been working in the barn since sunup," he said. "What's going on?"

I made the explanation as brief as possible, concentrating on the necessity of keeping Katie safe until the killer was caught. Rob didn't need much convincing.

"You sure your house is safe, and that cop can cover both of you at the same time?" He didn't wait for an answer. "I'll be there too, you know. No one will get by me to my little sweetie. I'll pick her up at the hospital as soon as they call, get the dog from the vet, and we'll see you at the station. Don't worry. We're in."

Pete put down his phone at the same time I did. "Is Marr all clued in?" I asked.

"Yep. He says no problem. He also says he likes that little clown. Doesn't want to see anything bad happen to her. He's on the way to WICH-TV now."

"Good. Let's go downstairs and run it by Aunt Ibby. I'm sure she'll okay it."

I was right about Aunt Ibby's okay. She was enthusiastic about the whole plan and wanted to know if there was anything the Angels could do to help. Pete tried hard to discourage any Angel involvement. "Everything here at the house should look as normal as possible. Except for the new dog, of course."

"Katie's trick dog?" Her enthusiasm appeared to dim

just a tad. She gave me a sideways glance. "Did you consult O'Ryan about that?"

"Not yet," I admitted.

"Guess we'll find out," she said. "I'll get the guest room ready. Fresh flowers, new magazines."

Pete and I walked together along the flagstone path toward the garage. I couldn't help looking at the bushes where the orange bike had been partially hidden the day before. I wondered if it was possible that the police would find any prints on it, but I was almost positive that they wouldn't. "Will they give the bike back to the owner as soon as they're through with it?" I asked.

"Sure. Probably this afternoon. Why?"

"You said it belonged to a kid. A nice bike like that stolen—he must have been devastated."

"You have a kind heart, Lee." He smiled and ruffled my hair. I pulled the key chain from my bag. Vowing to be much more aware of the importance of keys, I gave it a little buffing against the edge of my suede vest to shine it up, and unlocked the garage door. "I love you," Pete said. "I'll come in and take a quick look at your car before we leave."

"You don't think anyone—someone—he—might have gotten in here somehow and messed with it, do you?"

"No. I really don't think that. It's just that I love you so damned much I have to be sure. Will you open it, please, and wait here?"

I stood in the doorway, pulled the fob from my bag, and unlocked the car. Pete walked all the way around the Vette first, then climbed inside. After a moment he got out and waved me into the garage. "All set," he said. "Back her out and I'll be right behind you."

I got into the car and activated the garage door opener. Backing out onto Oliver Street, I made sure Pete's Crown Vic was close behind me. I checked the rearview mirror often, hoping nothing else would show up in the reflection. "So far, so good," I thought as I rolled into the WICH-TV lot and parked in my usual space beside the sea wall. Pete had parked closer to the building, next to Ariel's bench. He got out of his car and hurried across the lot to meet me. "Want to show me your new office?"

"Sure," I said. *He wants to be sure I'm safe in there.* I tapped my security code into the pad and we walked into the darkened studio. "Do you have time to see the stage where we'll be shooting the *Ranger Rob's Rodeo* show?"

"With the famous blue bull chute? Lead me to it."

I heard voices as we approached the set. "Some early risers beat us to it. It's probably Chester and Officer Marr. Hello!" I called. "That you, Chester?"

"Come on back, Lee," came the answer.

"You get to travel through my big blue creation," I bragged. "Plywood and closet poles. What do you think?"

"Impressive," he said. "We get to walk through it?"

"If Paco the wonder dog was here, he'd open the gate for us," I told him as I lifted the latch. "He knows how to close it too."

I led the way toward the sounds of voices and Pete followed close behind me through the short passage. "You could use a light in here," he said.

He was right about that. Some guests might be nervous about walking through the tunnel-like structure in near-darkness. I made a mental note. *Light for bull chute.* We walked past the plastic-covered costume racks and entered Chester's hideaway.

I introduced Pete to Chester. "Quite a setup you've got here," Pete said. "Looks like a professional carpenter shop."

"This young lady keeps me busy," Chester said. "She had us building a deluxe doghouse yesterday." He pointed to Paco's brightly painted new digs. "Besides that, me and my assistant here measured for drapes yesterday too. We were just wondering what's in store for us today."

"Don't worry. I'll think of something," I promised.

Pete and Officer Marr stood off to one side, speaking in low tones. Chester pointed to a large oblong brown cardboard box resting on top of a tall red toolbox. "Speaking of the drapes, looks like they arrived early this morning."

"That's great. Did you sign for them?"

"No. That new salesman must have got here just before I did. The curtain-store truck was just pulling out of the lot. He was standing there with the box. Guess he signed for them." He smiled. "Nice fella. He said he knew you were in a hurry for them."

Pete and Officer Marr had turned to face us, their conversation halted.

"I didn't know we had a new salesman. What does he look like?" I reached for the paper invoice tucked under a corner of the box.

"Nice looking dude. Suit, tie, vest. Even had those fancy leather driving gloves on. Gray hair, little skinny mustache, sunglasses, name of Al."

Al?

"Chester, did you see Al go inside the building?" Pete's tone was urgent.

"Nope. He just handed me that package and walked around toward the front. He's new. Probably has to go up to the reception desk. Takes a while before they give you a key code."

"That's true." I pulled the folded invoice from the top of the box. The signature scrawled at the bottom was A. J. Pridholm. Wordlessly, I handed it to Pete.

CHAPTER 36

"Marr, go up to the reception desk and see if Rhonda knows anything about this Al guy. See if she's seen anyone by that description this morning. Check the security camera on the front door and see if he came inside. Tell Rhonda to get on the horn and evacuate the building. Make sure everyone gets out." At Marr's questioning look he pointed to the package, then pulled his phone from his pocket. "Mondello here. I'm at WICH-TV. Suspicious package on the lower level. Get hold of Harry and June. I'll meet them in the parking lot." He put the phone in his pocket and with an arm around my waist, propelled me quickly back toward the bull chute. "Bomb sniffing dog and her handler," he explained. "Come on. Let's go. You too, Chester. Is anyone else apt to be on this floor this early?"

"Wanda is." I pointed to the lighted set at the opposite

end of the studio. "She's putting together Sunday brunch. Marty McCarthy is probably with her. There'll be staff in the newsroom too, getting ready for the morning news show."

It didn't take long to clear the building. Marr reported that the surveillance tape showed that Pridholm hadn't entered the place after all. We all moved our cars from the WICH-TV lot to the nearby Pickering Wharf guest lot. Neither Francine or Old Jim had arrived yet, so Rhonda and one of the sales people moved the van and the mobile unit. Yellow warning tape was soon festooned around the property, and one lane of Derby Street in front of the building was closed. I called Rob and told him what was going on and called Aunt Ibby so she wouldn't hear about it on the radio or TV.

A truck marked SPD Bomb Squad Special Operations pulled into the far end of the lot where Pete waited. Two men in heavily padded green and black suits with hoods and masks and carrying black equipment bags exited the truck, along with a leashed German shepherd. They paused to speak briefly with Pete, then ran toward the open studio door. Marty, with shoulder-mounted camera, filmed the action, and because neither Scott nor Howie was there, I was tagged to narrate. I shoved my fear down, Marty handed me my favorite stick mic, and we took a position across the street from the building where all of the station staff stood together. Wanda, wearing her pink sequined chef's hat and a white apron barely covering brief pink shorts and purple midriff halter top, posed for selfies with passersby. Marr directed traffic away from the area, while Pete did the same with pedestrians. I'd seen enough cop shows to wonder if the bomb guys would have to blow up the package and I'd have to re-

order the draperies. Mostly I wondered how A. J. Pridholm had managed to get this close to me again. I wasn't
sure how much information I should relate to the WICH-
TV audience. With my back to the building and no solid
information to go on, I had to wing it.

"A suspicious package was delivered to the WICH-TV
studios early this morning. Police have reason to believe
the person who delivered the package may be a wanted
suspect in an ongoing investigation. Two members of the
Salem Police Department bomb squad with their specially trained bomb-sniffing German shepherd, named
June, have just entered the building."

That's all I know! I saw the field reporter from the
local radio station, WESX, approaching from the direction of Pickering Wharf. I was sure she didn't know any
more about what was going on here than I did.

I looked to Marty for help. With a tilt of her head, she
indicated Pete, who'd crossed Derby Street and was on
the sidewalk only a few feet away. With full knowledge
that he wasn't going to appreciate it, I walked over and
stuck the mic in his face. "Detective Mondello, can you
tell the WICH-TV audience a little about what the dog
will do in there?"

Slight frown and official cop voice. "June is specially
trained to smell explosives. Dogs have extraordinary
noses, and she's been trained to detect certain odors. She
likes treats and knows she'll be rewarded if she finds an
explosive device. If the package we're interested in con-
tains one, June will sit and wait for her treat. If not, she'll
continue to pull on her leash and walk around. If the
squad team believes it's necessary to X-ray the thing,
they'll do it on-site. After that you'll probably see them
come out of the building carrying the package."

He stopped speaking. That was apparently all I was going to get. "Thank you, Detective," I said, then thought about my new draperies and tossed in another question. "Do you think they'll have to blow up the package?"

"We'll see," he said, and with a smile, went back to directing pedestrians past Wanda.

Marty aimed the camera toward the bomb squad truck, and to help fill the time while I tried to figure out where to go with this next, I read all of the lettering aloud— slowly. She focused the camera on the open studio door, and I gave a brief description of what the place looked like inside. Warming a little to the subject, I told the audience that the package in question was located behind the soundstage of an upcoming morning show featuring beloved WICH-TV alumni Ranger Rob and Katie the Clown. That gave me an opportunity to give an update on Katie's condition. "Katie, who was injured in a recent hit-and-run incident, is expected to be released from the hospital today and plans to return to work on rehearsals for the upcoming *Ranger Rob's Rodeo* show."

How much can I say about the suspect, A. J. Pridholm? Should I steer clear of the subject?

Fortunately, I didn't have to make the decision. A cheer went up from the group gathered on the sidewalk. I turned to see what was going on in the parking lot. June, the bomb-sniffing dog, tail wagging and prancing ahead of her master, was first out of the studio door, followed by the other squad member carrying the offending package, which he placed on the ground. Both men then faced in our direction, each giving a heavily gloved thumbs-up all-clear sign. Another even louder cheer went up. I was ready to cheer too, when I saw Scott on a dead run a little way down Derby Street, heading for the station. I realized how glad I'd be to hand over that day's field reporter duties.

"No bomb found, folks," I said. "That's a big relief for everyone. Stay tuned to WICH-TV for updates on this breaking news story."

Officer Marr, with Chester's assistance, removed the orange cones from the street, enabling traffic to resume normalcy, while Pete escorted the WICH-TV staff—beginning with Rhonda, Phil Archer, and Marty—a few members at a time, to the front door of the building. By the time I retrieved my Vette from Pickering Wharf and climbed the metal stairs to the reception area, Rhonda's whiteboard was up-to-date with assignments, Phil Archer was in his anchor seat at the news desk, Marty had nearly finished editing my hastily put together stand-up, and Scott and Old Jim were on their way to the police station for the chief's latest briefing. My draperies, still in the box, along with the invoice signed by A. J. Pridholm, had been transported to the police station for further examination. "Evidence, Lee," Pete explained. "You understand." I did understand and *Shopping Salem* could make do with the old drapes for a little while longer.

One of several things I *didn't* understand though, was why the curtain store had been in such a hurry to deliver my draperies, since I'd readily agreed to wait a day or two for them, and how A. J. Pridholm had managed to be in the parking lot at exactly the moment they arrived.

I called the curtain store. "Hello. This is Lee Barrett at WICH-TV."

"Oh, Ms. Barrett," came the reply. "Were the draperies there in time for your special event? We put a rush on the order the minute your associate called last night. Yours was the first delivery of the day."

That explained a lot. It was obvious that the curtain-shop people weren't wasting time watching daytime TV, and I didn't want to be the one to tell them that their rush order was now in the hands of SPD. None of this was their fault, so I just said, "Thank you," and wished them a good day. I'd give Pete the information. Maybe there'd be some sort of phone record to trace that call back to Pridholm, but I doubted there would be. He was much too devious to slip up on a detail like that.

My personal rush order by then had to be getting *Ranger Rob's Rodeo* in shape for the show's debut just a week away. The script for the show consisted of a series of events, reality-show style, rather than dialogue. Rob and Katie didn't have to memorize lines. They were each expert at staying on topic and involving their studio guests—Rob's "little buckaroos." Each show would have a theme and, hopefully, a worthwhile message for young viewers.

The theme we'd planned for the first show was "Our Animal Friends," giving us a chance to introduce Prince Valiant and Paco. Katie had offered to bring Percival to the studio too.

Wow! What if we could get June and her trainer to do a guest spot?

I'd make a few calls later and try to set it up. Meanwhile, Officer Marr and I stood at the window in Rhonda's office, watching the lot, looking for Rob's truck. He'd planned to pick Katie up from the hospital first, then get Paco from the vet, and then drive straight to the station.

"Here he comes," Marr said, pointing. "Don't worry. I've told Rob to stay in the truck until I get down there to escort them into the building." He dashed for the stairway leading to the lobby.

Would a single police escort be enough protection from a man who was clearly mad enough, devious enough, sick enough to aim an automobile at a tiny woman, to wrap a bleeding man in plastic and leave him to die in a trash bin, to terrorize me in my own backyard, and now in my workplace?

CHAPTER 37

Rob, Katie, and Paco, accompanied by the overall-wearing police officer, crossed the parking lot and entered the studio without incident. Katie was greeted with gentle hugs and loving well-wishes from just about everybody in the building. Paco, only slightly favoring the injured leg, enjoyed head pattings, ear scratchings, and probably way too many deftly palmed doggie treats.

If Katie was suffering any ill effects from her injuries, it didn't show in her performance. She didn't attempt to put Paco through his paces though, because the vet had said he should have a couple of days to rest. After checking out his new doghouse, Paco sat beside me on the kiddie bleachers, seeming to listen intently to Rob and Katie's patter. All was well onstage and the rehearsal didn't seem to require any input from me at the moment. Officer Marr was close by, just a short dash through the bull chute away, should any trouble arise, so I gave Paco an extra pat and left the brightly lighted set.

Once back inside the comparative privacy of my glass-walled office, I tried to piece together the events of the past twenty-four hours—at least the events that had so impacted my little corner of the world. The man had hidden a stolen bicycle behind our garage, but hadn't damaged or defaced our property. He'd signed for a package I needed for my work, but hadn't opened it or harmed it in any way, let alone planted a bomb in it. Why had Alfred J. Pridholm—if that was his real name—selected me as a target for his chilling pranks, if pranks were what they were? I knew it had to have something to do with Emily, but what?

This train of thought was getting me nowhere. I opened the briefcase, pulling out my copy of the spiral-bound presentation I'd prepared for Mr. Doan. I'd promised a PowerPoint demonstration to go along with it and hadn't even begun work on that. The plastic-bagged notebook Emily had returned to me slid out of the case, along with the poly-covered brochure. Good. It would provide a convenient place to make notes for my PowerPoint project—and to get my mind away from disturbing thoughts.

Picking up a purple WICH-TV pen, I opened to the first page. The blank notebook wasn't blank after all. Emily had written something in it—a series of numbers, decimal points, and commas. I squinted at the page. The numbers meant nothing to me—but why should they? Emily was an accountant. I was a B-minus business math student. I flipped through the rest of the pages, making sure there was nothing else written in it.

Okay. I'll tear out that page, give it back to Emily, and get busy on my own project.

Ever so carefully I removed the page, put it aside, and concentrated on *Ranger Rob's Rodeo*, with all its color and fun and excitement—its cute clown, beautiful horse, wonder dog, and bright blue bull chute.

I scribbled away in purple ink, quite happily filling page after page with partly formed thoughts, some badly drawn but understandable to me—staging suggestions, a couple of carpentry projects for Chester, even some doggy costume ideas for Paco. This was exactly the way I've always liked to work through any creative process. Get it all down on paper and sort it out later.

A *tap-tap* on my door broke my concentration. Somewhat annoyed, I looked up to see the smiling face of Captain Billy Barker on the other side of the glass. I hurried to let him in. I've always liked the jovial old fisherman, and besides that, he was about to become a major sponsor of *Ranger Rob's Rodeo*.

"Welcome, Captain Billy," I said. "Here to check on the progress of your new show? I think you'll be pleased. I know I am."

"I've heard good things about it so far," he said. "I know it's going to be great. Actually, I'm here to get an idea of the size of the space involved. Want to see if my miniature train—engine and caboose—will fit. I understand there's going to be a transportation-themed show."

"That's on the drawing board, along with lots of others," I promised. "Let me put this stuff away and we'll go on over to the soundstage. They're already rehearsing the debut show. Animal friends."

"Sounds good," he said, watching me shuffle papers into a pile. He pointed to the single page I'd put aside to return to Emily. "Planning a fishing trip?"

Huh?

"Fishing? No." I frowned, puzzled. "Why?"

He tapped the page with one finger. "LORAN bearings. Must be somebody's honey hole, right?"

Loran? Honey hole? What the hell is he talking about? My confused expression gave me away.

"A honey hole is fisherman's lingo for a favorite fishing spot." He smiled kindly and spoke slowly, as if talking to a kid. "I guess you're too young to remember LORAN. It stands for long range navigation. It's a system we used to find our way around on water before they came up with GPS."

"I see—sort of," I said. "So that's what those numbers and dots and commas stand for? Somebody's directions to someplace on the water?"

"Yep. You catch on fast."

"A friend wrote it in a notebook," I said. "I guess maybe she's a fisherman."

"If she's ever going to find that spot again, she'll need to convert it to GPS," he said. "It takes special software. I can do it if you want me to."

I didn't know how Emily would feel about it, but I knew I'd sure like to know what it meant. "Would you? I'd appreciate it."

"No problem," he said. "I'll just copy it down." I pushed my pad of sticky notes and the purple pen toward him. "Might even use it myself," he said with a broad wink. "I'm not above fishing somebody else's honey hole."

Putting my program director hat back on, I gave Captain Billy a good tour of the soundstage. Chester helped with measurements for the engine and caboose while Rob and Katie enthused about the possibility of repeating their long-ago "Cannonball Express" routine for a new generation of little buckaroos.

An hour or so later, Captain Billy thanked me for the tour, promised to get back to me with the new GPS data soon, and went upstairs to "talk money" with Mr. Doan. Back in my office, I retrieved my papers once again from the overworked top drawer and got back to work on my plans for future Ranger Rob shows.

Once again, there was a brisk *tap-tap* at my office door. Rhonda smiled through the glass and held up a small pink Neiman Marcus bag. "Come on in," I called. "It's not locked," I added, immediately realizing that perhaps it should be.

"Your friend Louisa dropped this off for you," she said. "It was open so I peeked. Hope you don't mind." She put the bag on my desk. "Looks like a stack of real estate business cards with a rubber band around them. You looking for a house? Like, do you and Pete have plans you haven't told me about?"

"No, nothing like that," I said honestly, and maybe a little regretfully. "My aunt and her girlfriends are working on a little—um—real estate project and I'm trying to help them out."

"Oh." She sounded disappointed. "Well, good luck with it. How'd it feel to be field reporter this morning during all the excitement? You looked as good as ever. Like riding a bike, huh?" The bicycle reference was unfortunate considering my recent experience, but I was glad she thought I'd done all right. Rhonda doesn't mince words and if she'd thought I'd lost my touch, she'd have let me know, politely but firmly.

"Something like that," I agreed, "and thanks." This

time I locked the door behind her, and as soon as she'd left, I dumped the contents of the pink bag onto my desk and removed the band. Almost all of the cards showed photos of beautiful waterfront homes, all with perfect landscaping and even a few with yachts parked in the foreground. I was surprised that these cards represented the Angels' idea of "less expensive" real estate. I guessed that meant under a million dollars. I fanned them out in a colorful half-circle. What was I looking for? What did I expect to find? I picked up the first card on my right, grabbed a piece of copy paper, divided it into two columns, and wrote down agent names and phone numbers. I went through the stack that way. By the time I'd gone through half of them I'd already seen one number come up several times, each with a different agent attached to it. I was on to something here. I knew it and my excitement level began to rise.

Was one person using a dozen different names, or were there a dozen people working the same scam? If it *was* a scam. I felt as though I had the proverbial tiger by the tail. What was I supposed to do with it?

Another tap at the door, and like a kid who'd been caught reading comic books in study hall, I swept the cards into the top desk drawer and looked up to see Katie and Officer Marr. I smiled a welcome and hurried to let them in.

"Glad to see you're keeping it locked up, Ms. Barrett." Marr stood back and let Katie enter the office first.

"How are you feeling, Katie?" I asked. "You looked as good as new at the rehearsal."

"Oh, a few little aches here and there. No biggie." She waved a white-gloved hand. "What I wanted to talk to you about is the plan for me to stay at your house for a little while. Is it true that I can bring Percival and Paco too?"

"Absolutely," I told her. "My aunt and I are looking forward to all three of you joining us."

"Will O'Ryan mind? I know he likes Percy, but how does he feel about dogs?"

I repeated something Pete had said to me earlier in the day. "We'll see."

CHAPTER 38

Katie wanted to go to her house to get some clothes and to pick up Percival, but Marr quickly vetoed that idea. "I can't be in two places at one time," he stated flatly. "Can't watch Ms. Barrett and you if you're in two different places. Give Rob a list of what you want. He can drop off the cat and your clothes and stuff at Ms. Barrett's place. I'll take you and the dog with me and we'll follow Ms. Barrett home. That's the way it has to be."

Katie looked as though she was about to argue, but closed her mouth and spoke a soft "Okay."

It was a logical solution. My gorgeous car is a two-seater. Room for Katie but not Paco. Marr said he often rode with a K-9 dog for backup and Paco was more than welcome to ride with him anytime. Rob readily agreed to pack whatever Katie wanted in her navy-blue suitcase and to remember to bring Paco's food, Percy's litter box and his special diet cat food. It was clear that Rob was familiar with Katie's house and knew where everything was. He kissed her on the cheek and told her that she needn't worry about anything.

Except maybe being murdered by a homicidal prankster.

I shook the bad thought away.

"Katie needs to change back into her street clothes," I said, "and I need to check out with Rhonda. If you get to my place before we do, Rob," I told him, "just ring the front doorbell. My aunt is expecting you."

As it turned out, Rob and Percy did arrive on Winter Street before we did. As soon as I'd parked the Vette in the garage and stepped out the side door onto the flagstone path, *two* cats ran out to greet me—one big yellow striped one, and one small black-and-white one. Percival had obviously been welcomed to the family. Minutes later Katie and Officer Marr joined me on the garden path, with Paco straining so hard at his leash when he sighted the advancing felines that Marr reached over and took the leash from Katie's hand.

"I'll hold him, Katie. Does he normally chase cats?"

"Of course not. Stay, Paco," she said. The dog immediately stood stock still, watching Katie as though waiting for his next command. Marr handed her the leash. "Guess you can handle this," he said.

"Paco is just happy to see Percy, that's all." She narrowed her eyes, peering at O'Ryan. "I think that's all."

I was sorely tempted to say "Stay, O'Ryan," but knew better. Cats don't take commands, even when they understand perfectly what you want them to do. *Especially* when they understand perfectly what you want them to do.

O'Ryan turned his back, tail straight up in what I believe is the cat version of a very rude gesture, walked slowly and regally back to his cat door, and disappeared inside. Percival looked back and forth a couple of times, then followed O'Ryan back into the house.

Crisis averted? I hoped so. "Come on, Aunt Ibby is expecting us. Would you like to come inside and meet my aunt, Officer Marr?"

"Sure thing," he said. "She's a friend of my mom's."

I pulled the key chain from my bag, selected the back door key. Before I could insert it into the lock, the whole thing slipped from my grip, falling with a clunk onto the granite step. Embarrassed by my clumsiness, I muttered an apology, and wiping the key against my vest, tried again. It slipped easily into the lock and we were in. O'Ryan was nowhere in sight as I knocked on my aunt's kitchen door. "It's me, Aunt Ibby," I called. "Katie and Paco and Officer Marr are with me."

"Be right there," she answered. "Rob and I are having a nice little visit." I heard the click of the lock and the three of us, plus dog, piled into the kitchen. Rob hurried across the room to Katie's side. Paco nuzzled his hand. "Ibby, this is Paco, the wonder dog," Rob said. "Paco, sit and shake hands with Ibby." Paco approached my aunt, and offered his uninjured paw.

"How sweet," she said. "What a good dog." She accepted the paw, then turned to Officer Marr. "You're Jimmy Marr," she said. "I haven't seen you since you were a boy. Your mother is so proud of you." She faced Katie. "Katie, dear, please sit down. You're just out of the hospital. How are you feeling? I have the guest room all ready for you. Rob has already put your things upstairs, and Paco and Percy's food is in the pantry along with O'Ryan's. Would you like to go upstairs now and take a little nap?"

"Thank you, Ms. Russell," Katie said. "I'm fine for now." She looked around the kitchen. "Did Percy come in here with O'Ryan?"

"Neither of them came back after they went outside to greet you. Maybe they went up to Maralee's apartment. The little scallywags seem to enjoy chasing one another up and down those stairs."

Katie looked distressed. No sense in having her worry about her cat. She'd been through enough lately. "I'll run up and get them," I offered, pulling open the kitchen door and stepping out into the back hall.

I didn't have to go far to find the scallywags. They were right across the hall in the laundry room. O'Ryan lay on the floor beneath the ironing board, looking the picture of innocence, while Percy was stretched out, sound asleep on my blue blouse. I noticed that a litter box had been discreetly placed in a corner beside the dryer. I picked up the black-and-white cat gently. "Come on, sleepyhead," I said. "Your mom is waiting for you." O'Ryan lay motionless, his green eyes following me. "You can stay here if you want to," I told him. "That dog is still in your house." He closed his eyes, pretending to be asleep.

Katie was clearly delighted to see Percival, and the feeling was noticeably mutual as she reached for him, cuddling him close to her face. Conversation momentarily halted while celebratory purring and face-licking took place.

"Well, looks like everything's under control here," Of-

ficer Marr said. "Good to meet you, Ms. Russell." He gave
a brief salute in my direction. "See you two ladies in the
morning."

"Good to see you too, Jimmy," my aunt said. Katie
lifted one of Percy's paws and made him wave. Cute.

I opened the kitchen door and walked with Marr to the
back steps. "Thanks for bringing Katie and Paco. I really
appreciate all you're doing for us."

"My pleasure," he said. "See you in the morning." He
started down the path, then turned and pointed. "Don't
forget to lock up."

"I won't," I promised, thinking of how much trouble
I'd caused so recently by not taking that simple action. I
pushed the lock button and went back to Aunt Ibby's
kitchen—through the door I'd just left ajar.

*No need to get paranoid about it. I was just across the
hall.* Once inside, I pushed that lock button and rejoined
the group. My aunt had just invited Rob to join us for dinner. "Nothing fancy," she insisted. "Hot dogs, macaroni
salad, and iced tea. An indoor picnic. Apple pie for dessert. I've already invited Pete. Around seven?"

"That sounds wonderful," Katie said. "Please stay,
Rob."

"You don't have to twist my arm," he said, "but Katie,
darlin, you need to rest a bit. Want to go up and take a little snooze before dinner? I'll take a ride over to the stable
and check on things and see you later."

"Sounds good to me," I said. "That'll give me time to
catch up on a little ironing. Come with me, Katie. I'll
show you your room." She stood and, still on his leash,
Paco cocked his head and looked at me with soft brown
eyes. "By the way, where does Paco sleep when you're at
home?"

"He sleeps at the foot of my bed."

"Well then," my aunt said, "that's exactly where he'll sleep while you're here." Brief hesitation. "I suppose he tells you when he needs to go out?"

"He does." Katie stood, put Percy on the floor and stroked Paco's smooth black fur. "I usually take him for a walk right after dinner and he's good until morning."

"I'll walk him tonight, darlin'," Rob said. "You get some rest."

"Okay," she said. "Come on, Paco. We're going to see our new room." Percy had already scooted out through the cat door. I walked ahead through the living room, out into the foyer, and up the stairs, Paco's claws *click-clicking* on polished wood. As Rob had promised, Katie's navy-blue suitcase was on the foot of the bed, and as Aunt Ibby had promised, there were fresh flowers in a crystal vase on the bureau.

"How pretty!" Katie clapped her hands together just the way she does on the show. "Thanks for inviting me. I know I'll sleep like a baby in this beautiful room." She unhooked the leash from Paco's collar. "We both will."

I showed her the bathroom and the closet. "Get some rest. I'll come up and tap on your door when dinner's ready." I retraced my steps back to the first floor. Rob had left and my aunt was deep in preparations for her justly famous macaroni salad. "I'm going to iron a couple of blouses," I announced. "Percy thinks the blue one makes a nice mattress."

"That's nice, dear," she said, more focused on chopping celery than on her favorite niece's overdue domestic efforts. I headed for the laundry room, where the cats had each assumed their previous positions—one under the ironing board, one resting peacefully on blue cotton. For the second time that day, I interrupted Percy's nap. This time I put him on the floor. He didn't seem to mind—shook himself and went directly to his litter box.

Unfortunately, he'd left some sooty little footprints on the back of my blouse. I'd need some kind of spot remover before rewashing it. Aunt Ibby is a staunch believer in the old-fashioned way—wet a bar of Fels-Naptha laundry soap and rub gently. There was a slightly used gold-colored bar of it in the soap dish over the deep sink. I reached for it and turned on the faucet.

Both cats reacted when I gasped and dropped the soap. Slowly, I picked it up and turned it over. I hadn't been mistaken—hadn't imagined the clear outline I'd seen there. Someone had pressed a key into the surface of that soap and the exact shape of the key remained. I could even read the backwards "Kwikset" letters on it.

What did it mean? I was pretty sure that if I got my key chain out of my bag, one of my keys would fit into the key-shaped indent on Aunt Ibby's soap. I remembered reading somewhere that a locksmith *could* actually make a key from an impression like this—but that an honest locksmith would never do it. If someone went to the trouble to press one of my keys into soap in order to duplicate it, I reasoned, why wouldn't they take the soap with them? Very carefully, I emptied a fabric softener box and placed the bar inside. Maybe Pete could find fingerprints on it—and if he could, I was sure they'd belong to Alfred Pridholm.

Once back inside Aunt Ibby's kitchen, I grabbed my bag from the back of one of the captain's chairs. "Calling Pete," I explained, and ducked back into the hall. He answered on the first ring. "Are you on your way here?"

"Yes. What's wrong?"

How does he know just from my voice when something is wrong? I answered truthfully, explaining what I'd found. "He must have been inside the house, Pete. He took my keys out of my bag. He made that imprint and left it where Aunt Ibby or I would find it."

CHAPTER 39

I waited there in the hall, just outside the laundry room, for Pete. Both cats were awake now, both watching me. When O'Ryan stood, stretched, and trotted to the cat door, I knew Pete was about to arrive. I followed, and waited on the back steps for the familiar Crown Vic to pull into the driveway.

We hurried toward each other and met halfway along the flagstone path. He pulled me close. Neither of us spoke for a moment. Two cats rubbed my ankles. "I'm scared, Pete," I whispered. "He's been in my house."

"Show me what you've found." His voice was ragged.

We walked together, his protective arm around my shoulders, into the hall. The two cats tagged along behind, then turned as one, and with O'Ryan in the lead, pushed through the cat door to my aunt's kitchen, leaving us alone with a washer and dryer, an ironing board and a soiled blouse, a basketful of Aunt Ibby's neatly folded clean laundry, an empty deep sink, a folding table, and one defaced cake of soap. I pointed to the fabric softener box with its cute teddy-bear graphics. *How inappropriate.* "I put it in there. Fingerprints."

"Good girl." He picked up a folded white hand towel from Aunt Ibby's basket and placed it, opened, on the folding table. Sliding the Fels-Naptha bar from its box, he peered closely at the incised key silhouette. "If someone was actually going to use this to duplicate a key, that someone would have made impressions of both sides, not one."

"Then why . . . ?"

Pete pulled a folded plastic bag from his jacket pocket. I'd seen bags like it before. An evidence bag. Using the towel to lift the soap bar, he slid it into the bag and pressed the locking seal. "The guy seems to have a warped sense of humor." He held the evidence bag up and turned it from side to side. "Maybe this was supposed to show you that he *could* get into the house if he wanted to."

"Like signing for my drapes—and making you call out the bomb squad? And leaving the bike behind our garage?" Red-head anger rising. "If these pranks are supposed to scare me, they worked pretty well. I'm scared. And mad."

He pulled out his phone. "I'm not about to leave you and Katie here without protection. I'll call for someone to pick this up. I'll ask for a fingerprint kit too, although I doubt seriously that there are fingerprints on the soap or the door handles or anything else. He's meticulous about that. I hate to mess up anybody's house with the powder we use if it's not necessary. That stuff's a bear to clean up. I'll see what the chief says about my doing it. Has your aunt seen the soap yet?"

"No. I called you right away. She thinks I'm ironing."

"We'll have to tell her about this. Maybe you two can close off this room, put off using it for a little while—at least until I hear what Chief wants to do. Are your keys in that handbag?"

"Yes." I opened the zippered compartment. "The laundry can wait, I'm sure, and we often close the door if we're having guests, but Percy's litter box is in here, so I can't close it off entirely." Pete nodded, then, turning away from me, spoke briefly into his phone in terse tones. I heard the words "evidence" and "fingerprints" and "killer." As soon as he'd finished, I handed him the jingling ring of keys. "They're all here. Front door, back door, garage, my living room, my kitchen, and my new office. The fob for my car and the overhead garage door opener are separate."

"Do any of these look or feel different??" He spread them out on the towel where the soap had recently been the center of attention. "Let's try the garage side door key first," he said. detaching it from the ring. "It's the only one that has that kind of a blank." He was right. "Kwikset" was spelled out on the rounded top section.

"That key felt funny when I used it this morning. I even wiped it on my vest," I remembered. "There was something wrong with that back door key too." I pointed to it. "It was slippery. I dropped the whole key ring on the steps."

"Could there have been another cake of soap out here besides the one you found?"

"Sure. My aunt buys them by the half-dozen from

Amazon. There are probably some more in the overhead cabinet."

Using the towel again, he pulled the cabinet door open. There were four of the wrapped bars among the detergents, bleach, spray starch, and fabric softeners. My heart sank. There was no way to know how many impressions he might have made. I said as much to Pete.

"Chances are he just took photos of whatever keys he wanted to duplicate. It's easier, and a dishonest locksmith can work with pictures better than with soap. I believe the soap thing was designed to let you know he's been in here. To scare you."

Yeah, well, it worked. A horn sounded from outside. "Wait for me here." He picked up the evidence bag and sprinted out the back door just as Aunt Ibby's door swung open and my aunt poked her head out.

"Everything all right here? I heard a horn." She glanced at the open back door. "I thought I heard Pete's voice."

"Everything's fine," I fibbed. "Another officer came by to leave something for Pete. He just ran out to get it. He'll be right back."

"The macaroni salad is chilling. Hungry yet?"

"Starving," I said. "What with all the bomb scare excitement, I skipped lunch again." I looked at my watch. "I'll knock on Katie's door in about fifteen minutes. I have a feeling she may have skipped lunch too."

"I wouldn't be surprised. Poor child."

Aunt returned to her cooking and Pete arrived back beside me in the hall. "That's done," he said, locking the door behind him. "They'll go over the soap and Chief will let me know about using the print kit. Shall we give your aunt a heads-up about the laundry room before Rob gets back?"

"Good idea," I said. With a backward glance at the ne-
glected blue blouse, I pulled the laundry room pocket
door almost shut—leaving just enough room for cats—
and knocked on the kitchen door.

"Come on in. It's not locked," she called.

Pete shook his head. Old habits are hard to unlearn. I
opened the door and when we were both inside, I made a
rather dramatic point of locking it.

"Oops." Aunt Ibby looked apologetic. "I knew you'd
be coming in right away," she explained. "Anyway, you
left the outside door wide open a few minutes ago."

"But Pete was coming right back in," I said.

"Exactly." Big smile. "Want to help me set the table?"

"Sure. But Pete needs to tell you something first."

So, gently but firmly, while I assembled the appropriate dishes and bowls and silver and glassware, Pete told
her what was going on. She paled a little when he related
the possibility that Alfred Pridholm might very well have
keys to virtually every door in the house, and put her
hand to her mouth and sat down when he got to the part
about the defaced cake of soap.

"We'll see to getting all the locks changed first thing
tomorrow," Pete said. "You have an excellent alarm system already in place, and I'll be right here with you. My
car is parked outside. By now he knows who I am. He
knows I'm here and he knows I'm armed. He won't try
anything tonight."

"I'm going to run upstairs and get Katie," I said, "and
I think I just heard Rob's truck. That big four-hundred-
and-fifty horsepower engine is hard to miss." O'Ryan's
fuzzy head appeared at the cat door. He wiggled through
and ran ahead of me toward the front hall.

"Where's Percy?" my aunt asked.

"Probably curled up sound asleep on my blue blouse," I muttered, and followed the cat.

O'Ryan stopped at the top of the stairs on the second floor while I proceeded down the hall toward the guest room. "You worried about that dog?" I asked. "Come on. Katie can control him." On reluctant cat feet, he approached the guest room.

I knocked. *Click-click*. Good. Katie had remembered to lock her door. It opened a couple of inches, just enough for a dog's nose to poke through. "Lee? Is that you?"

"It's me," I said. "O'Ryan is with me."

"Stay, Paco," came the command. The dog's nose withdrew, O'Ryan retreated to the stairs, the door opened and Katie, looking refreshed and rested in a pink jumpsuit, stepped out into the corridor. "I had a nice nap. Is Rob back yet?"

"I just heard his truck," I told her. Pete's downstairs too. Guess the gang's all here, safe and sound." *I hope we're all safe*. Katie and I started down the stairs, O'Ryan leading the way a few steps ahead of us.

"Where's Percy?" Katie asked. "He seems to have made himself at home here already."

"He was snoozing in the laundry room last time I checked," I said. "I think O'Ryan wore him out with the running up and down stairs game they've been playing."

"That's good. As long as he's happy."

All through the Winter Street house that summer evening, everyone seemed to be relaxed and happy—men and women, cats and dog. Conversation was light and easy. Aunt Ibby's indoor picnic meal was expectedly perfect. The TV was turned off and nobody seemed to miss the evening news. None of us even once mentioned mur-ders—past or present. There was no talk of bomb threats or hit-and-run cars or abandoned bicycles or stolen keys. Rob took Paco for an uneventful walk after dinner.

For me, the sense of unreality hung in the air like a Stephen King mist.

CHAPTER 40

Once Pete and I were in bed, I told him about Emily's cryptic series of numbers and punctuation marks on the notebook page. "It was something she wrote when she was still Janie," I said. "Captain Billy calls it LORAN bearings. Something fishermen used to find their way around the ocean back before we had GPS."

"That was along time ago," he said. "I wonder why she wrote them down. They wouldn't be much use to anybody these days."

"Captain Billy knows how to convert them to GPS. He's going to do it for me."

"Should be interesting. You say she had that notebook when she was Janie? Before she got her memory back?" He paused. "Allegedly."

"Right," I agreed. "That reminds me. I've been fooling around with numbers myself." I told him about Louisa's business-card collection and the names and phone numbers I'd found. "A few of the numbers match up, but none of the names. I have no idea what it means. A dozen people with the same phone number, or one person with a dozen phones? I'll give it to you."

"I'll take it," he said. "Any other clues to share?"

I told him about my phone call to the curtain store and how they'd confirmed the bogus call asking for early delivery. SPD had already covered that too. "Now we have his voice print," he said. "We're checking it against phone messages Sawtelle had with the men who set up the meeting at the conservancy. I'm pretty sure we'll have at least one match."

With the growing pile of evidence, how come this guy is still wandering around loose?

It wasn't necessary for me to voice that thought. I knew Pete and every member of the police department was agonizing over the boldness of this criminal and their thus-far inability to capture him.

As though he could read my thoughts, he held me close. "I worry about you every minute of every day that I'm not with you," he whispered. "I want to be with you—I want you with me—all the time."

I want it too. His kiss told me he already knew that. Safe in his arms, my sleep was peaceful and dream-free.

Aunt Ibby had already invited Katie to join her downstairs for an early breakfast of old-fashioned homemade oatmeal with raisins and brown sugar. O'Ryan scooted out the cat door to join them, leaving Pete and me alone in my kitchen, enjoying the last two slices of Aunt Ibby's apple pie with our coffee. Pie for breakfast is an old and valued New England custom. Out of consideration for my two-seater, Pete had volunteered to drive Katie and Paco to work. I'd drive the Vette and they'd follow me.

I really need to think about getting a full-sized car.

Maybe.

Not yet.

It was not quite eight o'clock when we were all assembled in the downstairs back hall. Katie, Pete, and I, along with Paco, were ready to leave. The chief had agreed to pass on the fingerprinting of the laundry room, so the sliding door was open wide once again. My blouse, still unwashed and un-ironed, drooped forlornly from the ironing board. I'd already returned the dream books to Aunt Ibby, who was scheduled for a half day at the library. "I'll wait here for the locksmith and the alarm company man before I go," she said. "They both agreed to be here at eight. I'll feel better when everything is secure again."

"We'll wait with you," Pete said, and I knew he wanted to be sure both locksmith and alarm installer were who they said they were—unlike my phony "assistant" who'd signed for the draperies. "Lee, why don't you back your car out now so we can get on the road as soon as I check these guys out. Don't worry, I'll walk with you to the garage to be sure everything in there is copacetic."

"Thanks. I'm still a little nervous about the key thing," I admitted. Pete made the same kind of careful inspection he'd made before. Relieved, I opened the overhead door, tossed my briefcase and handbag onto the seat, and carefully pulled the Vette onto the street, big engine purring, closed and locked the garage and rejoined the others.

"Paco needs to go out for a minute before we leave," Katie said. "Okay if I just walk him down to the corner of

Oliver Street and back?" She held a plastic bag in one hand and clutched Paco's leash in the other. "I think he really needs to go."

The front doorbell chimed "The Impossible Dream." "Oh-oh," my aunt said. "That's the front doorbell. It's probably one or the other of them."

"Okay," Pete said. "I'll get it. Lee, keep an eye on Katie and the dog. I'll be right back."

Katie and Paco turned left from our driveway, walking toward the common, opposite to Oliver Street's one-way traffic. She had nearly reached Washington Square when Paco paused to take care of business. When Katie bent for clean-up duty, a dusty maroon Chevy slowed beside her and tooted the horn—a friendly toot, not an annoyed blast—then slowed again as it approached me. The Chevy stopped beside the parked Vette, windows open. The driver wore a black knitted watch cap, completely covering his hair. He had a skinny mustache. The cruel eyes, the mocking smile were unmistakable. "Hey, sweetheart. I don't like clowns. Or dogs." He sped away toward Bridge Street.

I didn't hesitate—didn't stop to think—just pulled open the door of the Vette, jumped in and gunned it. I was on the tail of that Chevy and had no intention of losing it. I knew that Pridholm could track the Vette's every move, but so could Pete—thanks to the twin bugs under the hood. I knew my car was faster. I wouldn't, couldn't lose him. "Siri, call Pete," I commanded the phone.

"What the hell is wrong?" he demanded. "Where did you go?"

"Pridholm!" I yelled, executing a sharp turn onto North Street. "He knows where Katie is. I'm following

him. We're on Route 114 toward Peabody. Maroon Chevy."
I read the license plate number aloud.

He knows what Katie looks like now.

We were both exceeding the speed limit—by a lot. He
wove in and out of traffic. So did I. The Chevy turned
onto Orne Street.

"I'm coming," Pete yelled. "Katie and Paco are
with me."

The Chevy barreled between a pair of iron gates.

"He's turning into the cemetery," I said. "Greenlawn
Cemetery."

My grandparents are in here.

Greenlawn is huge. Maybe bigger than the common,
but it's crisscrossed with paths and streets, hills and
ponds, and many, many trees. Big, tall, view-obstructing
trees. I couldn't see the Chevy. I rolled down the windows so that maybe I could hear it. "Where did he go?" I
spoke out loud. "I don't know where he went."

*But Alfred Pridholm knows exactly where I am.
Damned GPS bug.*

I still couldn't hear the Chevy. Instead, I heard sirens.
Pete would find me. Pete would catch Pridholm and this
nightmare would be over.

Then I saw it—a giant maroon blur, speeding down-
hill, straight at me. I saw the man jump from the front
seat and roll away. He'd lost his hat. The hair was gray. I
jerked the wheel to the left. Too late. I heard the crash.
Felt it too. *Must be the airbag*, I thought as I went to
sleep.

CHAPTER 41

Mist. No, it was fog. Was I dreaming again? Not fog.

Smoke.

I turned my head left, then right. There were tombstones on either side of me. Tall, white tombstones.

Am I dead?

"Lee? Lee? Can you hear me?"

Pete. I wasn't dead and Pete was with me. "What happened?" My voice sounded funny.

"Accident. Can you move? Are you hurt?"

"My head hurts." I raised one hand, then the other. I wiggled my toes. Tried to sit up.

"Better not get up yet, Lee," came a soft voice. "The ambulance is coming."

"Katie?"

"Yes. I'm here. So's Paco. You had an accident."

"An accident," I said. "Yes. The airbag." Then, despite advice, I sat up, suddenly aware of a sea of blue uniforms around me." My car. Is my car okay?" I looked around. Couldn't see the Vette. "Where is it?" Paco's moist nose nuzzled my hand.

Pete knelt on the ground beside me. "We had to move you away from it. Smoke. Sorry, babe. The Chevy smashed one of those fiberglass fenders and a tree got the other one. The engine caught fire. The fire department is here and the tow truck is on the way." He touched my face, ever so gently. "Looks like your eye is bruised."

I lay down again as memory flooded back. "Did Pridholm get away again?"

"Looks that way."

"Any chance there are prints or anything in the Chevy?" My voice sounded normal again. "It's stolen, I suppose."

"It is. It'll be towed to the impound lot. We'll check for prints." He didn't sound confident.

Katie spoke up. "Pete, may I ask a question?"

"Sure, Katie," Pete answered.

"Would the man have left his scent in that car?"

"Probably. You're thinking Paco could help while the scent is still fresh?"

"He's awfully smart," she said.

"Pridholm doesn't like dogs," I put in. "He told me that, and Pete, his hat fell off."

"I've alerted K-9, but since Paco is right here . . . what does the hat look like?"

I gave a fast description. "Black, knitted, covered his hair."

Pete motioned to one of the uniformed cops. "Find a black knitted cap. It may still be in the Chevy or nearby. Give it to this lady. Katie, can you tell Paco what you want him to do?"

"Sure," she said. "I told you. He's really smart."

Pete spoke to the officer. "Escort this lady and the dog over to the Chevy. Katie, give the officer the leash. We can't involve you in a search."

"He doesn't like clowns either," I whispered. "Be careful, Katie."

More siren sounds. I felt very tired. And sad. And discouraged. I closed my eyes. The ambulance had arrived. I was loaded onto a stretcher along with my smoky-smelling handbag. I saw the WICH-TV mobile unit approaching just as the rear double doors swung shut and was thankful that there'd been no camera around to witness my helpless state. I even felt a flash of sympathy for some of the people I'd interviewed on camera when they were looking and feeling far from their best. Two kind EMTs rode with me to the hospital. Pete couldn't leave the scene and Katie needed to stay because of Paco. Someone had called Aunt Ibby and she was already waiting in the emergency room when we got there.

"Oh, Maralee, dear child. Are you badly hurt? What can I do?"

I patted her hand. "I feel all right. Just a little headache where the airbag hit me. I'm sure they'll let me go home with you." A little self-pitying sniffle. "I have no car anymore."

I was right about going home. After some prodding, a couple of X-rays, a sample package of extra-strength Tylenol, and a tiny round ice pack for my bruised eye—

which had turned out to be a real shiner—I was released and wheelchaired out to the Buick.

It was good to be safe at home in our house on Winter Street, especially since the locks had all been changed, the state-of-the-art updated alarm system was in place, and I'd replaced the old keys on my key ring. My aunt wasn't ready to let me climb the stairs to my apartment, so I showered in the downstairs bathroom while she went upstairs and brought me my soft and comfy gray sweats. With a big, purring yellow cat at my side, I lay on her living room couch with fluffy pillows, crocheted afghan, and a glass of cold ginger ale. For the first time in many hours, I began to relax.

The phone calls began. The first one was from Pete, of course, assuring me that he'd be with me just as soon as he could get away. He reported that Paco had indeed followed the scent of the fleeing man up and down streets and alleys, through backyards and vacant lots, right up until the scent disappeared at the corner of Larchmont Road. Not coincidentally, a vehicle was reported stolen in that vicinity. This time he'd grabbed a dry cleaner's truck the driver had parked with the motor left running. Fortunately, it was recovered intact a few blocks away. Rhonda called to tell me that Katie and Paco had returned to the station via police cruiser, and that rehearsal was proceeding as planned on the *Ranger Rob's Rodeo* set. Emily Hemenway called, and the Angels each called too, all expressing loving concern.

A number without any identifying name popped up. The number was vaguely familiar, so I answered. "Hello," I said. "Lee Barrett here."

"Hello, sweetheart," came the now-familiar voice. "So

you're not dead. I don't really care, one way or the other. I don't need the clown either, now that I know exactly how to get to that nosy bitch Emily. Give my regards to the dumb cop."

And he was gone.

Of course I called Pete immediately, repeated the chilling message and gave him the number. It turned out to be one of the ones I'd found in Louisa's card collection, and like the long trail of deliberate clues Pridholm had left, I had little hope that it would yield any information of value.

So much for relaxing.

I dislodged the sleeping cat, tossed off the afghan, and stood up. After what I'd just told him, I was sure Pete would be by my side very soon. Meanwhile, I might as well attend to my long-postponed laundry duties.

"Aunt Ibby," I said. "My headache is gone. I'll be in the laundry room."

She fussed a little, but conceded that I certainly *looked* better. Comforting thought. With O'Ryan leading the way, I crossed the hall. A tiny bit hesitantly, I unwrapped a fresh bar of Fels-Naptha and proceeded to treat and wash the stained blouse. While the washing machine whirred quietly, I mulled over Pridholm's chilling words— that he knew exactly how to get to Emily. He'd spoken with such confidence. *The misplaced confidence of a madman?*

I'd assumed all along that he believed I was the key he needed to get to Emily—the only witness to his killing of John Sawtelle. I remembered too, that there were some people, including the chief of police, who thought otherwise about Emily's connection to the crew-cut beachboy and the kindly school teacher. He wanted to get rid of witnesses, that was for sure. Katie had seen his partner plant the bug under my car, but since he'd eliminated the partner, Katie was no longer a threat, and if he didn't need me anymore to get to Emily—that left only Emily.

Could I have been wrong about her? Was Pridholm trying to get to Emily because she'd been part of their scam? Because she knew too much?

I was still in the laundry room, still pondering imponderables, when Pete arrived. He didn't say anything at first, just held me close. "Oh my God, Lee. I just got a good look at the front of your car. I didn't realize how close we came to losing you." His voice shook. There were tears in his eyes.

It took a moment for what he'd said to sink in. Other than a black eye, I felt fine. I'd been worried about my lovely blue Corvette, which from Pete's words, I assumed was totaled. It hadn't even occurred to me that I'd narrowly escaped death.

I didn't know how to respond. I said, "I guess I need a new car."

He stepped back a few inches, still holding my shoulders. "Yes, silly goose, you need a new car. Not another one of your foo-foo, fancy-ass convertibles either. You need a good, strong, dependable, all-weather, four-wheel drive, American car. Maybe a Jeep. Safe, sturdy, affordable transportation. Plenty of room for groceries and a dog and our kids."

Our kids? Had I heard him right? **Our** *kids?*

I said it out loud. "Our kids?"

"That's right. Our kids. Hey, I wasn't going to do it this way. I was going to ask your aunt first. I was going to take you to dinner. Champagne and all that. Get down on one knee. Whip out the blue velvet ring box. Damn it, Lee. Will you marry me?"

"Well, okay," I said. "Yes. I will."

"Good," he said. "That's settled."

CHAPTER 42

A few long, lovely kisses, and then Pete leaned against the dryer, arms folded, cop voice activated. "Now, what more can you tell me about Pridholm. Exactly what did he say to you? What does he look like this time?"

Real fast mindset adjustment—from hearts and flowers, blue velvet and diamonds, rainbows and unicorns, to murder. I made the adjustment.

"He slowed down first, right next to Katie. She had her back turned, and he tooted the horn. Just a little toot. Friendly-like. But then he slowed again, next to me. Actually came to a stop, I think. His window was open. He leaned toward me. Looked right at me." I actually shivered at the recollection. "He said 'Hi, sweetheart. I don't like clowns. Or dogs.'"

I remembered his face. "That hat covered his hair. He has a thin little mustache that looks fake." I closed my eyes, seeing the cruel eyes, the self-assured smile. "It might be glued on."

"So you decided to follow him."

"Sure. I was standing right next to my car. The engine was running. I knew he couldn't outrun me with that beat-up old Chevy. Of course I chased him. I knew you'd be right behind me." I watched his face. He frowned and shook his head. "I was right, wasn't I? If he hadn't turned in to the cemetery, we would have caught him this time."

"My love, chasing criminals isn't your job. It's mine." He held up both hands. "It was a reckless, thoughtless thing to do. You could have been killed. You have to promise me you'll never, ever, take a chance like that again." He shook his head. "I was sure when you changed jobs, this kind of thing would be over with."

"I thought so too." He'd had tears in his eyes when he'd talked about losing me. He was right and I knew it. "I promise, Pete, I'll never scare you like that again. I promise."

He pulled me close again. "I love you."

"I know." I smiled. "Now can we go tell Aunt Ibby that we're engaged?"

"I meant to do it old-school, you know. I was going to ask her for your hand in marriage." The frown was back. "Think she'll forgive me?"

"Of course she will. She'll probably say 'What took you so long?'" I took his hand, led him across the hall, and knocked on the kitchen door. "It's us, Aunt Ibby. We've got some good news."

The lock clicked. "We can always use some of that." she said. "Have you caught that dreadful man?"

"Not yet," I said, "but we . . . I mean . . . the police are getting close."

"He's certainly a devious one," she said. "The Angels have been putting a lot of time and effort into figuring out what in the world was going on in his real estate dealings."

"That was the right place to begin," Pete said. "Somehow those dealings have led to murders. Two of them."

My aunt wore her wise-old-owl face. "We'll figure it out, Pete. I'm sure of it. Now, tell me about your good news."

So we did. It must have been a disjointed recitation with both Pete and I talking at once. We knew from the joy in her eyes that it was good news to her too—and she didn't say "It took you long enough." She did manage to ask, though, if he actually *had* a ring in a blue velvet box stashed somewhere to mark the happy occasion.

Darn good question.

Pete looked down at his shoes. "Well, at this point, the whole blue velvet box thing is still what you might call imaginary, along with the champagne and the dinner." Broad smile. "Don't worry. I'll have that remedied by the end of the week."

Darn good answer.

I hadn't been without wheels of my own since I got my first driver's license. Call me spoiled. Aunt Ibby gave me a Toyota Corolla for my sixteenth birthday and it had lasted me through high school and four years of college. Once I started working though, I'd always bought my own cars. I admit the Vette was an extravagance, and Pete was undoubtedly right about my needing something less flashy and more practical. But meanwhile, being dependent on others for transportation was completely foreign to me and I didn't like it one bit.

As long as Pridholm was still on the loose, Emily, Katie, and I were all still considered possible targets, no matter what he'd said about not being interested in Katie or me anymore. Add to that the fact that since Katie and Paco were living at the Winter Street house too, they also needed transportation to and from work every day.

There were still two cars in the household—Pete's and Aunt Ibby's. Rob's big truck was an option on some days too, and Officer Marr was already scheduled to drive Katie, Paco, and me home after work. Since Pete's a.m. schedule varied so much, it was decided that we'd figure out our morning rides on a day-to-day basis.

The morning after my one day of rest, eye blackened and newly engaged, I was ready and anxious to resume my program director duties. Pete, however, had a six o'clock staff meeting scheduled and Katie and I didn't need to clock in at WICH-TV until nine. Since we'd all fit comfortably into the Buick, Aunt offered to drive, but Pete arranged for Officer Marr to pick us all up at eight thirty.

I thought that was an imposition and I told Pete so. "It's so far out of his way," I said. "He lives way over in North Salem. Aunt Ibby can just as well drive us. It's only a few blocks away, for heaven's sake."

"Babe, when we get this nutjob locked up, you can roller-skate to work if you want to," he said. "Meanwhile we do this my way."

Pete left at five thirty. O'Ryan and I stayed in bed until my alarm clock went off at seven. Aunt Ibby had invited Katie and me downstairs for breakfast, where there was a lot of discussion about engagement ring styles. Simple solitaire? Emerald cut? Heart shaped? Halo setting? At eight thirty sharp, when Officer Marr rang the doorbell, we were in the front hall ready for the day. So was Paco, fed, collared, and leashed, and though still favoring the injured leg, fairly prancing in doggie anticipation of an outing.

We were about to get into Marr's waiting car when Aunt Ibby dashed out the front door and down the steps to the curb. She carried a Friends of the Library book bag. "Maralee," she said, holding the bag out toward me. "I have a full day at the library today, and I promised to drop off these cozy mysteries for Emily. She's so bored, being house-bound and all. I've picked out Barbara Ross, Maddie Day, and Sofie Ryan for her. She'll love them, I know. Could you do it on the way home this evening—that is, if the officer doesn't mind?" She pointed toward the common, flashing her best Aunt Ibby smile in Marr's direction. "It won't be out of your way. Her condo is over there, just across Washington Square."

"No problem, Ms. Russell," he said. "Glad to oblige."

"No problem here either," I said, accepting the books. "It'll be good to see her. She sounded kind of down last time I spoke with her."

I rode up front with Officer Marr. Katie and Paco shared the back seat. I balanced the book bag on my lap along with an overstuffed medium-sized handbag. I wondered if the cleaners could get the smoky smell out of my trusty hobo.

We rode up in Old Clunky—mostly so Paco wouldn't have to manage climbing stairs with his wounded leg. Rhonda must have been watching for us from her window because there was quite a reception committee waiting for us—Chester, Marty, and Scott were there, along with Wanda and Rob. Even Mr. Doan joined in welcoming us back to work.

My black eye was much commented on, and maybe sort of admired by some. The group dispersed quickly, prompted by Mr. Doan's pointed glances at the gold sunburst wall clock. I waited until they'd left before I told Rhonda that Pete had finally popped the question.

Her eyes darted to my left hand, which clutched the book bag. "No ring yet," I hurriedly explained. "It was kind of a spur-of-the-moment thing. Maybe next week."

"Congratulations." Big smile. "It's about time."

We rode the elevator down again and cut through the lobby to the studio door. Chester had made amazing progress on the *Ranger Rob's Rodeo* set. The split-rail fence was in place and colorful advertising banners for sponsors were discreetly arranged along its length. Captain Billy had provided a realistic chuck wagon, and an American flag waved from the roof of Paco's dog house. I took the bull chute route backstage to thank Chester. Officer Marr called me aside.

"Just got a little update on that stolen cleaner's truck on Larchmont Road," he said. "The driver reported an order missing."

"What's missing?"

"A couple of medical scrub tops from an animal hospital." He looked at a piece of paper. "They're light blue with embroidered red letters, *Pet Docs*."

He has a new disguise.

CHAPTER 43

This wasn't the right time to think about a killer masquerading as a vet. Pete was right. Chasing criminals wasn't my job. It was his, and I'd sort of promised to stay out of the crime business. Anyway, I had quite enough to handle in my own job. I tried really hard to erase the image of a blue-scrub-wearing Pridholm from my mind, confident that there'd be an all-points bulletin out for him by now. He couldn't hide in plain sight forever.

Katie had selected one of her many clown suits from the backstage clothes rack, chosen a coordinating neck ruff for Paco, and prepared for a full dress rehearsal for the first performance of *Ranger Rob's Rodeo*—the "Animal Friends" show. Prince Valiant was on hand, along with a sweet alpaca from Bothways Farm in nearby Essex. We all had our fingers crossed, hoping the various animals would get along with one another. Paco was on his leash. Rob had a tight hold on the Palomino's reins, and the alpaca was safe in a high-sided pen.

Things progressed smoothly on stage with no major mishaps. Our four-legged cast members tolerated one another, so I left the colorful group and went to the comparative peace and quiet of my office. I unlocked my little fishbowl of a sanctuary, tried to avoid looking into the newsroom next door, and pulled the outline for the second show from the file cabinet. It was going to be about boats and fishing, with Captain Billy at the helm, so I wasn't going to have to do a lot of planning for that one. It would probably wind up being an hour-long toy commercial, but the kids would love it.

I called Captain Billy to confirm dates, and to inquire about Emily/Janie's notebook numbers. "I was just about to call you, Lee," he said. "Darndest thing about that LORAN bearing you gave me. Either your friend transcribed some part of it wrong, or her honey hole is right on the edge of Wingaersheek Beach, up Cape Ann way— pretty near on somebody's front lawn."

"Could you send me that GPS information anyway, Captain?" I asked. "It might be important." I wasn't sure exactly *how* it might be important, but I meant to pass it on to Pete right away.

That's what I did. I forwarded the captain's information to Pete the minute I received it. Then I phoned him. "Does it make any sense to you?"

"It does, Lee. Our team came up with the same result. It may be the most important piece in this puzzle so far."

"Care to explain that?"

"Can't right now. Later today, I promise. And, Lee, no more Nancy Drew on this one, okay? We're about to close in on this guy. You just stay put. Stay safe."

I replied with a tentative "Okay," and hung up. I mentally put Nancy Drew aside, as requested. But Lee Barrett still had questions. What harm could it do to ask Emily about the numbers? I needed to talk to her about the library books anyway. I was sure she'd have to tell the doorman to expect me. Before I could change my mind, I called her.

"Oh, Lee," she said, before I'd even said hello. "I'm so glad to hear your voice. I hope you're calling to invite me over for some TV watching. I'm not used to this house arrest thing. I don't get to talk to anyone except my parents, the police, and the cat these days."

I wished a TV show was the reason for my call too, and I told her so. "I wouldn't be surprised if we can arrange for a *Midsomer Murders* date real soon," I told her. "Pete says that the chief isn't opposed to the idea."

"That's encouraging." There was disappointment in her voice. "But I'm glad to hear from you anyway."

"Aunt Ibby has picked out some library books for you. Mysteries. If it's okay I'll bring them over tonight on my way home from work."

"That will be great." She sounded happier. "Something to look forward to. Thank her for me."

"One more thing, Emily," I said. "It's about a notebook you returned with my clothes."

"Oh, the one I put those numbers in." Short laugh. "You must have found it confusing."

"I did," I admitted. "Can you tell me what the numbers mean?"

"I wish I could," she said. "John Sawtelle had a piece of paper with those numbers on it—as close as I can remember them. He handed it to me when we were on the way to meet those men."

"He didn't tell you what they meant?"

"No. He said there might be more of a problem going on than we'd anticipated. Then he said the strangest thing. He said, 'It's okay though. I know where the big fish are.' He laughed, and asked me what I thought."

"Did you tell him you didn't get it?"

"I never got a chance. 'We'll talk about it later,' he said. 'Maybe these people have a good explanation for it.' He took that paper with him."

"You wrote in the notebook when you were Jane Doe," I pointed out. "You remembered those figures, but not your own name?"

"I know. I've thought about that," she said. "Maybe it was because studying that piece of paper so hard just before I saw—before I saw what happened—that memory was still fresh." A long sigh. "I've written them down again and again. I shared them with my dad."

"What does he say about it?"

"He says I'm overthinking it. He said it looks like some old numbers they used to use years ago when he and John went fishing together on John's boat."

"Have the police consulted him?"

"They haven't asked either of us about it. We think they've probably figured it out on their own, so they don't need our help. I gave your notebook back because I didn't need it. Even though there are things about that day I still don't remember, those numbers are burned into my brain."

They have figured it out. Maybe they don't need Emily. Or maybe they still just don't trust her.

"Whatever the numbers mean, it may have been the information that got John Sawtelle killed," I said, thinking out loud. "There's a chance his killers figured you have that information too."

"I know." Her voice was soft. "And I'm scared."

"You have good protection all around you, and I'll get back to you as soon as I can about the next get-together with the Angels," I promised. "See you soon."

It was four thirty when Officer Marr tapped on my office door. He did not look happy. "Ms. Barrett? We've got a little problem."

"What's wrong?"

"Got a flat. I've called the station and they're sending road service. Rob's got plenty of room in that big crew cab for all of us in his truck if that's okay with you."

"You'll come with us?"

"Of course. That's my assignment. Rob says we can take you and Katie home to your place. We can even swing by and deliver those books if you want to. It's right on the way. By then my tire should be changed, and Rob'll drop me off back here. Piece of cake."

I remembered the animal show. "What about the animals?"

"The alpaca-farm people have already taken their critter home. The Prince is all tucked into his trailer. Katie rides up front with Rob, you and me in the back seat with Paco. What do you say? It's only a few blocks."

"I know. I was just telling Pete that. It's only a few blocks. I say sure, why not? It might even be fun."

"Good deal. I'll go round up Katie and the dog. Meet you at Rhonda's desk at five?"

"I'll be there," I promised, and began the ritual end-of-day tidying of my work space—both on computer and in physical backup files. I realized belatedly that I'd already missed two opportunities to watch Wanda's Sunday brunch prep, and that I'd need a lot more books to fill the shelves on *Saturday Morning Business Hour*'s commodious new bookcase. I added a couple more of the hot-pink sticky-note reminders to the growing row of them arranged across the glass wall behind me. "Tomorrow's another day," I told myself, and with a relatively clear conscience, picked up my handbag and the bag of books, locked my office, and took the metal stairway to Rhonda's reception area.

Katie and Paco were already there, Katie still in costume except for the clown shoes and the ping-pong-ball red nose, and Paco still wearing his ruffled collar. "We worked right up until the last minute," she explained, with a toss of orange yarn hair. "I didn't have time to change and I don't want to hold you all up. Hope nobody minds."

I certainly didn't mind. I thought she looked adorable and told her so. The gold starburst clock showed exactly five o'clock when Officer Marr joined us in front of Rhonda's desk. "Rob's already out front with the engine running and my road service guy is on his way. We all set to go?"

We must have made an odd-looking crew—a program director with a purple, rapidly turning greenish black eye; a cop in paint-spattered overalls; an orange-haired rodeo clown; and a performing dog with a cast on one leg, all tumbling out of Old Clunky, then piling into a giant truck towing a horse trailer and driven by a ten-gallon-hat-wearing cowboy.

As Marr and I had both recently observed, Washington Square was only a few blocks away from the station. The Hemenways' condo was in one of Salem's handsome mid-1850s brick buildings—and there really was a uniformed doorman, brass buttons, white gloves and all—at the porticoed entrance to the place. Rob pulled the truck up in a parking spot marked GUEST right beside a 2015 black Jeep Renegade. Emily's dad's car. I wondered if it was the kind of Jeep Pete had in mind for me. And our kids. The thought of our kids made me smile. I picked up my book bag and opened the truck door. "This won't take long," I promised Officer Marr. "I know you need to get back to pick up your car."

"Just a minute, Ms. Barrett." He joined me on the pavement. "Mondello picked me to keep an eye on you—and Katie too. If you go in there, we all have to go in. Rob can't leave Prince Valiant unattended. He'll wait right here for us."

It seemed like an unnecessary precaution to me. All I needed to do was walk into what had to be one of the most secure buildings in the city, hand Emily a bag of books, say hi, and leave. But Marr was a cop following orders. I knew from personal experience that there was absolutely no point in arguing. "Might as well take Paco too then," I said. "Emily will get a kick out of it."

So like some kind of weird, mini-Mardi Gras parade, Katie, Marr, and me, along with Paco the wonder dog, approached the very proper doorman. To his credit, he didn't change his expression. Didn't even blink. "Good afternoon," he said. "Are you expected by one of our guests?"

I held the Friends of the Library bag up for his inspection. "I'm Lee Barrett. Emily Hemenway is expecting me. I'm delivering some library books she requested."

"Just a moment, Ms. Barrett." He consulted a tablet. "Yes. She is expecting you. But, the others . . . ?" Raised eyebrow. Dismissive wave of a gloved hand.

Marr reached into the overalls' front pocket and produced his badge. "Official business," he said, using his best cop voice.

"Yes, sir." Doorman snapped to attention. I almost expected him to salute. "Go right on in. First floor. Suite 101." With a sidelong glance toward clown and dog, he held the door open for us. "The Hemenways are popular this evening. Miss Emily's new kitten arrived today too."

"A new kitten," I whispered to Katie. "That's nice. She must have found a companion for Fred Astaire. She said he seems to be just as bored here as she is."

We trooped, single file, with Paco in the lead, sniffing his way along the very posh and elegant corridor where cream-colored damask wall coverings were interspersed with bronze wall sconce light fixtures. It occurred to me that the forensic accounting field must pay quite well.

Paco came to an abrupt halt in front of a paneled door. Above the brass knocker, matching brass numerals identified Suite 101. It was a beautifully polished, very shiny brass knocker. The flashing lights began.

Marr's voice seemed to come from a distance. "How'd he know that? Can he read?"

"Maybe," I heard Katie say. "He hasn't shown me all of his tricks yet."

I forced myself to look down at Paco, away from the

swirling colors. Paco sat, facing us, his back to the door, those big brown eyes focused on Katie.

"What's that all about?" Marr said. "Looks like he wants something."

"He does that after he's done a trick." Shrugging her shoulders, she reached into one of her many pockets. "He's expecting a treat."

The colors in the brass door knocker cleared. I saw a light blue shirt. Embroidered red words. *Pet Vet.* I knew who'd delivered Emily's new kitten.

"Wait a minute." I held up a warning hand, speaking softly. "Somebody brought a kitten in here today. June sits for a treat that way after she finds an explosive. The only thing we've asked Paco to find is . . ."

Marr finished my sentence. "Is Alfred Pridholm." He reached for his gun and moved to one side of the door, waving us off. Obediently, Katie and I, with a reluctant Paco, backed away. Marr knocked. No response. He knocked again, louder. "Police. Open up."

Sounds came from inside Suite 101. Crashing. Banging. A scream. Marr kicked the door. Again and again. Wood splintered and it swung open. A man and woman stood there. *The Hemenways?* "He's got Emily," the woman cried. "He's got a gun." The man put an arm around her shoulders, and pointed to an open door. "They went out the back. He's got my car keys." Marr rushed forward, gun in one hand, phone in the other. I knew he was calling for backup.

Katie and I, with Paco in the lead, turned and ran. We burst onto the landing, startling the doorman. "Call 911!" I shouted. "Hurry! Kidnapper!" Rob saw us coming, opened the truck door, jumped down from the high cab, and ran to meet us.

"What's wrong? Where's Marr?"

I pointed to the rear of the property where the gray-haired man in a light blue hospital scrub shirt pushed the woman ahead of him, her right arm twisted behind her at a cruel angle. A large gun was aimed at her head.

"They're heading for that black Jeep," I yelled as Marr raced from behind the brick building. I was right. We watched, horrified, as Pridholm pulled open the door of the Renegade, pushing Emily inside, the gun still leveled at her head. Shoving her over into the passenger seat, he jammed himself in behind the wheel. We heard the Jeep's engine start up.

"Get into the truck and keep your heads down," Rob commanded, positioning himself between the cab and the trailer. Katie and I climbed into the back seat, pulling Paco up with us. Keeping our heads down was another matter. I'd been a field reporter for far too long to miss the kind of action that I knew was about to play out in front of us. I saw the black Jeep lurch forward, nearly hitting a nearby lamppost. The engine quit. I knew right away what had happened.

Smart-ass, mastermind, never-makes-a-mistake, killer Alfred Pridholm didn't know how to drive a stick shift.

Disobeying orders again, I rolled down the window. I was too far away from Marr to warn him. "Rob," I yelled to the cowboy behind us. "He can't drive a stick shift. He's going to run."

It didn't take long for me to be proven right. The Jeep lurched a couple more times, then hit the lamppost. Sirens sounded nearby. The cavalry was on the way. The door of the Jeep popped open and Pridholm emerged, gun held in both hands, pointed straight at the advancing Marr.

The camera in my phone was better than nothing. I aimed it out the window.

A new sound. Close by and familiar. Hoof beats. Suddenly, it was classic vintage Western television. Ranger Rob, astride the great horse Prince Valiant, thundered toward the astonished criminal. A rope twirled, spiraled, hovered in circular perfection, and descended over Alfred Pridholm's head and shoulders. The gun spun out of his hands and onto the ground.

"Hog-tied that sucker!" Rob yelled. "Yee-haw!"

Hog-tied was right. Nobody was sorry to see Pridholm dragged a few extra yards in the dust before Prince Valiant slowed, stopped, and performed his triumphant, trademark, rearing up, front-hooves-in-the-air photo-op shot.

By then the cops had arrived, red, white, and blue lights flashing. I saw Pete get out of the lead car. Camera still recording, I leaned out of the open truck window and flashed him a fast thumbs-up sign so he'd know I was okay. Media vehicles weren't far behind the police. Pridholm, handcuffed, dirt streaked, with fake mustache askew, was loaded into a cruiser, accompanied by Pete and Officer Marr and driven away with sirens screaming. Emily, released from the Jeep, rushed into the welcoming arms of her parents. Katie and Paco posed for pictures and Rob, still mounted on Prince Valiant, answered questions from the press. At first I tried to hide from the microphones, aware of my makeup-free, discolored, swollen-eyed face, but decided this was way too big a promotional opportunity to pass up. I faced cameras and mics from CBS, NPR, and two Boston cable stations, along with Scott and Old Jim from WICH-TV, introduced myself as Lee Barrett, program director, and invited an estimated audience of several million viewers to join Rob, Katie, and Paco for the upcoming debut of *Ranger Rob's Rodeo*.

Doan was going to love it. Maybe I'd even get a raise. I could almost hear Rhonda laughing at that idea.

EPILOGUE

Black eye and all, I was the one who got the favored investigative reporter spot beside Buck Covington on the late news that night. I even got the photo credit for my cell phone video of Alfred Pridholm's dramatic, worthy of the Lone Ranger, capture by Ranger Rob and the great horse, Prince Valiant—with Old Jim's footage of the actual arrest tacked on. That was followed by some still shots of a large home on Cape Ann's pretty Wingaersheek Beach. It turned out that John Sawtelle had indeed known where the "big fish" lived, and that knowledge had cost him his life. The LORAN information, converted to GPS format, augmented by Google Earth's ground-level view, had given SPD's special weapons and tactics team—yep, that's the SWAT team—the exact location of Pridholm's crooked real estate operation. It felt good to tell the story, to tell the audience about the toy store owner whose fishing knowledge had helped to crack the case and that they didn't need to worry anymore about a crazed killer on the loose in Salem, that justice had finally won out.

I couldn't tell the WICH-TV viewers everything. For instance, I didn't reveal that three ladies of a certain age, with an interest in crime detection, had amassed the telephone numbers that were all connected to that Wingaersheek Beach home address. I did, however, use the primetime opportunity to give several shameless plugs for *Ranger Rob's Rodeo*.

Once in custody, Pridholm had confessed—bragged, actually—about his complicated string of crimes. He told, in an offhand way, how Sean Kiley, the red Mazda guy, had "chickened out" and was going to turn himself in, so he had to die. He even admitted to slashing Officer Marr's tire. Pete had been right about Pridholm not being top banana in the real estate fraud game. In fact, his clumsy and messy attempts at cleaning up his mistakes had given police enough ammunition to bring down the whole elaborate interstate multimillion-dollar scheme. Multiple arrests were made. Pridholm himself was charged with—among other things—two counts of murder, several counts of grand theft auto, real estate fraud, attempted murder, hit-and-run, kidnapping, stalking, resisting arrest, and breaking and entering. He'll be away for a long, long time.

I never did get to see Wanda's meal prep. Guess I'll have to wait for the book.

The kitten Pridholm had used to gain admission to the Hemenways' condo was one he'd actually bought and paid for in a pet store, so Emily was allowed to keep her.

She's an adorable orange cat, a sweet companion for Fred Astaire. Her name, of course, is Ginger Rogers.

The Angels have given up on my becoming a detective. They are now working on Joyce Rouse to assume that role.

I finally told Pete about the money—the fact that I have quite a lot of it. I should have realized what his response would be. A big smile and a hug. "You mean I can stop worrying about sending the kids to good colleges? That's fantastic!" What a guy.

My engagement dinner was everything I'd ever dreamed it could be. The black eye was all healed. My hair behaved. I wore a great Carolina Herrera off-the-shoulder sea-green silk sheath dress. (Oh, hush. It was on sale at Nordstrom.) Delicious dinner, top-shelf champagne, blue velvet box, gorgeous ring, bended knee proposal and all.

Oh, about that blue-gate dream—the one the book said meant I was close to the beginning of a new journey—a new phase in my life.

Dreams do come true.

Wanda the Weather Girl's Sunday Brunch

**CITRUS COMBO, EGG SCRAMBLE
CASSEROLE, SPINACH STUFFED TOMATOES**

(Serves eight)

This menu can be prepared the day before.

CITRUS COMBO

2 grapefruits
3 oranges
3 tangerines
½ cup sugar, divided
½ cup shredded coconut, divided

Section and seed the fruit. Place half the fruit in a bowl, sprinkle with ¼ cup sugar and ¼ cup coconut. Repeat layers, using another ¼ cup sugar and another ¼ cup coconut with the fruit. Chill at least one hour.

EGG SCRAMBLE CASSEROLE

2 tablespoons melted butter
2 tablespoons flour
2 cups milk
½ teaspoon salt
¼ teaspoon pepper
1 cup shredded American cheese
1 cup chopped Canadian bacon
¼ cup chopped green onion
3 tablespoons melted butter
1 dozen eggs, beaten
1 4-ounce can of mushrooms, drained
1½ cups buttered breadcrumbs
Dash of paprika

Combine butter and flour, blending until smooth. Cook over low heat until bubbly. Gradually stir in milk and cook until smooth and thickened, stirring constantly. Add salt, pepper, and cheese. Heat until cheese melts, stirring constantly. Set aside.

Sauté bacon and onion in three tablespoons butter until onion is tender. Add eggs and cook until set, stirring occasionally to scramble. Fold in mushrooms and cheese sauce. Spoon egg mixture into a lightly greased 12x7x2-inch baking dish. Top with breadcrumbs and sprinkle with paprika. Bake at 350° F. for 30 minutes. Can be prepared ahead and refrigerated until time to bake.

SPINACH-STUFFED TOMATOES

8 medium sized tomatoes
2 10-ounce packages frozen chopped spinach
1 cup breadcrumbs
1 cup grated Parmesan cheese
3 green onions, chopped
2 beaten eggs
3 tablespoons melted butter or margarine
½ teaspoon thyme
½ teaspoon Accent
¼ teaspoon garlic salt
Dash of Tabasco
Salt and pepper to taste.

Cut tops from tomatoes and remove pulp. Leave shells intact. Reserve pulp for another use. Sprinkle a little salt inside shells and invert to drain.

Cook frozen spinach according to package directions. Drain well. Combine spinach with breadcrumbs, Parmesan cheese, chopped onions, eggs, butter, seasoning, and Tabasco. Spoon into tomato shells and bake at 350 F for 25 minutes.

NIGEL'S MOTHER'S DATE SCONES

2 cups flour
$\frac{1}{2}$ cup sugar
2 teaspoons cream of tartar
1 teaspoon baking soda
$\frac{3}{4}$ teaspoon salt
$\frac{1}{2}$ cup butter
$\frac{1}{2}$ cup chopped dates
3 eggs

Combine dry ingredients, cutting in butter until mixture resembles fine bread crumbs. Add dates, tossing lightly. Beat 2 eggs slightly and add to mixture. Stir with a fork until the mixture forms a ball and leaves the sides of the bowl.

Roll dough to $\frac{1}{2}$-inch thickness on a lightly floured board. Cut out with a 2-inch biscuit cutter. Place on greased cookie sheets, spacing 2 inches apart. Slightly beat 1 egg, brushing top of each scone with this. Bake at 400° F for 15 minutes. Makes 20.

TABITHA TRUMBULL'S GIANT OATMEAL COOKIES

1 cup butter
1 cup sugar
1 cup firmly packed brown sugar
2 eggs
1 teaspoon vanilla
1½ cups flour
2 teaspoons ground cinnamon
2 teaspoons ground allspice
2 teaspoons ground cloves
1 teaspoon ground ginger
¼ teaspoon salt
½ teaspoon baking soda
3 cups quick-cooking oats

Cream butter, sugar, and brown sugar until light and fluffy. Beat in eggs and vanilla. Stir together flour, cinnamon, allspice, cloves, ginger, salt, and baking soda. Stir flour mixture into butter mixture. Stir in oats. Let dough sit at room temperature for two hours. Drop about 1/4 cup of dough at a time onto lightly greased baking sheets. Flatten cookies slightly with the back of a spoon. Bake at 375° F for 10 minutes. Do not overbake. Makes about two dozen large cookies.

RIVER NORTH'S ANADAMA BREAD

Nobody can say for sure where the idea for anadama bread came from, or even how it got its odd name. There are a couple of improbable stories about how it came about, but most folks agree that the yeast bread, made with wheat flour, cornmeal, and molasses, probably originated in Rockport, MA in the mid-1850s. In the 1940s, a Rockport restaurant owned by Bill and Melissa Smith (Blacksmith Shop Restaurant) started baking it for their customers. Everybody loved it and by 1956 there were 40 trucks delivering anadama bread all over New England. The bakery closed after Bill Smith's death in 1970. Now you can get it sometimes in restaurants around Gloucester and Rockport, but mostly folks bake it at home.

½ cup water
¼ cup cornmeal
2 tablespoons butter
½ cup molasses
1 (.25 ounce) package active dry yeast
½ cup warm water (110° F)
3 cups all-purpose flour, divided
1 teaspoon salt

Place ½ cup water and the cornmeal in a small saucepan. Bring to a boil over medium heat, stirring occasionally. Cook until mixture thickens, about 5 minutes. Remove from heat and stir in the butter and molasses. Let cool to lukewarm.

In a small mixing bowl, dissolve yeast in ½ cup warm water. Let sit until creamy—about 10 minutes.

Recipes

In a large mixing bowl, combine the cooled cornmeal mixture with the yeast mixture, stir until well blended. Add 2 cups of the flour and the salt, mix well. Add the remaining flour, ½ cup at a time, stirring well after each addition. When the dough has pulled together, turn it out onto a lightly floured surface and knead until smooth and elastic, about 8 minutes.

Lightly oil a large mixing bowl, place the dough in the bowl, and turn to coat with oil. Cover with a damp cloth and put in a warm place to rise until doubled in volume. About 1 hour.

Preheat oven to 375° F.

Deflate the dough and turn it out onto a lightly floured surface and form into a loaf. Place the loaf in a lightly greased 9x5-inch loaf pan. Cover with a damp cloth and let rise until doubled in volume, about 40 minutes.

Bake in preheated oven for about 30 minutes or until top is golden brown and the bottom of the loaf sounds hollow when tapped.

Delicious anytime, but wonderful served warm.

MACARONI SALAD FOR A CROWD

(Serves around twenty)

(Authors note: I could say this is Aunt Ibby's recipe, or maybe Tabitha Trumbull's, but it's really my mother-in-law Betty Perry's, and everybody loves it.)

4 cups small seashell macaroni, cooked (Betty says don't overcook it!)
1 large onion, diced
4 carrots, grated
1 large green pepper, chopped
1 cup celery, sliced
1 cup vinegar
$\frac{1}{3}$ cup sugar
2 cups mayonnaise
1 cup sweetened condensed milk
Salt and pepper to taste

In a large bowl mix all the liquid ingredients, the mayonnaise and the sugar with a whisk. Pour over the macaroni and prepared vegetables and mix thoroughly.

If you like, you can add a can or two of tiny canned shrimp, drained and rinsed. (That's the way my husband Dan's friend Dave Doughty liked it.) This will keep up to two weeks in a tight container in the refrigerator.

ACKNOWLEDGMENTS

For the most part, writing is a solitary business—bottom in chair, fingers on keyboard, creating scene after scene for the book. But behind the scenes of the writer's *real* life there are many helpers. They provide welcome encouragement along with gentle criticism. They are there to raise a glass in celebration or to lend a shoulder to cry on. I'm sure some of them have no idea how important they are and have been to me.

Here are the names of a few of this writer's valued helpers—in no particular order:

Laura Kennedy, Liz Drayer, Becca Johnson, Lee Summerall, Jacquie Luke Hayes, Dana Cassell, Marty Martindale, Andi Davis, Sofie Kelly, Susan Santangelo, Patzi Gil, Rita Moreau, Cheryl Hollon, Emily Gray, Dale Aden Sr., Lois Mercer, my kids—Allison, Debbie, and Steve—daughter-in-law, Mary and son-in-law, Pete, Kensington cheerleaders Esi Sogah and Larissa Ackerman, and of course my husband and best friend, Dan.

Connect with U(s)

Visit us online at
KensingtonBooks.com
to read more from your favorite authors, see books
by series, view reading group guides, and more.

Join us on social media

for sneak peeks, chances to win books and prize packs,
and to share your thoughts with other readers.

facebook.com/kensingtonpublishing
twitter.com/kensingtonbooks

Tell us what you think!

To share your thoughts, submit a review,
or sign up for our eNewsletters, please visit:
KensingtonBooks.com/TellUs.